One of the robbers saw Walker.

He swung the automatic rifle in his hands toward the Ranger. Flame geysered from the muzzle as he fired a burst. The bullets chiseled chips of granite from the building wall as Walker flung himself down and squeezed off a couple of shots of his own. He saw the robber jerk slightly as the bullets thudded into his chest, but the man kept moving. The slugs hadn't penetrated his body armor.

The truck's motor roared as it leaped away from the bank entrance and headed down the sidewalk. Walker and Trivette stood up as the armored truck headed down Houston Street at breakneck speed. The truck turned a corner and disappeared.

''We'll get them, Walker,'' Trivette said.

Walker looked around at the carnage in the bank lobby. ''Yeah,'' he said, his jaw tight. ''We will.''

Don't miss the first in the series . . .

Walker, Texas Ranger

The Novel

WALKER, TEXAS RANGER™

HELL'S HALF ACRE

James Reasoner

BERKLEY BOULEVARD BOOKS, NEW YORK

WALKER, TEXAS RANGER: HELL'S HALF ACRE

A Berkley Boulevard Book / published by arrangement with CBS Enterprises

PRINTING HISTORY
Berkley Boulevard edition / July 1999

Cover design by Mike Stromberg.
Cover photograph by Richard Twarog/CBS.

For information address: The Berkley Publishing Group, a division of Penguin Putnam Inc.,
375 Hudson Street, New York, New York 10014.

The Penguin Putnam Inc. World Wide Web site address is
http://www.penguinputnam.com

ISBN: 0-425-16972-3

BERKLEY BOULEVARD
Berkley Boulevard Books are published by The Berkley Publishing Group, a division of Penguin Putnam Inc.,
375 Hudson Street, New York, New York 10014.
BERKLEY BOULEVARD and its logo are trademarks belonging to Penguin Putnam Inc.

PRINTED IN THE UNITED STATES OF AMERICA

10 9 8 7 6 5 4 3 2 1

This book is dedicated to the memory of four great storytellers who spun some of my favorite yarns about the Texas Rangers:

A. Leslie Scott
Tom Curry
Walker A. Tompkins
Bennie Gardner

ACKNOWLEDGMENTS

Special thanks, as always, to
Chuck Norris, Aaron Norris, and Gordon Dawson;
Jeff Nemerovsky and Mary Ann Martin of CBS;
and Kimberly Waltemyer and John Talbot.

PROLOGUE

The Texas Ranger Hall of Fame

Cordell Walker paused in front of a large bronze statue of a man in Western clothes. He turned to the group of children following him and asked, "Does anybody know who this is?"

There were about twenty children in the group, and their ages—ten and eleven—and the attractive young woman accompanying them, who was obviously a teacher, marked them as a school class on a field trip. One of them, a lanky boy with bright red hair sticking out from under his baseball cap, leaned forward and read the plaque attached to the base of the statue. " 'Captain William "Wild Bill" MacDonald.' "

"That's right, Ricky," said Walker. "What else does it say?"

Ricky frowned a little as he concentrated on the words. " 'No man in the wrong can stand up against a man in the right who keeps on a-coming.' "

"And you'd all do well to remember Captain MacDonald's words," Walker told the kids with a smile.

The teacher moved to the head of the group. "Thank you, Ranger Walker," she said. "Now, we've taken up enough of your time, so . . ." She turned to the children. "Class, what do we say to Ranger Walker?"

"Tell us a story, Ranger Walker!" exclaimed the young boy called Ricky. Several of the others piped up as well, echoing the request for a story.

Clearly embarrassed, the teacher began, "No, that's not what I meant—"

"Don't worry about it," Walker told her, grinning broadly. "These kids have been here before. They know there are a lot of interesting stories in this building."

"Yeah, a story about the old-time Rangers," said Ricky. "A real shoot-'em-up!"

"Well, I don't know about that," said Walker, "but if you'll come over here, maybe I can remember one of the yarns about the old-timers." He led the children over to a wall packed with portraits of Texas Rangers from the past. "This is the Wall of Honor, and right here is one of the men who make it special." Walker pointed to the portrait of a man with a short beard and hair that fell to his shoulders. The man wore a fringed buckskin shirt and a Stetson.

"Was he a Ranger in the Old West?" asked Ricky.

"He sure was, but you know, the Old West lasted a little later than you might think. Texas was still pretty wild in the early days of this very century. That's why, even in 1901, they still needed Rangers like Hayes Cooper here." Walker pointed to the portrait again. "I remember hearing about a day in that year when Cooper was on the trail of a fugitive not far from here. . . ."

ONE

North Texas, 1901

He was getting too old for this, no doubt about it.

Hayes Cooper reined in on a wooded ridge overlooking the Trinity River and leaned forward in the saddle to ease muscles made stiff by the long day of riding. He took off his hat and used the sleeve of his buckskin shirt to wipe sweat from his forehead.

For more than a dozen years, he had been riding these back trails, spending days in the saddle and nights rolled up in a blanket on the cold, hard ground. Never knowing when a bullet would come from ambush, never knowing if the next tree or rock hid a man who wanted him dead. And it wasn't much better in town. He had walked the streets of countless settlements, from Dalhart to Del Rio, from El Paso to Texarkana, all too aware that the mouth of every dark alley could conceal death in its shadows. He asked himself sometimes why he still did it.

But he knew the answer. He was a Texas Ranger, a manhunter, the last of a breed. The men who had come before him, lone wolves like Slade and Hatfield, Gillette and Aken, their day was done. But Hayes Cooper still wore the silver star on a silver circle. He wasn't ready yet to put away the badge and hang up his six-guns. Not as long as he was still needed.

Right now there was no question about him being needed. Somewhere up there in front of him was a man named Doyle Parnell, who had robbed the bank in Decatur. That was just the latest in a series of bank jobs Parnell had pulled. Cooper had been on his trail for a month but had always been just a little too late to stop Parnell before he struck again.

But this time it was going to be different, Cooper told himself as he put his hat back on and heeled his horse into motion, heading down the slope into the river valley. This time his gut told him that he was close to Parnell.

Maybe too close.

Post oaks and cottonwoods grew thickly along the banks of the Trinity, and as Cooper rode toward them he suddenly saw the late-afternoon sunlight reflect off something in the shadows under the trees. The glint of that stray beam of light was enough warning to make Cooper kick his feet free of the stirrups and throw himself out of the saddle as a rifle cracked. His hat flew off his head as he fell, but he didn't know if a bullet had plucked it off or not. He landed hard, knocking the breath out of his lungs, but that didn't stop him from immediately rolling behind a clump of brush.

When he came to a stop, he realized that his Colt .45 was in his hand. Cooper didn't even remember drawing the gun. Instinct had taken over, just as it had prompted him to dive out of the saddle.

The horse pranced off to the side, made nervous by the shot. Cooper lay motionless where he was, waiting for the bushwhacker's rifle to speak again. The brush where he was hidden wouldn't stop a high-powered bullet, and he was surprised that the ambusher wasn't already raking the thicket with rifle fire.

Parnell. The rifleman had to be Parnell. All day long, Cooper had felt like he was closing in on the outlaw. Parnell had been on the dodge long enough that he probably had the same sort of instincts that would warn him when a lawman was catching up to him. So he had stopped and hidden in those trees on the riverbank, waiting to see who would come along.

Parnell would have recognized him at first sight, thought Cooper. They had seen each other at Parnell's trial in Austin several years earlier, when Cooper had been one of a group of Rangers who had corralled Parnell after a bank robbery in Round Rock. Parnell had been sent away for twenty years in that trial, but the penitentiary at Huntsville had held him for less than three years before he broke out. He had immediately gone back to his bank-robbing ways, and Cooper had been on his trail ever since. He knew that Parnell would take particular pleasure in killing him if he got the chance.

Cooper looked at his horse and saw the stock of the Winchester sticking up from the saddle boot. He wished he had the rifle right now; he could put up a lot better fight with it. The Colt in his hand was a magnificent weapon, but not at the range involved here. Parnell could keep him pinned down all day.

Suddenly Cooper wondered if Parnell thought he'd been hit by that first, and so far only, shot. True, Cooper had left the saddle before the sound of the rifle reached his ears, but the two things had been almost simultaneous. The gap had been so small that Parnell might not have noticed. And Cooper hadn't had to roll very far to reach this brush. To Parnell's eye, it might have looked as if the momentum of his fall had carried him out of sight.

So it was possible, Cooper decided, that Parnell was sitting down there thinking he had already killed the Texas Ranger who was following him. Under the circumstances, that was exactly what Cooper wanted Parnell to think. If he lay here motionless long enough, that might draw Parnell closer, close enough for Cooper to make a play. . . .

Or Parnell might just ride off, Cooper thought disgustedly as he heard the faint sound of hoofbeats in the distance. He lifted his head just enough to peer through a small gap in the brush and saw a rider leaving the trees and moving through a pasture on the far side of the Trinity.

Cooper scrambled to his feet and lunged out from behind the cover of the brush, heading toward his horse. He had taken only a couple of steps when another shot rang out and something that felt like a giant fist clipped him on the left hip. The impact spun him around and made him fall. He hung on to his gun, though, and even as he fell he triggered a couple of shots toward the river. The bullets would fall short, but Cooper's nature wouldn't let him just lie there and not fight back.

He rolled again, not toward the brush this time but toward his horse. He had to get his hands on that Winchester if he was going to have a chance to survive. Another bullet slammed into the ground less than a foot from his head, kicking dirt into his eyes. Cooper blinked rapidly to clear his vision and surged to his feet. He lunged at the horse, which shied away from him. Cooper was able to get his hand on the stock of the rifle and yank it free from its sheath.

He threw himself down as something tugged at the fringe on the right shoulder of his shirt. Lying prone, he worked the level of the Winchester and fired toward the river. He saw a faint puff of smoke from the shadows under the trees as Parnell returned the shot, so he was able to concentrate his shots in that direction. Cooper fired half a dozen times as fast as he could jack the lever of the rifle and squeeze the trigger.

Then he was moving again, rolling over and coming up into a run that was made a little awkward by the bullet crease on his hip. At least, Cooper wanted to think it was just a crease and not something more serious. His hip didn't hurt much; in fact, it was almost numb. That was from the shock of the bullet striking it, he knew, and the feeling would wear off sooner or later. When it did, he would probably hurt like the dickens, so he planned to take advantage of the numbness while he could.

He didn't head for the brush this time but back up the slope instead. More slugs thudded into the ground around his feet, but he was moving too fast for Parnell to draw a bead on him. He reached the top of the rise and dove over it.

Cooper twisted around so that he could poke his head and the barrel of the Winchester over the top of the hill. He saw a man on horseback burst out of the cover of the trees along the Trinity. This time, he knew it was really Parnell. He had realized too late that the outlaw had fooled him the first time.

Parnell had two horses, one of the things that had made him difficult to catch. Not knowing whether he had hit Cooper with his first shot or not, he had sent one of the mounts galloping riderless out of the trees, hoping to draw the Ranger out. And Cooper had fallen for it, not realizing as he peered through the brush that the horse's saddle was empty. Cooper's jaw tightened in anger at himself. He was too damned old, too experienced a lawman, to be falling for such tricks.

Maybe that was another sign that he ought to get out of this business, before he got himself—or somebody else—killed.

This time Parnell was really gone. From the top of the hill, Cooper got a good look at him as he rode off. Parnell had realized that he had lost his advantage when Cooper reached the top of the slope with the rifle. At that point, the ambush had turned into a standoff, and Parnell didn't have the stomach for that. He had run instead.

Cooper stood up. He could still see Parnell, a dwindling figure on horseback in the distance. For a moment, Cooper thought about trying one more shot at the outlaw, but Parnell was too far away. Cooper would just be wasting a bullet. With a sigh and a grimace, Cooper went to catch his horse. That was what Parnell would be doing about now, he thought, rounding up that spare mount he had used to fool Cooper into thinking he was fleeing.

Parnell was heading southeast, toward the booming settlement of Fort Worth. That was probably his destination, Cooper decided. In the past couple of decades, the arrival of the railroad had changed Fort Worth from a sleepy little prairie village into a bustling community that was also known as Cowtown. Ranchers from all over Texas drove their cattle to the stockyards on the north side of Fort Worth, and at the other end of town there was such a proliferation of saloons, gambling halls, and whorehouses that the area had come to be known as Hell's Half Acre. Parnell probably thought that it would be easy for a man like him to lose himself in such a place.

Cooper didn't intend to let that happen. He planned to stick to the outlaw's trail like a burr.

• • •

After Cooper caught his horse, he tied the reins to a small oak tree and pushed down his denim trousers to examine the wound on his hip. There was only a small rip and not much blood on the trousers, which was encouraging, and when Cooper exposed the wound, he saw that it was very shallow and only a couple of inches long. It was hardly more than a bullet burn . . . which didn't stop it from smarting a considerable amount. Cooper took a bottle of whiskey from his saddlebags, poured a goodly splash over the scrape, tied a bandage over it, then thought about taking a swallow internally. He told himself the whiskey was for medicinal purposes, replaced the cork in the neck of the bottle, and stowed it away again.

Riding was downright painful, he quickly discovered. He improvised a pad from a spare shirt and draped it over the edge of the saddle so that it cushioned the wounded hip. That threw him out of balance, however, so he gave up and shoved the shirt back into his saddlebag. He'd just put up with the pain, he told himself. Fort Worth wasn't more than half a day's ride away.

By the time he reached a smaller settlement late that afternoon, Cooper was mighty glad to see it. He reined the horse to a halt in front of a squat building made of large chunks of reddish sandstone. The roof was of red tile and had apparently given the place its name: the Red Top. It appeared to be a combination café and saloon.

Cooper swung down from the saddle and knotted the reins around a wooden hitching post. He glanced around the settlement, which was little more than a single dirt street with a dozen or so buildings on either side of it. There was a grocery store across from the Red Top, and a few doors down on the same side of the street was a two-story white frame building that housed a drugstore on the first floor and the local Odd Fellows hall on the second. A few wagons were parked at the store, but the Red Top seemed to be the busiest place in town. Several wagons were parked there, too, and more than half a dozen horses were tied to the hitching post.

The Red Top had a sidewalk, also made out of chunks of sandstone, with a wooden awning over it. Cooper stepped into the shade of the awning and crossed the sidewalk to the door. It was dim and cool and smoky inside the place, the air thick with the smells of tobacco, whiskey, coffee, and fried food all mixed together. Cooper had been in hundreds of places like this during his years as a Ranger. Stepping into one was like coming home.

There was an L-shaped counter on the left side of the room. The short leg, nearest to the front, served as a lunch counter, with a swinging door in the wall behind it leading to the kitchen. To the right, where the long leg of the L ran toward the back of the room, was the bar area. Men were lined up there on stools, leaning on the counter and drinking beer from glass mugs. A domino game was going on between four cowboys at one of the tables scattered around the right side of the room.

A couple of men in overalls and work boots were sitting at the lunch counter, and that was where Cooper headed. Behind the counter was a burly, balding man in a long white apron. He rested knobby-knuckled hands on the counter and nodded pleasantly as he said to Cooper, "What can I do for you?"

"Chicken-fry me up a good-sized chunk of steak with plenty of potatoes on the side. And biscuits if you've got 'em."

The man grinned across the counter at Cooper. "We got 'em," he said. "Cream gravy?"

"As much as you can pour on there," said Cooper.

"Comin' right up. Have a seat. Coffee?"

Cooper nodded. He settled onto one of the empty stools at the counter and sighed with weariness. He hoped that the coffee and the food would go a long way toward perking him up. He hadn't decided if he wanted to try to ride the rest of the way into Fort Worth tonight or not.

The proprietor pushed the swinging door open and called Cooper's order back into the kitchen. A woman's voice replied, "Comin' up." Probably the proprietor's wife doing the cooking, thought Cooper. The man filled a chipped china cup from a coffeepot and placed it on the counter in front of the Ranger.

"Got some cream and sugar, if you'd like."

Cooper shook his head. "I take it black." He lifted the cup, sipped the strong brew. He could almost feel strength flowing back into him as he drank.

The proprietor was eyeing Cooper's long hair, the buckskin shirt, and the gun belt around his waist. "Don't recall ever seein' you in here before," he ventured.

"Never been here," said Cooper. His tone was mild and unchallenging, but it didn't give anything away, either.

"Passing through on business?"

"You could call it that." Cooper hesitated. His Ranger badge wasn't pinned to his shirt. He normally carried it on a special pocket on the back of his wide belt, because he had found that folks usually talked more freely when they didn't know he was a lawman. He left it there now, deciding not to reveal his identity. Instead, he went on, "I'm looking for a man."

"Somebody who lives around here? I know most everybody in these parts."

Cooper shook his head. "No, this fella's from up in the Panhandle originally. I think he's on his way to Fort Worth and I'm trying to catch up to him. We're supposed to do some business together."

"Tall gent, lanky, curly brown hair, big friendly smile?"

Cooper tried not to stare at the proprietor of the Red Top. The man had just described Doyle Parnell perfectly. Parnell didn't look particularly vicious or dangerous, which was one of the things that made him deadly.

"That sounds like him, all right," said Cooper, taking pains to keep his voice casual. "Have you seen him around here?"

"He sat right there on that same stool where you're sittin' and ate a big meal, not more'n an hour ago. Friendly sort of fella, said he was a cattle buyer on his way to Fort Worth to pick up some steers at the stockyards."

"That's him," Cooper said, "and that's the deal I'm going in on with him. Did he say where he's going to be staying?"

"Nope, I'm afraid not." The proprietor dropped his voice to a confidential level as he leaned across the counter closer to Cooper. "But he did say that he was going to pay a visit to some place in Hell's Half Acre called the Golden Garter. Pleasure before business, he said." The proprietor dropped one eyelid in a lazy wink.

"Much obliged. Maybe I'd better try to catch up to him." Cooper started to stand up.

The proprietor straightened. "Aren't you goin' to eat your chicken-fried steak? It ought to be just about ready."

Cooper hesitated. This was a much better lead to Parnell's whereabouts than he had expected to stumble over in this small town. And he'd had a long day, not to mention the blood he had lost from that bullet crease. The food would help considerably in restoring his strength.

He settled back down on the stool. "Sure. Bring it on."

"I'll freshen up that coffee for you, too. There's a good road between here and Fort Worth. If you push on after you eat, you can be there well before midnight."

That seemed like a good idea to Cooper. He sat there and waited for his food, listening to the sound of dominoes being shuffled and the good-natured gibes of the cowboys as they played.

The Golden Garter, he thought. He had never heard of the place, but he was willing to bet that it wouldn't be hard to find. Somebody would be eager to point it out to him.

After all, in Hell's Half Acre, the easiest thing to find was sin.

TWO

Fort Worth was really two towns in one, divided by the Trinity River. The military post that had given the town its name had been built on a wooded bluff overlooking the river. The settlement had grown up next to the fort and remained when it was abandoned by the army. The downtown area now stretched for over a mile, running north and south.

North of the river was the area where the meat-packing companies had built their plants, and this was a flourishing neighborhood as well, complete with saloons and hotels and a wide variety of other businesses. It might have been expected that Fort Worth's red-light district would grow up here, too, but for some reason it hadn't. When the cowboys who brought the herds into Fort Worth wanted someplace to spend their wages on whiskey, women, and games of chance, they headed for the southern end of downtown, an area that had once been known as the Third Ward.

Now everybody just called it Hell's Half Acre.

That night, Hayes Cooper rode down Main Street, which ran straight as an arrow from the Tarrant County Courthouse at the north end to the Texas & Pacific depot on the south. Gas streetlights burned on nearly every corner, and Cooper had to be careful not to let his horse trip over the rails in the center of the street where electric streetcars ran. Brick buildings that were three and four stories tall lined the street. Telephone wires were strung on poles. Cooper's mouth tightened a little as he looked around at all the indications of so-called progress. Times were changing, and he wasn't sure he liked what they were changing into. As he looked up and down the street he saw plenty of horse-drawn buggies parked along the sidewalks, but his was the only saddle horse in sight. He wondered if the cowboys who patronized the establishments in the Acre rode the streetcars over here from the stockyards.

It was almost ten o'clock, so there weren't many people on the streets. Cooper turned his horse toward the sidewalk when he spotted a man walking along there. The man was moving at an unsteady pace, and Cooper figured he was drunk. The Ranger asked anyway, "Hey, mister, can you tell me where to find the Golden Garter?"

The man stopped short, hiccuped, and peered intently at Cooper, coming to the edge of the sidewalk to get a better look at him in the glow from a nearby streetlight. After a moment, the man exclaimed, "My God, it's Buffalo Bill Cody! Is your Wild West show back in town, Bill?"

"I'm not Bill Cody," Cooper said curtly, trying to rein in his impatience. "I'm looking for the Golden Garter."

"Have you checked aroun' the thigh of a lady?"

"It's a saloon," grated Cooper. "Either that, or a sporting house."

"Oh. *That* Golden Garter." The drunk swayed a little, steadied himself, and pointed down Main Street. "That way. Just before you get to Twelfth Street, I believe."

"Obliged." Cooper heeled his horse into motion again.

The drunk called after him, "Are you sure you're not Buffalo Bill?"

Cooper ignored him and rode on.

The sounds of tinny piano music and laughter grew louder as he proceeded along Main Street. More people were on the sidewalks, though most of them stayed in the shadows close to the buildings. Cooper glanced warily at the dark mouths of the alleys he passed, not liking them. Parnell could be waiting in any of them with a rifle.

Cooper frowned. From what the proprietor of the Red Top had said, Parnell hadn't sounded too worried. Parnell had stopped at the cafe long enough for a steak and some casual conversation. That didn't sound like a man who thought that a Texas Ranger was right on his tail.

Parnell had seen him fall when that slug clipped him on the hip. He had seen the way Cooper had hobbled over the top of the hill, too. So Parnell knew Cooper was injured. Maybe he thought that would slow Cooper down enough so that he wouldn't have to hurry for a while. If that was the case, it was dangerous overconfidence on the outlaw's part, a foolish mistake.

But Cooper had made some mistakes of his own today. Everybody did, Rangers and owlhoots included. If Parnell wanted to hand him a lucky break on a silver platter, Cooper was damn sure going to take it.

He wasn't sure which street was which, and the infrequent signs were poorly placed and hard to read. He found Tenth Street, however, and assumed that the next one was Eleventh. So that put Twelfth just ahead of him, and sure enough, on the left-hand side of the street was a brightly lit establishment with fancy gilt letters in the window announcing that it was the Golden Garter. The entrance, complete with old-fashioned swinging batwing doors, was at the corner of Main and Twelfth. The drunk had known what he was talking about, even if he had mistaken Cooper for Buffalo Bill Cody.

There was no hitch rack in front of the place. Cooper swung down from the saddle and tied his mount's reins to one of the wooden poles that held up the telephone lines. At least the pole was good for something, even if it was only tying up horses. Cooper had talked on a telephone only a few times, and he hadn't liked it. It made his ear tingle unpleasantly.

He stepped up onto the sidewalk and went along it to the entrance of the saloon. As he did so he peered into the place through the windows. The Golden Garter had an unusual amount of them, and the glass was even clean, which meant it was more high-class than a lot of the saloons down here. Busy, too, noted Cooper. He paused at the door, looking over the batwings and studying the crowd at the bar, as well as the people at the tables.

There were actually two bars, one on each side of the room. The area in between was closely packed with tables, except for an open space at the rear that was likely used as a dance floor. Nobody was dancing at the moment, though. A stairway at the far end of each bar led up to a balcony that ran all the way around the room, overhanging the dance floor and both bars. Up there would be the cribs of the working girls.

Cooper counted six bartenders in white shirts, string ties, fancy vests, and sleeve garters. They were evenly divided between the two bars. In addition, several young women in low-cut spangled dresses that reached only to their knees were delivering drinks to the tables. At the far end of the left-hand bar stood a blond woman in a red gown that was considerably more decorous than the outfits worn by the saloon girls. The dress came up high on her throat and swept all the way down to her ankles. For all of that, however, it was tight enough to be rather scandalous, revealing the blond woman's lovely figure. She turned her head as one of the bartenders spoke to her, giving Cooper a glimpse of her profile.

Cooper turned his gaze away from her, reminding himself that he wasn't here to look at pretty women. The dull ache in his hip was reminder enough of that. He wasn't able to get a good look at everybody in the room, but so far he had seen no sign of Doyle Parnell. That didn't mean Parnell wasn't here, though. The outlaw could be hunkered at one of the tables in a corner, or he might be upstairs in one of the little rooms where the soiled doves plied their trade.

Standing here all night wasn't going to do him any good, Cooper told himself. Besides, somebody was liable to get suspicious of him. Moving easily and gracefully despite his injury, he pushed the batwings aside and stepped into the saloon. There was an open spot about halfway down the left-hand bar, so he headed for it.

Before he could get there, he felt eyes on him and saw that the blond woman in the red dress had spotted him. She was watching him with a look that seemed casual, yet Cooper knew she wasn't missing a thing about him. He was glad he had his badge safely stowed away in its hiding place. He wouldn't get much cooperation in a place like this if everybody knew he was a lawman.

One of the bartenders came over as Cooper stepped up to the bar. Cooper didn't wait for the drink juggler to ask him his pleasure. He said, "Beer," and the bartender nodded and reached for a mug. He filled it at the closest tap and turned to place it on the bar in front of Cooper, who reached into his pocket for a coin.

"No need for that," a voice said, quiet but still managing to cut cleanly through the hubbub of conversation and laughter that filled the room. Cooper looked and saw the blond woman standing beside him. She had glided along the bar so smoothly that he hadn't even seen her coming. She smiled and went on, "The first one's always on the house in the Golden Garter."

"The first one tonight, or the first one ever?" asked Cooper.

"You haven't been here before," she said. "I'd remember you." She extended a slim, long-fingered hand. "I'm Tess Malone. This is my place."

Cooper took her hand, folding its softness into his roughened palm. "Call me Cooper," he said.

"First name or last?" asked Tess Malone. Her hand was still in his.

Cooper shrugged. "Only, right now."

She slid her fingers out of his grip. "All right, Cooper."

Lord, she was a beautiful woman. Thick blond hair, blue eyes that a man wanted to dive into, a small birthmark on her cheek, a red-lipped mouth made for smiling—or kissing . . .

Cooper took a deep breath and reminded himself yet again why he was here. If Tess Malone was the owner of the Golden Garter, she likely kept a pretty close eye on the people who came and went in the place. She could tell him whether or not Parnell was here—but only if he asked the right way. Saloonkeepers had to be discreet if they wanted to stay in business.

Cooper picked up his beer with his left hand and sipped from the mug as Tess asked, "What brings you to Fort

Worth? Or are you as tight-lipped about that as you are your name?"

"Business," Cooper said. "Cattle business. I'm a buyer."

Tess favored him with a sardonic smile. "Everybody's either a buyer or seller of something, Cooper."

"Yeah, well . . . cattle's my line."

"Then you've come to the right town. There are more cattle in Fort Worth than people. Unfortunately, cattle don't drink or play poker."

A new voice said, "But if they did, they'd be welcome here, isn't that right, Tess?"

A slender, handsome black man in an expensive suit, a ruffled white shirt, and a silk cravat had stepped up on Tess's other side. He wasn't wearing a hat, and Cooper recalled seeing him sitting at one of the tables playing cards a few minutes earlier. The game must have ended. The gambler crooked a finger at the nearest bartender and said, "Sherry, please."

The bartender sighed in exasperation and rested his palms on the polished hardwood. "I've told you I don't know how many times, Yance, we don't have any of that fancy stuff," he said. "It's beer or whiskey."

"Oh, all right. I'll have a beer." The gambler turned and reached in front of Tess to offer his hand to Cooper. The affected air he had put on a moment earlier vanished as he grinned and said, "I'm Yance Shelby, professor of the pasteboards. I'll gladly take your money if you're in the mood for a game, friend."

"This is Cooper. That's all, just Cooper," said Tess as the Ranger shook hands with Shelby. "And he's here for business, not pleasure."

"Pleasure *is* my business," said Shelby. "The pleasure of genteel conversation and a stimulating game."

Cooper shook his head. "I'll pass."

Shelby picked up the beer the bartender had drawn for him. "I'll leave you to your drink, then," he said. He lifted the mug in a salute. "To your health, sir."

Cooper was about to return the informal toast when he saw Shelby's eyes widen in surprise. Tess Malone suddenly looked equally shocked as she peered over Cooper's shoulder at something behind him. Cooper was experienced enough in reading people's reactions to know that neither of them was faking. Something bad was about to happen.

Cooper twisted around, the mug of beer still in his left hand, his right flashing to the butt of the Colt on his hip. A man who had been sitting at one of the tables about fifteen feet away was starting to stand up. He was dressed like a cowboy, and his beard-stubbled face was contorted with rage and hatred. He spat out, "You! Cooper!"

The man looked familiar, and in less than a heartbeat, Cooper's nimble brain had put a name with the ugly face: Dave Reavis, a horse thief from Waco. Cooper had arrested him a couple of years earlier. In the past, horse thieves had been hanged, but Reavis had gotten off with a two-year prison sentence. From the pallor of the man's skin, Cooper judged that Reavis had just been released from Huntsville.

And he was holding a grudge, too, because as he straightened he clawed at the butt of the pistol tucked behind his belt and yelled, "I'm gonna kill you, Cooper!"

THREE

The last thing Cooper wanted in this crowded saloon was a shoot-out with some crazy jailbird bent on revenge. But that looked like what he was going to get. He yelled, ''Everybody down!''

Most of the Golden Garter's patrons paid heed to the warning, either diving for the sawdust-littered floor or scurrying for cover behind some of the tables. Two men didn't hide, though. They stepped up boldly behind Reavis, and one of them, the shorter one, said, ''Hold on, friend. You don't want to do that.''

The suggestion was reinforced by the metallic clicking of the guns being cocked in the hands of the two men.

Cooper stood stiffly at the bar, his own fingers brushing the smooth walnut grips of his Colt. He didn't want to take his eyes off Reavis, yet he had to glance at the two men who had intervened. They were dressed similarly, in pin-striped suits and derby hats, and both sported mustaches. The taller one was lean and solemnly handsome, while the shorter, stockier one flashed a cocky grin at Cooper.

''Sorry if we're interrupting something you'd rather do yourself,'' this one called to Cooper. ''Looked like this gent might get his gun out while your back was still turned, and we couldn't have that.''

''Much obliged,'' Cooper said.

''You want us to back off?'' asked the taller of the derby-wearing men.

Cooper smiled tightly. ''You look like you're doing just fine.'' He glanced at Tess Malone. ''Those two work for you?''

She shook her head. ''I never saw them before in my life.''

The shorter one flashed his grin again and tipped his hat to her without ever letting the gun in his other hand waver. ''We're newcomers to Fort Worth, ma'am, but I can already see that we're going to enjoy visiting your fair city. Plenty of excitement for a couple of country boys like us.''

Reavis was trembling slightly, Cooper saw. The man's jaw worked back and forth. He wanted to draw his gun so badly that he couldn't stand it, yet the two men had the drop on him.

The shorter one put his hat back on and said to Tess, ''With your permission, ma'am . . . ?''

She waved a slim hand. ''Go ahead and get him out of here.''

Reavis yelled, ''Damn it!'' and tried to yank his gun out, but the taller man stepped up smoothly and slapped him across the side of the head with his pistol. Reavis's hat flew off. He slumped toward the table where he had been sitting, but the shorter man caught his collar and hauled him upright. Placing the barrel of his gun under Reavis's chin, the man abandoned his jaunty pose and said in a cold voice, ''Don't you ever come in here again, mister. And don't you even think about trying to ambush that gent at the bar. If anything happens to him, I'll hunt you down and kill you like the dog you are.''

''He means it, too,'' the taller man said dryly. ''He hasn't killed anybody in almost a month.''

Reavis's eyes were unfocused from the clout on the head by the taller man's gun. The pressure of the gun barrel against his throat cleared his brain quickly, however, and he managed to jerk his head in a nod as the man holding him asked, "Do you understand?"

The taller man grabbed the back of Reavis's neck and shoved him roughly toward the door of the saloon. "Get out of here, then," he said. "The next time I see your face, I'll put a bullet in it."

Reavis stumbled toward the door, propelled by the push. He lost his balance and almost fell, then caught himself and practically ran out of the Golden Garter. The batwings flapped behind him after he knocked them aside.

The two men in derby hats waited until Reavis was gone, then holstered their guns in cross-draw rigs under their coats. They stepped over to the bar, and the shorter one nodded to Cooper and said, "Sorry again if we butted in, friend. I just can't stand to see a man bushwhacked."

"If he wanted to kill me, he shouldn't have yelled out that way," said Cooper. "I would have taken him. But I appreciate the help anyway. I didn't want a bunch of lead flying around in here."

Tess Malone gave a ladylike snort. "Neither did I," she said as she gestured at the long mirror behind the bar. "You know how much it costs to replace something like that?"

"No, ma'am," said the shorter man. "But then, I never did have much of a head for money." He stuck out a hand. "Name's Parker. This is my friend Harry. . . ."

"Harry Long," supplied the taller man. "We're, ah, cattle buyers."

"There certainly are a lot of those in here tonight," Yance Shelby said. The gambler's tone made it clear that he didn't necessarily believe any of the newcomers were in the cattle business. But he didn't particularly care, either.

Cooper said, "Then all that talk about not killing a man for almost a month . . . ?"

"Just talk," replied Parker breezily. "But it got that hombre to listen, didn't it?"

"Considering the way you gave me a hand, I reckon I ought to buy you a drink," Cooper said to the two men.

"That's an offer I'll not refuse," said Harry Long.

Shelby said, "Could I interest you gentlemen in a few hands of cards as well?"

Parker grinned in anticipation and said, "Now, that sounds mighty interesting. What about you, Cooper? You game?"

Cooper hadn't intended to get involved in anything like this, but he might be able to turn it to his advantage, he decided as he quickly considered his options. He said, "I might be . . ." He glanced at Tess. "If the lady plays, too."

Shelby hooted with laughter. "Cooper, you don't know what you just let yourself in for," he declared.

Tess was looking at Cooper, meeting his level stare. Without taking her eyes away from his, she said, "Pick up your drinks and find a table, boys. Let's play poker."

A shrill ringing sound interrupted Walker's story and brought groans of disappointment from the children gathered around him. He said, "Sorry, kids," and brought the cell phone out of his shirt pocket. He flipped it open. "Walker."

The voice of his partner, Ranger James Trivette, came from the phone. "They've hit again, Walker." Trivette was under control, as usual, but Walker could hear the undercurrent of excitement in his words.

"The same bunch?"

"Yeah, but one thing is different this time." Trivette paused, then said, "It went wrong for them. They're holed up in the bank with hostages."

Walker tensed. "Where?"

"In Fort Worth." Trivette named one of the major downtown banks.

"I'm on my way," said Walker. He snapped the phone closed and slid it back into his pocket.

As he turned back toward the children the one called Ricky asked plaintively, "Do you really have to go, Ranger Walker?"

"I'm afraid so," Walker said with a smile.

"Are you going after some bad guys?"

"Yeah. Some real bad guys."

"But you'll tell us the rest of the story some other time, won't you?"

Walker nodded. "I'll finish the story. And that's a promise."

Five minutes later, Walker was speeding smoothly down the highway at the wheel of his heavy-duty pickup, its lights flashing to indicate that he was on official business. As he drove he thought about what Trivette had told him and the events of the past few months that had led up to this newest crime.

In the past ten weeks, there had been eight bank holdups in the Dallas/Fort Worth metroplex. Each time, what seemed to be the same gang had pulled off the job. There were half a dozen men in the group, all of them heavily armed and wearing body armor and armored helmets. Their robberies were carried out with surgical precision. They struck late in the day, when there was plenty of money on hand. Using a van stolen just before the robbery, they drove up to the bank openly, piled out of the boosted vehicle, strode boldly inside, and took over the lobby by tossing flash-bang grenades into it, incapacitating everyone inside without actually harming them. Refractive visors on the helmets and ear protectors shielded the robbers from the effects of the grenades. Tellers' cash drawers were cleaned out by two of the men, while two more looted the vault. The remaining two stood guard. In each of the previous robberies, the thieves had been in and out of the bank quickly, spending no more than five minutes inside. Then, as calmly as they had entered, they always left and got back in the stolen van, driving off before police could respond. The van was always ditched quickly. So far, the only serious injury suffered by anyone in the course of the robberies had been a concussion. A guard had been pistol-whipped when he had tried to fight back despite being blinded and deafened by the flash-bang.

Because of the smoothness and efficiency of the holdups, not to mention the high-tech weaponry and body armor, Walker suspected that the thieves might have some military connection. Trivette had been working that angle, but so far he hadn't come up with anything.

Now, something had gone wrong on the gang's latest job,

and hostages were involved. People's lives were in danger. Walker's hands tightened on the steering wheel. He hoped he could reach the bank in time to help. The voice of the dispatcher on the radio under the pickup's dashboard told him that the robbers were still holed up inside the bank.

When he reached downtown Fort Worth, he found that Weatherford Street was blocked off. A couple of the cops posted there recognized his truck and pulled one of the sawhorse barricades aside for him when they saw him coming. Walker sped through with a grim nod of appreciation to the policemen, one of whom yelled after him, "Go get 'em, Ranger!"

Walker wheeled the pickup onto Houston Street and veered to the curb. He saw the police cars blocking the street a couple of blocks ahead, their lights flashing brightly. Beyond them, at the end of the next block, were more patrol cars. In between was the bank building. Walker knew that more police cars would be covering the other side of the bank building, over on Main Street.

As he dropped from the pickup and started running forward along the sidewalk, which had been cleared of all pedestrians, he was reminded of the story he had been telling the kids at the Texas Ranger Hall of Fame. The area that had been known as Hell's Half Acre had been at the other end of downtown, where the Tarrant County Convention Center and the Water Gardens were now. But this part of Fort Worth had been pretty rugged in those days, too. Instead of high-rise hotels and financial centers, saloons and gambling dens had lined these streets.

But times changed, and so did outlaws. Now they carried automatic weapons and wore body armor and used high-tech armament more suited to an antiterrorist squad. Sometimes, progress wasn't such a good thing.

Walker spotted Trivette crouching behind one of the patrol cars with a high-ranking officer from the Fort Worth Police Department beside him. Bending low, Walker hurried over to join them. "Any movement?" he asked.

"Walker!" exclaimed Trivette. "I'm glad you're here. No, they're still in there."

"Has anybody talked to them?"

"We've had one of our hostage negotiators on the phone," said the captain from the FWPD. He shook his head. "No dice. They won't even pick up the receiver on their end."

"Casualties in the bank?"

Trivette shook his head. "We don't know, Walker. We don't know anything except that all hell broke loose in there about an hour ago. There were gunshots reported, and when the first patrol units arrived less than a minute later, they encountered heavy fire from inside the bank."

"Our fast response bottled them up in there," said the police captain. His face was grim. "We were lucky we had units so close. But it got one of my men killed, too. They cut him down before he could get behind his vehicle."

Walker's jaw tightened. Like all law-enforcement officers, he hated it when any innocent person got hurt. But in the close-knit community of men and women who wore the badge, it was even worse when a cop went down.

He tilted his head back and squinted up at the top of the bank building, glad that the brim of his Stetson shaded his eyes. "Any way in up there?"

"We've discussed lowering men to the roof from a helicopter. They'd be sitting ducks if they rode down to the lobby in the elevators, though."

"How many stairwells in the building?"

"Four."

Trivette said, "If there's half a dozen of them, as usual, they could cover all the stairs."

"But it would only leave a couple to watch the hostages," Walker pointed out. "I don't think they'd do that." He looked at the police captain. "You've got a chopper standing by?"

The officer nodded. "At our helipad across the river."

"Come on, Trivette," Walker said. "We're going for a helicopter ride—"

Before he could finish, a startled shout came from one of the other policemen kneeling behind the cars parked in the street. "What's that?"

Walker heard a popping sound coming from several blocks

behind them. Trivette said excitedly, "That's gunfire!"

The little radio attached to the police captain's shoulder crackled. "Shots fired at barricades on Belknap," came the dispatcher's voice. Though she was trained not to show emotion in her calls, a little strain crept into her voice. "Vehicle identified as an armored truck has broken through the barricades and is proceeding west on Belknap."

"Not any more," Walker muttered as he turned and looked over his shoulder, staring back down Houston Street toward Belknap. The armored car that had broken through the police barricades had just careened through a tight turn and was now on Houston. Its engine roared with power as the driver stomped down on the accelerator and sent the armored vehicle racing forward. . . .

Straight toward the patrol cars blocking the street, with Walker, Trivette, and the police captain crouched behind them.

FOUR

Walker grabbed the .45-caliber Sig P-220 semiautomatic pistol clipped to his belt and dropped to one knee as he opened fire on the speeding armored truck. Beside him, Trivette and the police captain started shooting, too, as did the officers kneeling beside the other patrol units blocking the street.

Unfortunately, none of the lawmen were firing armor-piercing rounds. The bullets either bounced off the onrushing truck's grille or chipped small stars in the thick bulletproof glass of the windshield. Given enough time, Walker knew they could bust through that glass, even with small-arms fire.

But time was something they didn't have much of, because the truck had already covered a couple of blocks and was less than a block away from them now, still bearing down on them.

"Get ready to jump!" yelled Trivette.

"No," snapped Walker as his hand shot out to grab his partner's arm, pulling Trivette back as the younger Ranger started to fling himself toward the sidewalk.

The wheels of Walker's brain were turning at top speed. He knew the driver of the armored truck had to be connected with the gang of robbers holed up inside the bank. This was probably a desperate, last-ditch attempt to rescue them. That armored truck would withstand the fire of the police, but it wasn't heavy enough or powerful enough to knock aside the patrol units parked in the street, not without risking engine damage that could disable it. So the driver had to have something else in mind.

The sidewalk was wide in front of the bank and dotted with small live-oak trees planted in decorative wooden pots. At the last second, just as Walker thought he would, the driver of the armored truck wrenched the wheel to the left and took to the sidewalk. Walker snapped off a couple of shots at the vehicle's tires as it roared past, but he knew the tires were the type that were practically impossible to puncture. The truck slammed into the live oaks, exploding the planters in a shower of wood and potting soil, sweeping the obstacles aside. A hail of police gunfire still raked the truck as it skidded to a stop in front of the bank entrance, but none of the shots were effective.

Walker leaped to his feet and ran toward the armored truck with Trivette right behind him. The police captain yelled, "Cease fire! Cease fire!" as the Rangers charged forward. Walker veered toward the wall of the bank building, hoping to get an angle where he could see the door of the bank. The armored truck had it blocked from view.

That was so the members of the gang inside the building could dash out and climb into the truck, Walker knew. As he reached the outside wall of the building, he could see between the truck and the entrance and spotted a couple of armor-clad figures clambering into the vehicle.

One of the robbers saw Walker, too, and swung the automatic rifle in his hands toward the Ranger. Flame geysered from the muzzle as he fired a burst. The bullets chiseled chips of granite from the building wall as Walker flung himself down and squeezed off a couple of shots of his own.

He saw the robber jerk slightly as the bullets thudded into his chest, but the man kept moving. The slugs hadn't penetrated his body armor, but he'd probably have a couple of painful bruises underneath it. That knowledge was little comfort to Walker. He and Trivette scrambled for cover behind some of the larger pieces of debris from the destroyed planters and threw a few more ineffective shots toward the truck and the men climbing into it. Then the truck's motor roared again as it leaped away from the bank entrance and headed down the sidewalk.

Up ahead, one of the cops was trying to pull his cruiser up onto the sidewalk to block the truck, but he wasn't fast enough. The truck's right front fender crashed into the front of the police car. Sparks flew and metal screamed as the truck squeezed through the gap between the police car and the wall of the building, scraping on both sides. Then it popped free like a watermelon seed and bounced down off the curb into the street again. The driver floored the gas pedal.

Walker and Trivette stood up as the armored truck headed down Houston Street at breakneck speed. Several officers leaped into their patrol cars to pursue it. The truck turned a corner and disappeared.

The captain was shouting orders into his radio as he hurried over to Walker and Trivette. "We'll get 'em," he told the Rangers. "We've got a cordon all around downtown."

"That armored truck's going to be hard to stop," Trivette said grimly.

"We'll stop it," the captain promised.

Walker wasn't so sure. Those thieves were a determined bunch.

In the meantime, there had been hostages in the bank, and Walker wanted to make sure they were all right. He hadn't seen any civilians being taken from the bank and put into the armored truck, but he supposed it was possible the robbers had taken one or more hostages with them. He kept his pistol ready and headed toward the bank entrance.

The glass in the doors was pocked with bullet holes. Walker jerked one of the doors open and went in quickly, just in case one or more of the thieves had been left behind for some reason.

The lobby of the bank was chaos. Light fixtures had been shot out, leaving broken glass lying on the floor. There were approximately twenty people in the lobby, all of them frightened out of their wits. There were casualties, too: Walker spotted a couple of men in gray-and-tan uniforms lying motionless in pools of blood. On the other side of the room, in front of the marble counter where the tellers' windows were located, a woman was sprawled on her back, the middle of her blouse dark with blood.

Shouting questions and begging for help, the terrified former hostages surrounded Walker and Trivette. Trivette tried to calm them down as best he could, while Walker knelt to check on the wounded guards. He couldn't find a pulse in either man. They were both dead.

Walker stood up and strode across the lobby, glass from the broken light fixtures crunching under his booted feet. He went to a kneel beside the woman. She was about thirty, he saw, and would have been quite attractive in a suburban-housewife sort of way had her features not been set in a rictus of agony. Her eyes were open and staring sightlessly at the ceiling. Knowing it was futile, Walker rested a couple of fingers against her throat, searching for the tiny flutter of life that would tell him her heart was still beating.

Nothing. She was dead, too.

Gently, Walker closed her eyes and then stood up. Trivette came up beside him and said, "Gone?"

Walker nodded.

"Damn," Trivette said softly.

"That's four," said Walker. "The cop outside, two guards, and the woman in here."

"Their record of never killing anybody didn't last very long, did it?"

Emergency personnel had swarmed into the bank lobby by this time. Paramedics quickly checked the bodies of the people who had been killed, then moved on to the ones they could still help, the hostages who had cuts from flying glass and the ones who were having hysterical reactions now that the danger was over. Uniformed cops secured the lobby as others began a systematic search of the building, including the upper floors. If anything had been left behind that might help to trace the robbers, the police wanted to find it.

The captain made his way through the confusion toward Walker and Trivette. The Rangers could tell from his expression that he didn't have good news. As the captain came up to them Trivette said, "Don't tell me they got away."

"They managed to get on I-30 and headed west. We were still right behind them when they got off at University. Traffic was heavy, but that didn't slow them down any. They just ran everybody who got in their way off the road. We had wrecks all over the place, and that slowed my men down."

"They got away," Trivette said heavily.

"We lost them somewhere down around the zoo," the captain admitted. "Hell, we couldn't go in there with guns blazing, anyway. There were kids all over the place. . . ."

"Get roadblocks up and search every vehicle leaving that area," said Walker. "They'll steal a car and switch over from that armored truck as soon as possible."

"They may have even had another vehicle waiting for them," added Trivette. "Any word on where that armored truck came from?"

The captain nodded. "It was stolen off the street about forty-five minutes ago. The two-man crew was picking up receipts from a discount store on the north side when somebody jumped them and gunned them down. They were both killed."

Walker and Trivette exchanged a glance. "Six," Walker said.

The captain knew what he meant. "That's right. I figure the gang's driver was outside in a stolen van when he heard shots inside the bank. He took off right away, before any of our units arrived, and went looking for something he could use to bust the rest of the bunch out. He probably had an armored truck in mind from the get-go."

Walker nodded. The way the captain laid it out made sense. "They had it all worked out as a backup plan," he said. "They had all the contingencies figured."

"That ties in with what you thought about them having some sort of military background, Walker," said Trivette.

"In the meantime, they're gone, six innocent people are dead, and we're no closer to them than we were before."

"We'll get them, Walker," Trivette said.

Walker looked around at the carnage in the bank lobby. "Yeah," he said, his jaw tight. "We will."

• • •

Kyle Forrest's hands were slick with sweat on the steering wheel of the car as he drove along Lancaster Avenue in the shadow of the elevated freeway that cut across the southern end of downtown Fort Worth. He clamped his fingers tighter on the wheel as he made a right, dipped down below a railroad overpass, and came up into an industrial area. He turned right again, into a narrow alley that ran alongside a massive warehouse that stood the equivalent of three stories tall and occupied an entire block. He followed the alley to a small rear entrance. Three other cars were parked there. Kyle was the last one to arrive.

That was all right, he told himself. The extra time had given him a chance to calm down a little. He had to stay under control. Everything could slip away so easily if he let it, everything that he had worked for. . . .

Of course, in a way it was all ruined now anyway. All he could do was make the best of a bad situation.

Kyle parked the car and got out. He was in his early thirties, a little over medium height, with short, sleek dark hair and the sort of open, honest face that made people like him almost immediately. He was wearing jeans and a lightweight jacket over a knit shirt. He went to the steel door and used a key to unlock it, then stepped inside the warehouse and pulled the door shut behind him.

It was a lot darker inside than out, and Kyle had to pause for a moment to let his eyes adjust. But then he began to make out the looming shapes that filled the warehouse. False-fronted buildings that were almost full size had been erected inside the high-ceilinged warehouse. Dirt had been spread on the concrete floor and packed down to create the illusion of a street running between the rows of buildings. There was even a cross street, with a few buildings on either side of it. The buildings were fronted by plank boardwalks, and hitch racks made of peeled wooden poles bordered the boardwalks. Wooden water troughs sat every twenty feet or so on alternating sides of the street. Signs were painted on the false fronts of the buildings: SALOON, BLACKSMITH, APOTHECARY, GENERAL STORE, BARBERSHOP AND GENERAL DENTISTRY, MIL-

LINERY, LIVERY STABLE, GUNSMITH, SADDLE SHOP. . . .

More than anything else, the interior of the warehouse resembled a Hollywood soundstage where a low-budget Western TV series might have been filmed. Nick Adams as Johnny Yuma might have once strode along these boardwalks, or Don Durant as Johnny Ringo, or Clayton Moore as the Lone Ranger. That was exactly the look Kyle Forrest had been after when he designed this place. He even had a name for it: North Fork, after the town where Chuck Connors as Lucas McCain, the Rifleman, had lived.

Every time Kyle walked through the streets of *his* North Fork, he felt as if he had come home at last. Not that he had grown up watching those TV shows when they were new; that had been a little before his time. But thanks to the miracle of reruns and local independent TV stations, he had spent hours and hours as a kid sitting cross-legged in front of his parents' twenty-five-inch Zenith, living vicariously in the Old West. That had led him to the movies, especially that wonderful magnum opus written by William Goldman and directed by George Roy Hill and starring Paul Newman and Robert Redford, and that had taken him in turn to the myriad books written about the real thing, the bold band of friends who rode outside the law, but not too far outside.

He remembered being bitterly disappointed when he rented the videotape of that other film, the one by Sam Peckinpaugh. It was too bloody, and it wasn't about the real Wild Bunch at all. He'd had to watch *Ride the High Country*, starring Randolph Scott and Joel McCrea, a couple of times after that just to get the bad taste out of his mouth.

Kyle paused and took a deep breath. They were waiting for him up ahead, rendezvousing here according to plan after they had split up at the zoo, five of them sitting on ladder-back chairs on the front porch of North Fork's only hotel, Mitch leaning on the hitch rack beside the porch.

Mitch was grinning. *Grinning*. As if everything was all right.

Kyle almost lost it then. Anger welled up inside him. He wanted to grab Mitch Graham by the neck and wipe that smirk off his face. Mitch must have seen that on Kyle's face, because he straightened from his casual pose and tensed his muscles, ready to move in case of trouble.

Kyle stopped in front of his second-in-command and took a deep breath, reining in his anger. In a voice that he kept deliberately flat, he asked, "What the hell happened back there in the bank, Mitch? Why'd you start shooting?"

Mitch was a little shorter and stockier than Kyle, with pale hair that grew in tight curls against his head. He looked at Kyle defiantly and said, "You saw what happened. That guard pulled his gun. I didn't have any choice but to shoot." Mitch hesitated, then added, "Unless you'd have rather I let him gun you down."

"You were ten feet away from him," snapped Kyle. "Buddy was within arm's reach. He could have knocked the guard out."

One of the men sitting on the porch spoke up. "I didn't see the guy in time, Kyle. He might've gotten a shot off before I could have put him down. Then we would've still been screwed."

Kyle was still looking at Mitch. "But then you shot the other guard, too."

"Once he saw his pal was hit, he couldn't just stand there," Mitch said with a shrug. "He went for his gun, too."

Kyle hadn't seen the second guard make any move toward his pistol. He knew perfectly well what had happened.

Once Mitch had started squeezing the trigger, he hadn't wanted to stop.

"And the woman?" Kyle asked tightly.

Another shrug from Mitch. "She was in the ol' wrong place at the wrong time, pard."

Mitch's derisive tone was more than Kyle could stand. Without thinking about what he was doing, he launched himself forward, his hands going around Mitch's neck. "Butch never killed anybody, not once!" he yelled as the force of his charge drove Mitch back against the hitch rack. Mitch was bent backward over the wooden railing.

The other five men exploded out of their chairs and leaped down off the boardwalk to stop the fight. A couple of them grabbed Kyle's arms and pulled him free from Mitch's throat.

They dragged him back into the middle of the dirt street. The others got between the two men so that Mitch couldn't go after Kyle.

Trembling with rage as his friends held him back, Kyle shouted, "I told you how it was supposed to be! I told you all! No killing! We're supposed to outsmart the law, not outgun them. Just like Butch and Sundance and the Wild Bunch!"

Mitch rubbed his bruised throat with one hand and pointed at Kyle with the other. "You're out of your freakin' mind," he said. "No matter how you made this place look, this isn't the Old West, and you're not Butch Cassidy!"

"You didn't have to kill those people!"

"We're bank robbers, Kyle. It's a violent business." Mitch glowered at his friend, the man who had put this gang together. "Hell, we're lucky we're not all dead ourselves. Those cops tried hard enough to kill us. If Fulton hadn't come up with that armored truck, we'd still be trapped in that bank."

"It was Kyle's idea," pointed out one of the other men. "He said if we ever got in a bad spot, to look for something like that."

"Like that armored stagecoach in *The War Wagon*," said Kyle. "It worked, too." Since he seemed to be calming down again, the men who had been holding his arms let go of them. Kyle straightened his jacket and glared at Mitch, but he didn't make any move toward him.

"All right," said Mitch, making a slashing gesture with his hand. "It's over. We're all still alive, and we got the money. Next time things will go better."

Kyle jerked his head in a grudging nod. "Yeah. Next time." He rubbed a hand over his close-cropped hair. "I'm going up to the office to think." He turned and walked toward the front of the building.

As Kyle walked away Mitch reached over onto the boardwalk and picked up a peculiar-looking weapon with a fat barrel. It was air-powered, because he pumped it, then pointed it toward Kyle's retreating back. "Bam," he said softly. "You're dead."

Buddy put a hand on the barrel of the gun and pushed it down. "Don't kid around like that, man, not even with a paintball gun."

"One of these days . . ." Mitch began.

Buddy shook his head firmly, and the rest of the men looked like they agreed with him. "Kyle's the boss, even if he does have that bug up his ass about being like Butch Cassidy."

"He doesn't want to be *like* Butch Cassidy," muttered Mitch. "He's starting to think he *is* Butch." He looked around at the other men. "But this is the 1990s, not the *1890s*. I plan on becoming a rich man—and if anybody who gets in my way winds up dead, that's just too bad. . . ."

FIVE

Fort Worth, 1901

Hayes Cooper leaned back in his chair and studied the cards in his hand. Yance Shelby had dealt him a pair of eights and a pair of fives, a pretty good hand in itself. And he still had the draw to try to fill the full house.

He would need that third eight or five if he was going to recoup any of what he had lost so far tonight. He was down about forty dollars, a month's wages for a cowhand in the old days. He wasn't the only loser. Harry Long had lost about the same amount as Cooper, and Parker had dropped over two hundred. The losses didn't seem to bother Parker. He was still grinning as big as ever, talking garrulously, and evidently enjoying himself hugely.

The big winner was not Yance Shelby, as might have been expected from a professional gambler, although Shelby was slightly ahead for the evening. The largest pile of chips and coins and greenbacks was in front of Tess Malone. Just as Shelby had indicated, she was a good cardplayer. At some time in the past, probably before she owned the Golden Garter, she had likely made her living with a deck of pasteboards in her hands.

"Cards, gentlemen?" asked Shelby. "And lady?"

Harry Long was to his left. "Two," he said as he tossed a pair of cards onto the discard. Parker was next, and he took three, wiggling his eyebrows dramatically as he looked at each of them.

Cooper slid his discard, the deuce of hearts, onto the table. "I'll take one," he announced.

"Obviously a good hand," Shelby said as he gave Cooper a single card.

Cooper picked it up. Eight of clubs. He had his full house. Maybe that meant his luck was changing.

He hoped so. He had been playing for almost an hour, waiting for an opportunity to bring up Doyle Parnell. Waiting, as well, on the off chance that Parnell might just come moseying down from those upstairs rooms. So far, that hadn't happened, and Cooper was growing impatient.

Something else was bothering him, too. The more he looked at Parker and Long and thought about them, the more he felt as if he ought to recognize them.

"I'll take two cards," Tess Malone said quietly.

Shelby dealt her the cards, then said, "And the dealer takes two, as well."

The betting went around the table a couple of times, the pot in the middle growing to a goodly size. Long folded, and Parker raised ten dollars. He seemed to have plenty of money, and he wagered like he wasn't worried about where his next meal was coming from.

Cooper saw Parker's ten, and so did Tess. Shelby threw in his cards and shook his head ruefully. "Never throw good money after bad, that's my rule," he said.

"There's no such thing as bad money, my friend," said Parker. "It all spends just fine."

"I don't know about that," said Cooper.

Parker laughed. "Don't tell me you believe those old sayings about money being the root of all evil."

"The Good Book says that 'love of money' is the root of all evil."

"Well, I certainly do love money," said Parker, "so I guess that means I'm a bad fella." He pushed another stack of gold pieces forward into the center of the table. "So bad that I'm going to raise you another twenty, Mr. No-Other-Name Cooper."

Cooper didn't have twenty more dollars to spare. If he saw the bet and lost, that would clean him out. But he didn't like the way Parker's eyes shone with the anticipation of him folding, so he reached into his pocket and brought out the last of his coins. "I'll see your bet," he said as he laid them on the table.

"And so will I," said Tess. "Call, Mr. No-Other-Name Parker."

Parker placed his cards faceup on the green felt in front of him. "Two pair, jacks and treys."

"Not good enough," said Cooper as he showed his own cards. "Full house."

"Sorry," said Tess. "I have a flush, gentlemen."

"The lady wins again," Shelby murmured with a smile.

Cooper shook his head. "That does it for me," he said, not minding the loss so much now that he had seen how to put it to good use. "I'm going to have to go hunt up my partner and borrow some money just to get a hotel room, or I'll be sleeping in a livery stable tonight."

"Where's this partner of yours?" asked Shelby as he gathered up the cards and gave them to Tess to shuffle. He had played into Cooper's hands by asking the question, whether he knew it or not.

"I don't know," Cooper said as he looked around the room. "I figured I'd run into him here tonight. All he's been talking about lately is paying a visit to the Golden Garter when we met up in Fort Worth." He looked innocently at Tess. "Maybe you saw him earlier tonight. Tall, lanky gent with curly brown hair. Laughs and grins a lot, he's the friendly sort."

"His name's not Parnell, is it?" asked Tess.

Cooper was careful not to show the surprise he felt. "That's right," he said.

"He was in here earlier tonight, but he wasn't so friendly. In fact, he got pretty rambunctious when one of my bartenders told him to leave. I thought we were going to have to throw him out."

Cooper let his eyebrows lift in puzzlement. "What happened?"

"He was under the impression that the Golden Garter was still being run by the previous owner. I only bought the place last year," Tess explained. "It seems that some of the girls who used to work here were young. Very young."

"And that's what Parnell wanted?" Cooper felt his hands trying to tighten into fists.

"That's right. I won't pretend that I'm some kind of saint, but there are some things I won't allow in this place and that's one of them."

Long said, "Sounds like your friend Parnell's a pretty low-down character, Cooper."

"I never said he was my friend, just a business associate." Cooper didn't bother trying to hide the disgust in his voice as he went on, "Maybe it's time I stopped doing business with him. I want to collect the money he owes me first, though. Did he say where he was going when he left here?"

"There's a place over on Rusk Street," said Tess. "Harrigan's. He might have been able to find what he was looking for over there." She made a face. "I don't know for sure, and I don't want to know."

Cooper started to shove back his chair. "Maybe I'd better go try to look him up—"

A hand came down heavily on his right shoulder. "Don't get in such a doggone hurry, friend," said a hard voice.

Cooper turned his head, fighting down the instincts that would have had him leaping up and spinning around to confront this new threat, if indeed it was a threat. He saw an older man standing behind him and to the right. The man's left hand still rested on Cooper's shoulder. The thumb of the man's right hand was hooked in the vest that he wore under a brown tweed suit. A watch chain was looped from one breast pocket of his coat to the other, and Cooper would have been willing to bet that there was a derringer attached to one end of that chain. It was an old trick.

But then, J. P. McCormick was an old dog.

Cooper's eyes met McCormick's, and for a couple of seconds, neither man said anything. Then McCormick took his thumb out of his vest and extended his right hand to Cooper. "I'm J. P. McCormick," he said, "chief of detectives, Fort Worth Police Department."

Cooper had no choice but to shake McCormick's hand. "Name's Cooper," he said.

Of course, McCormick knew that. He also knew that Cooper was a Texas Ranger. The question remained, was he going to say anything about what he knew?

"Glad to meet you, Mr. Cooper." McCormick kept his left hand on Cooper's shoulder but leaned across the table to offer his right to Long and Parker. "I know Tess and ol' Yance here, but who might you boys be?"

Parker took the police detective's hand. "I'm Parker, and this is my friend Harry Long."

"Well, I'm mighty pleased to meet you both," said McCormick as he shook hands with them. He turned his head to look at Tess and went on, "I hear tell there was a spot of trouble in here earlier tonight."

"It didn't amount to much," Tess told him. "Somebody thought he had a grudge against Mr. Cooper."

McCormick looked down at Cooper with interest. "Did he have a reason for feelin' that way?"

"He thought I skinned him on a deal involving some horses a couple of years ago," said Cooper, knowing that McCormick would probably understand what he meant. "I hadn't seen him since then, though, so I didn't know he was gunning for me."

"Some fellas have a long memory. Didn't have to kill him, did you?"

Parker spoke up. "Nobody got killed. Harry and I just put the fear of God into the galoot and ran him out of here."

"Why'd the two of you take a hand?" McCormick wanted to know.

Long lit a cigar, then said around it, "We're peace-loving types, Detective. Can't stand to have any trouble going on around us."

McCormick nodded. "I see. Well, I heard rumors, thought

I'd better check 'em out. I can see I ain't needed here, though."

"Stay and have a drink, J. P.," Tess said.

"Maybe you'd like to sit in on the game," offered Shelby.

McCormick frowned. "You two are just funnin' me. You know I can't be guzzlin' whiskey and playin' cards while I'm on duty." He closed one eye in a lazy wink. "Reckon I'll just have to come back later, when my shift's over."

Tess laughed and said, "You do that, J. P. You know you're always welcome at the Golden Garter."

McCormick finally took his hand off Cooper's shoulder. He lifted it in a casual wave and turned to head for the door of the saloon. Parker watched him go, then said quietly to Tess, "You're mighty friendly with that old man, considering he totes a badge."

"J. P.'s all right," said Tess. "He knows that my gamblers all run clean games, and he knows that I don't allow anything too unsavory to go on upstairs. As long as no blood gets spilled on the sawdust in here, he pretty much leaves us alone."

"Except when the temperance ladies and the local ministers get in one of their periodic snits," said Shelby. "Then the police have to act like they're cracking down on us for a while. But nothing ever really changes."

Long shook his head. "Maybe not, but I can't see being that friendly with a lawman."

Why not? Cooper wondered. If Parker and Long were cattle buyers, as they claimed to be, why would they care one way or the other about the law?

He put that question aside for the moment and was thankful that McCormick had been quick enough mentally to realize that Cooper probably didn't want his real identity revealed. He and McCormick had known each other for years; McCormick himself had been a Texas Ranger for a while, in his earlier days. McCormick must have seen Cooper sitting there at the table, not wearing his badge and playing poker, and figured that he was working incognito. It had been a good guess on the detective's part.

Tess riffled the cards and said, "Well, gentlemen, shall we resume?"

Cooper shook his head. "I'm out, in more ways than one. I don't have any more money to lose to you, Miss Malone, so I'd better go see if I can find Parnell." He pushed his chair back.

To his surprise, so did Parker and Long. "We'll go with you," said Parker.

"That's not necessary—" Cooper began.

"We insist," said Long. "This can be a rough part of town. What do they call it? Hell's Half Acre?"

"I can take care of myself," Cooper said flatly.

"Sure, we know that," said Parker. "We just thought you might like a little company. Come on, you can't be afraid that we're going to rob you, or anything like that. You said yourself that you don't even have any money."

Cooper stood up and shrugged. "All right, come on, then." It would be better to let them tag along, he decided, than to cause a scene in here. Besides, if he did run into any trouble over at Harrigan's place, his two erstwhile companions had already demonstrated that they knew how to handle themselves.

Both men stood up and tipped their derbies to Tess. "Good evening to you, dear lady," Parker said. "I'm sure we shall return on another occasion."

"You do that," said Tess with a smile. She indicated the pile of winnings in front of her. "I'll play poker with you boys anytime."

Chuckling, Parker and Long fell in alongside Cooper, and the three men strode to the entrance and pushed out through the batwings.

Behind them, near the bar, one of the young women in a spangled dress set her serving tray down on the hardwood and called to the nearest bartender, "I'll be back in a few minutes, Ed."

He gave her a disapproving look and said, "Whatever you're up to, make it quick, Dora."

"I will, I promise." Dora went through a small door at the end of the bar.

On the other side of the door was a short corridor that led into a storage room full of crates of liquor. It was dark back here, but Dora knew the path well enough to thread her way through the crates and reach another door. This one let out into a shadowy alleyway behind the Golden Garter.

Dora made her way along the alley, trying to ignore the things she stepped in, giving her high-buttoned shoes a shake from time to time. When she reached Rusk Street, a block east of Main, she turned south. A couple of men she passed on the street reached out for her, but she shook off their grasping hands and growled curses at them. A few moments later, she reached a two-story brick building and opened a door to reveal a narrow staircase that led steeply up to the second floor. The stairs were lit by a single gas bulb at the top.

Dora hurried up to the landing. Another door let her into a small room that had a bar along one wall with kegs of whiskey and beer behind it. There were no tables here; the room was too small for that. Besides, nobody who came to Harrigan's was interested in sitting down for a drink. They took their liquor at the bar, either coming or going.

Harrigan himself was behind the bar, a bald-headed man with a sweeping mustache and jowls that hung loose beneath his weak chin. He glowered at Dora and said, "What're you doin' here? I ain't hirin' no girls as long in the tooth as you."

"Shut up, old man. I don't have much time. Fella who came over here about an hour ago, is he still here?"

"Lots o' fellers come here . . ."

Dora moved closer to the bar and reached under her short skirt. The yellow glow from the dingy chimney of the room's only lamp reflected on the blade of the knife she held to Harrigan's loose-skinned throat.

"I'll carve those jowls off you like wattles off a turkey, old man," she hissed. "Is he here or not?"

Harrigan turned pale all the way over the top of his bald pate. "R-room Seven," he said. As Dora started to turn away he said, "What's in it for me?"

She threw a glance over her shoulder. "Another few minutes of this miserable existence you call a life."

"You're a fine one to talk," he muttered to himself as she

hurried down the short hall with doors opening off each side. "Saloon girl. Whore."

If Dora heard him, she ignored him. She went to Room Seven and rapped sharply on the thin panel. "Mr. Parnell?" she called. "Mr. Parnell, you in there?"

For a moment there was no response then she heard footsteps on the other side of the door and it was opened a couple of inches. "What?" asked an unfriendly voice. "This better be damned important."

"It's Dora, Mr. Parnell," she said quietly. "From the Golden Garter. You gave me a five-dollar gold piece as you were leaving, told me to run over here and tell you if anybody showed up looking for you."

Now the door was jerked open several more inches, and Doyle Parnell peered out at her. He was wearing jeans but was barefoot and had no shirt on. Behind him on the narrow bed that was the room's only piece of furniture lay a nude, bored-looking girl who was no more than fifteen years old.

"Who was it?" demanded Parnell.

"A fella named Cooper, I heard him say. Medium height, long hair and a beard, buckskin shirt. Hard-looking sort of man."

Parnell grimaced. "Damn! He still over at the Golden Garter?"

Dora shook her head and said, "He's on his way here with a couple of friends of his. I came the back way so it'd be quicker."

Parnell's eyes widened. "On his way here now? Damn it, why'd you waste so much time jabberin'?" He whirled around and lunged for the shirt and boots and hat and gun belt he had left lying on the floor at the foot of the bed. He buckled on the gun belt and jammed his bare feet into the boots, but he was still carrying the shirt and hat in one hand when he used the other to open the window on the far side of the bed.

"Hey!" Dora said as Parnell started to climb out onto the newfangled fire escape. "You promised me more money if I warned you—"

"Jabberin' that way, you're lucky I don't . . ." The rest of

Parnell's words were lost in the clatter of his booted feet on the metal fire escape. Dora stared at the now empty window with her mouth open, her expression a mixture of surprise and anger.

"Ain't that always the way," said the naked girl on the bed. "Men promise you somethin', and then you don't never get it."

SIX

Cooper, Parker, and Long left the Golden Garter and walked east on Twelfth Street toward Rusk. Cooper asked, "Either of you know where this place called Harrigan's is?"

His two companions shook their heads. "Nope," said Long. "Sounds like too much of a place where shady characters hang out."

"Not our kind of establishment," Parker added dryly.

Cooper got the feeling the two of them were poking fun at him. All evening long, in fact, he had felt a growing unease about Parker and Long. He wasn't afraid of them, not by any means. Curious, was more like it. And he was tired of feeling that way, so he said bluntly, "You boys aren't cattle buyers."

Parker chuckled. "Neither are you."

Long said, "We've been mixed up in some deals that involved cattle."

"But we're more partial to banking," Parker went on. "In fact, we're down here in Fort Worth with some friends of ours who do some banking with us from time to time. We're not here on business, though. Reckon you could say it's more of a vacation for us."

Cooper stopped short on the sidewalk. Parker and Long

stopped, too, and looked at him curiously. "Something bothering you, Cooper?" Long asked quietly.

"You seem like a pretty good hombre, Cooper," said Parker. "That's why we're talking to you this way. I pride myself on being able to size up a man, and I reckon you're the sort we can trust."

Good Lord, thought Cooper. Parker . . . Long . . . Suddenly he knew who they really were. He had seen their real names a few times on wanted posters. George Leroy Parker and Harry Longabaugh, better known as . . .

"Where are you boys from?" Cooper asked tightly.

"Oh, up north a ways," Parker replied in a casual voice. "Wyoming, Idaho, Nevada, that's our usual stomping ground."

That clinched it, thought Cooper.

He was standing here on a sidewalk in Hell's Half Acre with Butch Cassidy and the Sundance Kid.

And he was a Texas Ranger.

What the hell was he supposed to do *now*?

Doyle Parnell had left his horses at a livery stable just down the street from Harrigan's, but it took him a while to get there since he had to stay in the back alleys and keep to the shadows. He didn't want to risk running into that damned Ranger.

Parnell hated Hayes Cooper more than he hated any other man in the whole world. Cooper had helped bring him in once, and now, ever since Parnell had busted out of Huntsville, Cooper had been dogging his trail and making his life miserable.

Twice today, Parnell had thought that Cooper was finally done for. First when Cooper had gone off his horse there on that hill overlooking the Trinity River. But he had fallen just a hair too soon, and Parnell, despite his high hopes that Cooper was finally dead, had been cautious enough to whack his spare mount on the rump and send the horse galloping out of the thicket where he had hidden to bushwhack the Ranger.

Sure enough, Cooper had come out of the brush to give chase, and Parnell had opened fire on him again. Then, for the second time in only a few minutes, he had dared to hope that Cooper was mortally wounded. He knew this time that he'd hit the Ranger.

But then Cooper had gotten up and hobbled over the hill, and Parnell had had to settle for hoping the bastard was hit bad enough at least to slow him down. Maybe his leg was even busted.

Parnell had let himself be seduced by that hope, so much so that he had stopped in some jackass of a little town to have himself a good hot meal for a change. Then he had pushed on to Fort Worth, anxious to have a few drinks and a girl and relax a mite before he met up with the fella who had sent for him.

And *that* hadn't worked out, either. The Golden Garter had changed considerably since the last time he'd been in Fort Worth. But it was still Hell's Half Acre down on that end of town, and a gent could buy just about anything he wanted somewhere in the area, if he had the money. Even if he had to go to a filthy dive like Harrigan's.

Parnell was just glad he'd had the foresight to bribe one of the gals at the Golden Garter to keep an eye out for anybody looking for him. Nora, Dora, whatever her name was, she'd earned the coin he'd given her.

But now he knew that Cooper wasn't hurt bad. That blasted Ranger was still after him, and Cooper's presence in Fort Worth threatened to ruin everything. Parnell didn't know exactly what the plan was, but he knew it was something big, something that would finally give him the big payoff he had always been looking for. . . .

Parnell reached the back door of the livery stable. He opened it quietly and slipped inside, hoping he could reclaim his horses without anybody seeing him. It was late, and the hostler was probably sound asleep in the tack room. Parnell went down the wide aisle in the center of the barn. A small lamp hanging on a nail driven into one of the pillars that supported the hayloft provided enough light for him to see by. He found the two stalls, side by side, where his horses were stabled. His saddle and blanket were hanging on the gate of one of the stalls. Parnell lifted them down quietly and opened the gate.

It took him only a few minutes to saddle up the horse. When he was done, he got the spare bridle and bit on the other horse so that he could lead it. He had his foot in the stirrup, but before he could swing up into the saddle, door hinges squeaked behind him and the hostler came out of the tack room, rubbing his eyes sleepily.

"Oh, howdy," he said when he saw Parnell. "Come to get your horses?"

"Anything wrong with that?" Parnell asked tensely.

The hostler yawned widely and shook his head. "Naw, I reckon not. You already paid, so you can have your horses back anytime you want. It's the middle of the night, though. Most folks're asleep now."

"Well, I ain't."

The hostler yawned again and started to turn away. "That's fine. Reckon I'll go back to my cot."

Parnell started to let him go. But then he thought about all the people he had left behind him who must have pointed Cooper on his trail. He thought about how nothing seemed to work out for him anymore, how bad luck dogged him just like that Ranger did. How he'd had to climb out that window at Harrigan's before he was anywhere near finished with that little gal. . . .

Parnell palmed out his Colt and said, "Hey."

The hostler stopped and turned back toward him. "Yeah?" Then his eyes widened and he threw his arms up to try to block the blow as he saw the gun barrel coming at his head.

Parnell hit the young man hard on the left temple with the Colt. The hostler staggered, and Parnell hit him again. Then the hostler fell, and Parnell leaned over him, the gun rising and falling, rising and falling, the blows sounding like someone chopping into a ripe watermelon with a butcher knife.

Parnell wasn't even breathing hard when he finally straightened and went into the tack room to find a rag to wipe the blood off the barrel of his gun. He hoped he hadn't gotten anything in the barrel that would clog it up.

A few minutes later, he opened one of the big front doors of the barn just enough to lead both horses outside. Then he closed the door and mounted the horse he had saddled. Holding the reins of the other horse, he rode around the corner of the stable and into an alley. The street was dark and fairly quiet behind him, although the sounds of merriment could still be heard coming from some of the saloons a few blocks away.

Parnell followed a roundabout route until he reached an area of good-sized houses just west of downtown. The homes here had large lawns dotted with trees and flower beds behind picket fences. Parnell was out of place in a neighborhood like this, and he knew it. But this was where he had been told to come.

He found the street number he was looking for and rode around to the back of the house. A dog started barking somewhere nearby, and Parnell grimaced, wishing that he could put a bullet in the mutt. Shooting off his gun would just attract more attention, though, and that was something he and his new partner didn't want.

He swung down from the saddle and left the horses tied in the shadow of a small barn where the owner of the house undoubtedly kept a fancy buggy. Parnell catfooted his way up to the rear door of the house and knocked three times, waited, then knocked twice more. It was a simple signal, but it was what the owner of the house had told him to do.

A moment later, the door swung open, and a man whispered from the darkness inside, "Parnell?"

"That's right," said Parnell.

"I expected you before now."

"I'm here now," Parnell snapped. "You want to do business or not?"

"Come inside," the man said. "We have a lot to talk about."

"That's fine," said Parnell as he stepped into the house. "As long as it makes me rich."

The unseen man chuckled. "Beyond your wildest dreams, my desperado friend. Beyond your wildest dreams . . ."

"You two are a long way from home, then," Cooper forced himself to say.

"That's the whole point of a vacation, isn't it?" asked

Parker—Butch Cassidy, Cooper reminded himself. He went on, "You want to get away from all the usual places and the usual people, see some new sights, rest and relax for a while."

"Where nobody expects anything of you," added Harry Longabaugh.

Cooper's emotions waged war inside him. These men were two of the West's most notorious outlaws . . . and yet, to Cooper's knowledge, no warrants had ever been issued in Texas for their arrest. They had never committed any crimes in the Lone Star State.

But they had robbed trains and banks in plenty of other places. The railroads wanted them, the Pinkertons wanted them, state lawmen in Wyoming and Idaho and Nevada wanted them. Cooper could arrest them, send a few wires, and within a day or two the Fort Worth authorities would have badge toters from all over clamoring that Butch and Sundance be turned over to them.

And in the meantime, Doyle Parnell, who *had* robbed banks in Texas, who *had* gunned down innocent Texans in cold blood, could be getting away.

There was a time and place for everything, Cooper told himself. Even the Good Book said that, where the fella talked about a season unto every purpose under heaven. Cooper drew a deep breath and said, "Sometimes I think I wouldn't mind a vacation myself. But right now I've got to find that fella Parnell."

"Come on, then," said Butch Cassidy. "Let's go hunt up that place called Harrigan's."

They turned onto Rusk Street, Cooper trying not to think too much about how he had just allied himself with a couple of owlhoots.

They had gone less than a block when they came to a man sitting on the sidewalk with his back against the wall of a building and his legs stuck out in front of him. Soft snores came from him. Cooper kicked the man in the ankle and said, "Hey. Wake up, mister."

The drunk snorted and sputtered and sat up straight. "Wha . . . wha . . ." he managed to say.

"We're looking for Harrigan's. Wake up and tell us where it is."

The drunk scrubbed his hands over his face. "H-Harrigan's?" he said.

"That's right."

"Couple blocks down . . . across the street. Second floor. Wh-white door, flight of stairs behind it."

"Know the place well, do you, friend?" asked Butch.

"Been thrown down them stairs a time or two."

"Obliged," said Cooper. He stepped over the drunk's legs and headed on down Rusk Street.

He was just glad *this* boozer hadn't mistaken him for Buffalo Bill Cody.

There were several buildings along the street with doors that led to staircases. After Cooper, Cassidy, and Longabaugh had gone a couple of blocks, Cooper tried the first such door on the other side of the street. If this wasn't the right place, he and his companions could keep looking.

At the top of the stairs was another door. Cooper opened it and stepped through into a small room with a bar to the left. A bald-headed old man was behind the bar, and coming out of a corridor on the other side of the room was a young woman in a short, low-cut, spangled dress. Cooper had a good memory for faces, and he recognized her immediately. He didn't know her name, but he knew the last place he'd seen her was the Golden Garter.

She stopped short, eyes going wide at the sight of him, and said, "Oh!" Clearly, she had recognized him, too.

Cooper knew what that meant.

Without hesitating, he sprang across the room and grabbed the woman by the shoulders. "What room?" he grated.

For an instant, he thought she wasn't going to tell him, but then her eyes flashed with anger and she said, "Seven."

Cooper pushed her aside, trying not to be too rough about it, and started down the hall. Behind him, the old man said querulously, "Hey!" He reached under the bar.

Cassidy and Longabaugh both had their guns out in less than the blink of an eye. "Better not be reaching for a greener, old-timer," warned Cassidy.

The old man backed against the kegs of liquor behind the bar, hands lifted so that Cassidy and Longabaugh could see they were empty. "Good," grunted Longabaugh. "Keep 'em that way."

Then he and Cassidy pushed past the young woman and went after Cooper.

The door to Room Seven was open. Cooper stepped out of it, a disgusted look on his face. He pulled the door shut behind him to give the young prostitute some privacy as she pulled a cotton shift over her tangled blond hair. Cooper shook his head at Cassidy and Longabaugh. "Parnell's gone," he said. "He could be anywhere out there in that rat's nest."

Cassidy shrugged and tucked his gun away. "Tough luck, Cooper. What are you going to do now?"

Cooper caught a glimpse of movement from the barroom and strode quickly along the hall. He reached the landing at the top of the stairs in time to close his left hand around the upper arm of the young woman who worked in the Golden Garter. She gasped and tried to pull away, but Cooper's grip was firm without being brutal.

"How much did he pay you?" he asked.

She looked up at him defiantly. "A dollar."

He thought of the way she had told him so quickly which room Parnell had been in. "Doesn't buy much loyalty, does it?"

"He promised me five if somebody came looking for him and I warned him," she shot back. "And then he just ran out and didn't pay me a dime."

"You put your trust in the wrong kind of man."

She laughed humorlessly and pushed the fingers of her free hand through her thick brunette hair. "Tell me something I don't know, mister." She looked down pointedly at his hand on her arm. "You hold on to me much longer and you're going to have to cough up some dough yourself."

Cooper let go of her but didn't step back. He still crowded her on the small landing. "Did Parnell say where he was going when he left here?"

"He was in too much of a hurry to say much of anything.

I'd help you if I could, mister, honest. I don't owe that son of a bitch anything now."

Cooper hesitated, gauging the look in her eyes, then nodded. "Go on back to the Golden Garter," he told her. "But if you see Parnell around anywhere, let me know."

"Why should I?"

"Because I asked nicely . . . this time."

After a couple of seconds, she shrugged. "Like I said, I don't owe Parnell anything. Where'll you be?"

"Right behind you," Cooper told her, "when you least expect it."

She looked at him out of the corner of her eye, then turned and went quickly down the narrow staircase.

"Well," Butch Cassidy said jovially from behind Cooper, "what are you going to do now?"

Cooper looked back at the two outlaws. That was a mighty good question.

SEVEN

Trivette looked up from his computer screen and said, "I may have a lead."

Walker was seated nearby at his desk in Ranger headquarters, going over some of the paperwork on another case. Crime never took a holiday, and when a lawman ran into a dead end on one case, there was always another—or a dozen more—demanding his attention.

But the killers who had committed those bank robberies and been responsible for the deaths of six innocent people were never out of Walker's thoughts for very long. Nor had he forgotten his vow to bring those men to justice, although over a week had passed since the last robbery, the one that had turned so violent and tragic.

Walker stood up quickly and moved to stand beside Trivette's desk. "What've you got?" he asked.

"Nothing on the members of the gang themselves," said Trivette, "but I've been digging through all the information I can find about illicit high-tech weaponry. You can't go into just any gun store and buy unmodified automatic rifles and flash-bang grenades, not to mention all that body armor."

Walker nodded, resting one hand on the desk and one on

the back of Trivette's chair as he leaned over to get a better look at the computer monitor.

Trivette tapped the mug shot he had pulled up on the screen. "This is Frank Kilbride. He was released from Huntsville six months ago after doing seven years of a ten-to-fifteen for trafficking in illegal weapons."

Walker nodded as he looked at the photos of a balding, middle-aged man with a thick mustache and prominent nose. He said, "I remember him. I arrested him once."

Trivette grinned and turned his head to look up at his partner. "Are there any criminals in North Texas you *haven't* arrested at one time or another?"

"Way too many," Walker said with an answering grin. "What do you have on Kilbride?"

"Like I said, he was released from prison six months ago, made his first two meetings with his parole officer, then dropped out of sight."

"So he's wanted again."

"Yeah, but you know as well as I do how many parole violators are out there, Walker. As long as it's not a high-profile case, it may take months before anybody gets around to seriously looking for this guy. Unless he gets picked up for some other crime, or stopped for speeding or something like that, so that he's run through the computer, he can roam around for a while without having to worry too much."

Walker nodded. Trivette was right; the system was overloaded, and felons such as Frank Kilbride sometimes fell through the cracks. All too often, in fact. "But you've gone looking for him."

Trivette nodded. "I figured he might be able to tell us where the gang got their armament—if Kilbride didn't sell it to them himself."

"How do you know he's back in that line of work?"

"I don't, but it's all Kilbride's done for the past twenty years. And he wouldn't have broken his parole if he was staying on the straight and narrow."

Walker indicated the computer screen. "So, did you find him?"

"No. But I found his sister. And here's the interesting

thing, Walker. Three months ago, she rented a warehouse on Hemphill. Paid cash for the deposit and six months' rent. She works as a cocktail waitress.''

Walker straightened and reached for his hat. ''Let's go see Alex.''

It took almost an hour for the two Rangers to pay a visit to the office of Assistant District Attorney Alex Cahill and then wait while she found a judge to sign the search warrant she had drawn up. But then she handed the folded document to Walker and said, ''I hope you find what you're looking for.''

''So do I,'' Walker agreed.

With Trivette beside him, Walker drove his pickup down Hemphill Avenue, out past Seminary Drive almost to Interstate 20. The Federal Archives were located in this area, row after row after row of red-brick buildings that housed government paperwork dating back decades. There were also a lot of fast-food joints, used-car lots, pawnshops, consignment stores, and older residences, some of them run-down, many fixed up neatly despite their age. Walker had the address of the warehouse that had been rented by Frank Kilbride's sister, and he found it to be a large stucco building, once painted beige but now wearing a coat of grime that had turned it gray. The warehouse took up half a block; the rest of the block was a weed-grown vacant lot. Several cars and a rusty old van were parked on the lot next to the loading dock that ran along the side of the building.

''Think we should have brought along some backup?'' asked Trivette as Walker parked next to the curb.

''Hard to justify when this could be a totally legitimate operation,'' said Walker.

Trivette looked doubtful. ''Where would Kilbride's sister get that much money in cash working as a cocktail waitress?''

''Big tippers?'' Walker asked with a tight smile.

Then his expression became all business as he stepped out of the pickup and started toward the warehouse.

Half a dozen concrete steps bordered by a railing made of metal pipe led up to a small concrete landing in front of an office door. Walker and Trivette walked openly up the steps.

Walker tried the doorknob and found it unlocked. He exchanged a glance with Trivette, then stepped into a windowless room. Inside was a gray metal desk, a swivel chair with upholstery that sported several duct-tape patches, a file cabinet, and a fluorescent light fixture that was buzzing from a faulty ballast about to go out. A man with salt-and-pepper hair pulled back into a ponytail held with a rubber band was sitting at the desk poking at a computer keyboard. He wore a T-shirt with the Texas Rangers logo emblazoned on it—the American League baseball team, not the law-enforcement agency. He looked up at Walker and Trivette with a friendly smile and said, "Hey, guys, what can I do for you?"

"We're looking for Frank Kilbride," said Walker.

The man shook his head and tapped a few more keys. "Sorry, I don't think I know him. Is he supposed to work here?"

"His sister rented this warehouse three months ago," said Trivette.

"You mean Maggie Blanchard?" the man asked.

"That's right."

"She's our landlady. She's subletting to my buddies and me."

"What sort of business do you have here?" asked Walker.

"Wholesale plumbing supplies."

"You don't have a sign on the building," Trivette pointed out.

The man shrugged. "We get good word of mouth." He started to look a little impatient. "Look, I can tell you gentlemen are the authorities, so I've been cooperating. But if you're looking for Frank Kilbride, you're out of luck. I told you, I don't know him, and he's certainly not here."

Walker placed the search warrant on the desk. "This says we can take a look around."

"Right now?" The man sounded aggrieved as he tapped a few more keys on the computer. "I've got all these invoices to get out—"

"Walker, he just typed *cops*!" Trivette exclaimed. "He's on a network with another computer in the building!"

Walker didn't wait any longer. He spun toward the door

leading into the rest of the warehouse and kicked it open.

At the same time, the ponytailed man lunged for something under the desk. Trivette didn't give him a chance to reach whatever it was, most likely a gun. He shoved the computer and monitor off the desk, right into the man's lap. The monitor popped and sizzled as it toppled off onto the floor and the screen shattered. Trivette leaned across the desk and threw a hard right fist into the man's face that sent him and the swivel chair slamming against the wall behind him. Trivette grabbed the man's shirt and hauled him out of the chair, spinning him across the room well out of reach of whatever weapon was hidden under the desk.

Meanwhile, Walker went into the warehouse in a crouch, his .45 already in his hand. His keen eyes darted to the left and then the right as he took in the scene before him. The interior of the warehouse was longer than it was wide, high-ceilinged, with dirty windows running down each wall just under the roof. Those windows let in enough light for Walker to see the stacks of wooden crates that filled at least half the warehouse.

He saw, too, the man who came out from behind a stack of those crates firing an Uzi at him.

Walker flung himself to the side behind some more crates as the bullets stitched across the floor toward him. He was reluctant to return the man's fire. For one thing, there was no telling what sort of explosives might be in here, and for another he wanted Frank Kilbride alive. In the brief glimpse he'd had of the gunman, he had recognized Kilbride.

"Texas Rangers!" he shouted, his voice echoing in the warehouse. "You're under arrest, Kilbride!"

The arms dealer's only response was another chattering burst of automatic fire. Walker crouched low behind the crates, hoping that Trivette would stay in the office and call for some backup.

A rush of footsteps made Walker turn to his right. A stocky man was charging toward him from the shadows near the wall of the warehouse. The man had a wickedly sharp metal hook in his hand, the sort used to catch hold of crates as they were being unloaded, and he slashed viciously at Walker with it.

Walker dropped back to avoid the hook and caught himself on his left hand. At the same time, he kicked out with his right leg and buried the heel of his boot in the attacker's soft belly. The man gasped and doubled over. Walker swept his feet out from under him with a leg thrust.

The hook went spinning away as the man toppled. He wasn't the only one attacking Walker, though. With a yell, another man came at him from the other side, swinging a crowbar. Walker rolled aside as the crowbar came sweeping down. The bar slammed into the concrete floor with a loud clang, and the man wielding it yelled in pain as the impact shivered back up both his arms.

Walker came surging to his feet and used the edge of his left hand to chop at the second man's neck. The man staggered and dropped the crowbar. Walker hit him again, this time with a closed fist that jerked the man's head sharply to the side. He folded up, stunned.

"Look out, Walker!" Trivette shouted from the doorway. He crouched there and snapped off two shots.

Walker ducked as another blast from the Uzi hammered chips of stucco from the wall where his head had been a second earlier. Kilbride had managed to dart closer and get the burst off before Trivette's shots drove him back behind another stack of crates.

"Trivette!" Walker called. When his partner glanced at him, Walker made a slashing motion with his hand that Trivette knew meant to stop firing. Walker had a plan of his own, and Kilbride had just placed himself in a perfect position for Walker to put it into action.

Walker put his gun back in its belt clip and leaped up onto one of the crates. Another leap took him to a higher crate, and then he launched himself into space feet first, aiming straight for the tall stack of crates behind which Kilbride was hiding. He hit the top two crates, one with each foot, and sent them sliding off the stack. Kilbride let out a scream as the heavy wooden boxes toppled and fell right on top of him.

Walker dropped back to the concrete floor, landing lightly on his hands and feet. He straightened as Trivette came rushing into the warehouse, tracking right and left with the pistol in his hand in case there were any more enemies lying in wait. "You okay?" he said to Walker.

"Fine," replied Walker. "Better than Kilbride." He drew his gun again and went around the stack of crates where he had last seen the arms dealer.

The crates had broken open when they fell on Kilbride, so that he lay sprawled beneath a pile of excelsior packing and automatic rifles wrapped in sheets of plastic bubble wrap. Walker spotted the Uzi Kilbride had been using lying on the floor, and he kicked it away before Kilbride could recover enough to make a grab for it.

It didn't look as if that was very likely anyway, Walker saw as he covered Kilbride with the Sig P-220. Kilbride was moaning in pain and seemed to be only half-conscious. Walker reached down with his left hand, grasped Kilbride's collar, and dragged him out from under the mound of debris. Kilbride groaned louder as Walker moved him, but the Ranger didn't waste any time feeling sympathy for him.

"You're under arrest for attempted murder and trafficking in illegal arms, Kilbride," Walker told him. "The attempted-murder part is new, but you've heard the other charge plenty of times." Walker recited the Miranda rights, then asked, "Do you understand?"

Kilbride was coherent enough to nod and say, "Yeah, I understand." Then he muttered, "You . . . you're crazy . . . I didn't do anything wrong. . . ."

Walker prodded one of the automatic weapons with his foot. "And this is just a BB gun. Not to mention that Uzi you were shooting off at me a minute ago." Walker grabbed Kilbride's shirt again and pulled him into a sitting position, propping him against one of the crates. "I bet once we start opening these boxes, we'll find all sorts of goodies."

Kilbride closed his eyes and moaned.

Trivette came up beside Walker and said, "I cuffed the other three. The place is clean except for them, and the police are on the way."

"Good work," Walker told him. "Now let's see if Frank here can tell us what we want to know."

''Only thing I'll tell you,'' rasped Kilbride, ''is to go f—''

''None of that, now,'' said Walker. ''You're already going away for a long time. No point in adding a public-nuisance charge on top of it.'' He hunkered on his heels in front of the battered arms dealer and continued, ''We want to know if you've sold any guns to a group of men lately. Say, three months ago, about the time you set this place up.''

Kilbride spat blood onto the floor. ''Sold lots of guns, man. That's what I do.''

''Told you,'' said Trivette.

Walker said, ''Guns, and flash-bang grenades, and body armor and helmets. Any of that ring a bell, Kilbride?''

Walker was watching Kilbride's eyes. He saw the look of cunning that appeared there for an instant, only to be carefully concealed. Kilbride said, ''I don't know anything about that sort of stuff. But if I did, what would it be worth to me?''

Walker shook his head. ''I don't make deals with scum, Kilbride.'' He paused, then said, ''But if you cooperate, that'll go in the report. What the district attorney and the judge and all the lawyers do with it from there is none of my business.''

Kilbride spat out more blood, shifted a little, then cursed and clutched his right shoulder with his left hand. ''I think one of those damn crates broke my arm,'' he complained. ''You gotta get me to a hospital.''

''Sure. When you've told us what you know about selling that stuff.''

Kilbride closed his eyes and sighed. ''All right. I've sold a bunch of automatic rifles, but the flash-bangs and the armor went to one bunch of guys.''

Walker tried to restrain his excitement. He had hoped that Kilbride could furnish them a lead to whoever had supplied the gang, at the very least. Now it appeared that Kilbride himself had been the supplier. Trivette's hunch had been a good one.

''What were their names?''

Kilbride gave an ugly laugh. ''Names? What, you think

they wrote me a check or paid by credit card? This is a cash business.''

''Then describe them.''

Kilbride closed his eyes, as if he was thinking back to the sale of the weaponry. He might lie, might make up anything he said, thought Walker, but it wasn't likely. Kilbride knew how much trouble he was facing, not to mention the pain he was in. He would probably spill the truth, even though it might gain him only a minuscule advantage when it came time for his trial.

''White guys,'' he said after a moment. ''Four of them. Those are the only ones I saw. If there were any others, I don't know about 'em.''

''That's not much of a description,'' said Trivette.

''They were in their thirties. Kind of . . . clean-cut looking, you know? Hell, I deal mostly with gang-bangers and drug pushers.'' Kilbride's mouth stretched in a bleak grin. ''Those guys are better armed than you cops these days.''

''The ones who bought the grenades and the armor,'' Walker prodded. He heard sirens in the distance and knew that the Fort Worth police would arrive shortly.

Kilbride tried to shrug and winced instead. ''This arm's broken, I tell you. Anyway, that's all I know about those guys.''

''How'd they find you?'' asked Trivette.

''They didn't say, I didn't ask.''

It wasn't much to go on, Walker thought as he stood up. The bank robbers were white, at least some of them, and their age and the fact that Kilbride had described them as clean-cut tallied with his suspicion that they might be ex-military.

''There was just one other thing, sort of odd,'' said Kilbride.

''What's that?'' asked Walker.

''One of the guys, he had these stains under his fingernails. They were red.''

''Like blood?'' Trivette asked with a frown.

Kilbride shook his head. ''Naw. I saw spots of the same stuff on his pant legs, too. I swear, it was red paint. Bright red paint.''

EIGHT

It was amazing how few *clean* crimes were left these days, Kyle Forrest thought as he sat in his office at the warehouse he called North Fork. Back in the days of Butch and Sundance and the Wild Bunch, a man could rob a bank or hold up the express car of a train and know that innocent people wouldn't be hurt by it. Well, not too much, anyway. Bankers and railroad magnates had more money and power in those days than the government, Kyle thought.

Now the railroad didn't do anything but haul freight, so they didn't make good targets for holdups. Banks, though, were another story. They were all insured, and many were owned by huge multinational corporations, and stealing from them didn't hurt the little folks at all. That was why Kyle picked the ones he did to rob. He'd never hit a small, locally owned bank, insured or not.

Unfortunately, whenever there was shooting, innocent people were at risk. That was why he'd made the rule that no one was to open fire unless it was absolutely necessary.

Mitch had ignored that rule, and ever since then, Kyle had been thinking long and hard about whether or not he wanted to continue the arrangement as they had in the past. Breaking up the gang would be hard; they had all been friends ever since their days together at Fort Hood. But if Mitch crossed the line even once more, he would have to go.

The door between the office and the front counter was open, so Kyle could hear if any customers came in. The sound of voices broke into his reverie, and he stood up and went out to see who was there. He wasn't surprised to see a group of eight teenage boys. The place was popular among teenagers, although given the Western atmosphere, it appealed more to baby boomers who had grown up in the fifties and early sixties, when dozens of Western series had been on television.

"Howdy," Kyle greeted the youngsters. "Come to play paintball?"

"Yeah, that's right, dude," responded one of the kids. The sides of his head were shaved, but the hair in the middle grew long and was slicked back so that it hung down the back of his neck. He wore a T-shirt depicting the latest industrial-metal band.

"Two teams of four each?" asked Kyle. The boys nodded.

Kyle rang up the admission prices and the rental fees for their equipment, then outfitted them. Four of the teenagers got pale blue coveralls, and four got yellow. All of them received matching helmets with visors that lowered over their eyes. Then Kyle handed out the paintball guns and ammunition and went over the rules of the game with them. When they were ready, he sent them through the double swinging doors into the warehouse proper, where they would spend the next couple of hours stalking each other through the Old West town. As they moved into the warehouse Kyle heard them making sarcastic comments about how the place looked, and he felt a twinge of anger mixed with regret. Kids today just didn't get it. They didn't understand how important it was to remember the past. The world had become a dememorized society, in which nothing that happened more than a month earlier had any importance. . . .

"Hey," said a voice as a hand came down on Kyle's shoulder. "You're fading out again, man."

Kyle gave a little shake of his head and looked over at

Mitch Graham, who stood there grinning. "What are you doing here?"

"Good to see you, too," Mitch said dryly. "Come on in the office. I've got an idea, and I asked the guys to meet us here so we can talk about it."

Kyle frowned. "I've got customers in there. . . ."

Mitch pushed one of the swinging doors open a few inches, and both men heard the whoops and yells coming from the teenagers firing paintballs at each other. "They don't have the slightest idea what's going on out here, and they wouldn't care if they did. You think a bunch of kids gives a damn about anything?"

Kyle had to admit Mitch was right, at least about how the teenagers weren't paying any attention to anything except the game. With a shrug, he said, "All right." He went into the office with Mitch following him.

Over the next fifteen minutes, the other members of the gang arrived. The office was crowded with seven men. Kyle looked around at the others: Mitch and Buddy, his lieutenant and sergeant, respectively; Rockley and Dane, the weapons experts; Dobie, the communications and computer wizard; and Fulton, the wheelman. Good men, each and every one of them. They had been the backbone of the company Kyle had commanded.

Those days were gone now. No more ranks, no more Captain Forrest. The downsizing of the military had seen to that. But really, that was all right with Kyle. When he hadn't been able to make a career of the army, as he had planned, he had been forced to look around and find something else to do with his life. This Old West paintball arena had become his dream, and he had financed it with the proceeds of the first holdup he and the men had pulled. But the jobs had been so easy, so seductively easy, and everything had gone so well until this last time. . . .

"What is it you've got for us, Kyle?" Buddy asked when they were all there. "Doesn't seem like it's been long enough for us to be pulling another job."

Kyle inclined his head toward Mitch. "This is Mitch's

show. He'll have to explain, because I don't know any more than you do.''

Mitch leaned his hip on a corner of Kyle's desk and said, ''Buddy's right, it's too soon to hit another bank, at least the way we've been hitting them.''

''What's that mean?'' asked Fulton. ''How else can you rob a bank except by holding it up?''

Mitch wiggled a finger at him. ''That's the question, all right.'' He looked over his shoulder at Kyle, who was seated behind the desk. ''You didn't like the way things went down last time, so I thought we should try something different. We'll get the bank to just give us the money without ever going there.''

''Why would they do that?'' asked Dane.

''Because we're going to grab the family of the bank president and tell him to get the loot for us if he doesn't want anything to happen to them.''

Kyle came up out of his chair, his palms resting on the desk. ''Kidnapping?'' he said angrily. ''You want us to become kidnappers?''

Mitch looked at him again, and this time some anger of his own glittered in Mitch's eyes. ''Just listen a minute, all right? Nobody gets hurt this way. It's just leverage to make the guy cooperate with us. Sure, his wife and kids will be pretty scared, but nothing will happen to them.''

''How can you be sure of that?'' Kyle demanded.

''Because you've got my word on it,'' snapped Mitch. ''Time was, that was good enough for you, Kyle.''

Kyle straightened. He still didn't like the sound of what Mitch was proposing. It certainly wasn't the way Butch and Sundance would have done things. He started to say as much, but then he saw how the other members of the gang were looking at him. They were expecting that exact reaction from him, he realized. Buddy confirmed that by saying, ''This isn't the Old West anymore, Kyle. Maybe Mitch is onto something.''

For a long moment, Kyle didn't say anything. Then: ''What bank did you have in mind?''

Mitch shrugged. ''We'll have to research that, find out who

the bank officers are at the ones we haven't hit and what their families are like. Dobie can hack into their computers and come up with that stuff."

Dobie, a small man with outsized ears, nodded confidently.

"Once we come up with a likely target, we'll do enough recon so that we know the best time and place to pull off the snatch. The less chance there is of anything going wrong, the less chance there is of anybody being hurt."

"You guaranteed that nobody would be hurt," Kyle pointed out.

"I mean to back it up, too," said Mitch. "That's why we have to take our time with this and be fully prepared."

"What sort of payoff can we expect?" asked Rockley.

Mitch grinned. "The biggest yet. Because we won't be running out of there with cash, no, sir. We'll have the ultimate inside man doing whatever we tell him, and he's going to electronically transfer as much money as he can to the account we'll set up in a Swiss bank."

"They'll find out what he's doing and stop him," said Kyle.

"Not until it's too late. Not until he's practically looted the whole bank and dumped millions of dollars into our account."

Kyle looked at Dobie. "Can this be done?"

The little man shrugged and said, "You'd be amazed how little time it takes to move around a bunch of money between computers."

"But there are bound to be safeguards—"

"And if the guy is the president of the bank, he'll know how to either go around them or override them," said Mitch. "Think it through, Kyle. We can do this."

Kyle looked around the room at the other men. Dobie nodded immediately, agreeing with Mitch. Fulton, Rockley, and Dane followed suit after a moment. Finally, Buddy nodded, too, signifying his acceptance of the plan.

He would lose them, Kyle suddenly realized, unless he allowed Mitch at least to try to put this scheme into operation. They were eager to attempt it, and they didn't want him holding them back.

''All right,'' he said. ''Start the preliminaries. But keep me updated on what you're doing, and if you run into any snags, I'm shutting the thing down.''

''There won't be any snags,'' Mitch said with a confidence that bordered on arrogance. ''This is going to make all of us richer than we ever dreamed of being. And I dream pretty damned big.''

''Red paint,'' mused Walker.

''Could've come from anywhere,'' said Trivette.

''Maybe they're housepainters,'' suggested C. D. Parker as he placed bottles of beer on the bar in front of the two Rangers.

Trivette laughed as he picked up his beer. ''Yeah, right,'' he said. ''Housepainters slash bank robbers. You see that all the time.''

''You got any better ideas?'' C. D. challenged him belligerently.

Walker leaned an elbow on the bar and sipped from the longneck. He was thinking, so he didn't pay too much attention to the usual wrangling going on between Trivette and C. D.

They were in C. D.'s Place, the combination bar and restaurant owned by retired Ranger C. D. Parker—although C. D. was quick to point out that he hadn't really retired. Anytime he was needed, he was always glad to pin on the silver star on a silver circle that he had worn during several decades of distinguished service to the state of Texas.

Four days had passed since the raid Walker and Trivette had carried out on Frank Kilbride's warehouse. Enough illegal munitions had been found in the warehouse to outfit a small army. Kilbride was going to prison for a long time and knew it, and he was eager to cooperate. He couldn't tell Walker any more than he already had about the men who had bought the grenades and the body armor, however, and Walker was more convinced than ever that the arms merchant was telling the truth. Neither the ponytailed man, nor either of the other two men who worked for Kilbride, had been able to shed any light on the matter, either.

Trivette had been searching the records of military personnel who had been discharged, either honorably or dishonorably, within the past year and then gone on to get in trouble with the law. That was just the beginning of a job that might prove to be both endless and futile, because there was no guarantee the robbers had a military connection, even though it seemed likely. And if they had been in the service, their discharges might have come more than a year earlier. Still, Trivette kept plugging away at it, for lack of any leads more promising.

Walker had checked the personnel records of paint manufacturers and distributors in the area, looking for employees with criminal histories that might make them suspects. That was pretty much a shot in the dark, too, just like Trivette's computer searches. Almost anybody could work with paint: from housepainters, as C. D. had pointed out, to people who worked in lumberyards and discount stores, all the way down to somebody who just happened to have painted a doghouse right before he went to buy a batch of illegal weapons. If that was the case, then the clue, such as it was, was essentially meaningless.

But something was nagging at Walker's brain, an instinct that told him there was an angle to this that none of them had thought of yet.

His musings were interrupted by Alex Cahill, who came into C. D.'s and took the stool next to Walker. She rested her head on his shoulder for a moment, then said, "Any luck on those bank robbers?"

"Nothing," replied Walker.

"We may have to wait until they hit again and try to grab them then," said Trivette.

Walker shook his head. "That's no good. Somebody else could be hurt."

"It's a shame there's no way you could bait a trap for 'em," said C. D. "Like I do with the mice in this place."

Alex looked around quickly. "There are *mice* in here?"

C. D. held a finger to his lips and said, "Shhh. I'm dealin' with 'em. I think there's just one, really. You don't want to get the health department down on me."

"C. D.," Alex said, "I'm an assistant district attorney. Or have you forgotten? I can't just ignore a violation of the health code."

C. D. drew himself up haughtily. "I'll have you know that this place passed its last inspection with flyin' colors." He paused, then added sheepishly, "It's just that since then, this little fella gnawed himself a hole somewhere and decided to move in."

"You've seen him?" asked Trivette.

C. D. nodded solemnly. "Yep. Can't seem to catch him, though, or find where he's been gettin' in and out."

"I don't think I'll be eating here in the future," Trivette said.

"Dang it, Jimmy, the mouse ain't been in any of the food. All the edibles are closed up tighter'n a new pair of shoes. It's just that the little son of a . . . the little varmint sometimes acts like he's laughin' at me. Like it's all just some sort o' game he's playin' with me."

Walker frowned as something tugged at his thoughts.

"Well, I won't mention anything about this to anyone in the health department . . . for now," said Alex. "But you'd better get rid of that mouse, C. D." She shuddered. "I don't care if it is a female stereotype. I . . . don't . . . like . . . mice."

"Maybe you should keep a loaded shotgun around, C. D.," suggested Trivette. "That way, the next time you saw the mouse, you could blow its head off."

C. D. glared at him. "You want me to go firin' off a greener in my kitchen? What kind of lawman are you?"

"I don't like mice, either."

C. D. turned to Walker. "Cordell, did you ever hear such foolishness?"

Walker sighed. Whatever the idea was that had been flitting around in the back of his head, it was gone now. It had been too nebulous for him to grasp. But given time, it might come back.

He just hoped that he had time, before the killing started again.

NINE

Fort Worth, 1901

Hayes Cooper had heard the old saying about the needle in the haystack all his life, but he was beginning to understand it now. He had spent the past several days scouring the area known as Hell's Half Acre for any sign of the bank robber named Doyle Parnell, but so far he had come up empty.

He had made the Golden Garter his headquarters, returning there from Harrigan's place with the two men he was convinced were Butch Cassidy and the Sundance Kid. But although they had hinted as much, they hadn't come right out and admitted that they were the famous outlaws, so Cooper put that worry aside for the moment and concentrated on finding Parnell. Later, when Parnell was behind bars where he belonged, Cooper could decide what to do about Cassidy and Longabaugh.

Tess Malone had been more than willing to rent him a room upstairs for the duration of his stay in Fort Worth. "I could even arrange for some company to go with it," she had offered.

Cooper just shook his head as he stood at the end of the bar with her. "No, I reckon I'll pass on that," he said.

She laid a hand on the sleeve of his buckskin shirt. "I wasn't talking about just any of the girls," she told him in a throaty voice as she leaned closer to him.

Cooper had been sorely tempted. He was a man with appetites just like any other, and Tess Malone was both beautiful and intelligent. But for the time being he had other things on his mind, so he had reluctantly shaken his head. "Maybe later."

"The offer may not be good forever," she warned.

"Reckon I'll have to take my chances."

"You're a stubborn man, Mr. No-Other-Name Cooper."

"Yes, ma'am."

She had laughed at the directness of his response and bought him a drink.

Since then, Cooper had become something of a nocturnal creature, dozing in his upstairs room during the day and coming out at night to prowl through the area bounded by Throckmorton Street on the west, Calhoun Street on the east, and Ninth Street on the north. From Ninth, Hell's Half Acre ran all the way south to the railroad tracks and the Texas & Pacific depot, although most of its activity was concentrated between Ninth and Thirteenth streets. He looked for Parnell in every hole-in-the-wall bar, every gambling den, every sporting house. He drank bad whiskey, lost a little money at crooked card games, and turned down countless invitations from overly painted-up women in scandalous clothes. He didn't run across Parnell anywhere, and no one would admit to knowing the bank robber or seeing anyone who fit his description.

It was possible, Cooper thought, that Parnell had moved on and was by now hundreds of miles away—and getting farther away by the minute. But as he thought back on the trail he had followed for the past few weeks, Cooper realized that Parnell had been heading for Fort Worth all along. Why would he have done that if he had no real reason for coming here? There hadn't been any bank robberies in town since Parnell's arrival; Cooper would have heard of them if there had been.

So he found himself sitting at a table in the Golden Garter

with Yance Shelby after several futile days, not knowing where to turn next.

Shelby was dealing hands of solitare, since it was only late afternoon and the evening's crowd wasn't on hand yet. A few drinkers were at the bar, but the place would be much more crowded later. Shelby gathered up the cards, began to shuffle them, and said to Cooper, "You're sure I can't interest you in a game? Your markers are good with me."

"You're too good for me in a regular game," said Cooper. "I'm sure not going to play you two-handed."

Shelby shrugged. After a moment, he said quietly, "You know, Tess is mighty curious about you."

Cooper glanced at the bar, where Tess was going over the liquor supply with a couple of her bartenders. "Is that so?"

"Yeah. She wants to know what brought you to Fort Worth."

"I told you, I'm a—"

"Cattle buyer, yeah, I know. But you haven't bought any cattle since you've been here, Cooper. In fact, you haven't done anything except roam around the Acre and ask questions about that so-called business associate of yours."

Cooper tensed slightly, not caring for the direction this conversation was taking. "So? I have to find him before I can settle anything else."

"Right," said Shelby, sounding as if he didn't believe that for a second. "Maybe you're just a drifter, taking advantage of the fact that Tess feels sorry for you. You're supposed to be renting that room upstairs, but I remember you saying you didn't have any money left after the game that first night."

"She's running a tab for the rent."

"As well as for drinks and food. It's because she likes you, Cooper."

"Anything wrong with that?"

Shelby sat up straight and placed the deck of cards on the table in front of him, their edges perfectly aligned. "Just this," he said in an even quieter voice. "Tess Malone is my friend. She lets me run my game in her place when a lot of other saloonkeepers in town wouldn't even let me in the back door. I don't want to see her hurt."

"You don't have to worry about me," Cooper assured him. "I'd like to think that Tess is my friend, too."

"She'd like to be more than that to you. So you just remember . . . I'm looking out for her best interests."

"A woman like her can usually look out for her own interests," Cooper said coolly.

"Just remember what I said."

Cooper shrugged and nodded, then looked at the entrance to the saloon as two men came in. "Now, there's the pair you should be worried about," he said to Shelby as he nodded toward the newcomers.

"Who? You mean Butch and Sundance?"

Cooper looked sharply at the gambler. "I thought their names were Parker and Long."

Shelby chuckled and said, "That's what they're calling themselves, but they've dropped enough hints that I know who they really are. They're down here with the rest of the Wild Bunch."

"They'd better be careful. They'll get themselves arrested."

"Why? They haven't broken any laws in Texas, and they're a long way from Wyoming and Idaho. Seems to me like they've been behaving themselves like model citizens."

Unfortunately, what Shelby said made sense to Cooper, who was left wrestling with the same dilemma that had been in the back of his mind for the past several days. He could arrest the two men, but doing so would reveal his identity as a Texas Ranger and effectively end whatever cooperation he might hope to get from the inhabitants of Hell's Half Acre. As long as Cassidy and Longabaugh behaved themselves, he wouldn't press the issue, he decided.

But they would have to stay on the straight and narrow, and Cooper had a hunch that was going to prove difficult for Butch Cassidy and the Sundance Kid.

The two men saw Cooper and Shelby sitting at the table, waved, and came across the room to join them. As they pulled back chairs Cassidy said, "Any luck finding that fellow, Cooper?"

"Not so far," Cooper said with a shake of his head.

"Better give up and get on with your own business," advised Longabaugh.

"Maybe so," said Cooper, although he knew he wasn't going to let go of this case. He was going to find Parnell no matter what it took, or how long.

Tess Malone came over from the bar and rested a hand companionably on Cooper's shoulder. He enjoyed the feel of it there.

"Well, good evening, gentlemen," she said to Cassidy and Longabaugh. "It appears that the Golden Garter has become a regular stop on your rounds of the area."

"You offer the most congenial company in the entire city, my dear," said Cassidy.

"And the coldest beer," added Longabaugh.

"Speaking of which, if you'd tell one of your lovely serving girls to bring us a pitcher . . ."

"Right away," promised Tess. She went back to the bar, and right away Cooper found himself missing her touch on his shoulder.

Cooper engaged in small talk with Shelby, Cassidy, and Longabaugh for a few minutes, and then one of the young women who worked in the Golden Garter delivered the pitcher of beer to the table. Cooper glanced up and saw to his surprise that the woman was Dora, the one who had warned Parnell to flee Harrigan's place. He had seen her around the saloon a few times since then, but neither of them had gone out of their way to speak to each other.

Now she gave the occupants of the table smiles all around as she placed the pitcher in front of Cassidy. Then she surprised the hell out of Cooper by leaning over his shoulder, rubbing her hand on his chest, and nuzzling his ear with her lips. The other three men laughed at the way he sat up straight, his eyes widening.

"He's still around," Dora whispered in Cooper's ear.

Immediately, he knew who she meant. He turned his head and lifted a hand to cup her chin so that he could look into her eyes. What he saw there confirmed his guess.

She leaned still closer, brushed her lips across his, and

moved her mouth back to his ear to murmur, "Upstairs in five minutes."

Cooper let his fingers trail off her jaw as she straightened. She smiled at him and sashayed away toward the bar.

"Now, how in blazes does he manage that?" Cassidy said into the silence that followed Dora's departure. "He's not only friends with the lovely Miss Malone, but now he's got the second prettiest woman in the place throwing herself all over him."

"Just lucky, I guess," said Cooper.

Longabaugh snorted. "Luck's got nothing to do with it, friend. Some gents are natural-born ladies' men."

"Nobody ever accused me of that," Cooper said.

"Well, then, you just haven't been paying attention. Look at the bar," said Cassidy.

Cooper glanced over his shoulder. Tess was standing there looking at him, a slight frown on her face. She had to have seen the way Dora was carrying on with him, and of course she had no idea what had prompted the young woman's actions. Cooper swallowed hard and turned his attention back to the table. He hoped he wasn't going to lose that free room he had been "renting."

But either way, he had to go upstairs in a few minutes and meet Dora. He hoped she could tell him the things he needed to know.

Like where to find Doyle Parnell . . .

Nobody would ever suspect him of hiding out in a fancy place like this, Parnell thought for maybe the hundredth time as he lit a cigar and flicked aside the lace curtain over the window of the upstairs bedroom in his partner's house.

He had been holed up here for several days, and he got considerable pleasure from knowing that damned Ranger was probably still down in the squalor of Hell's Half Acre, searching for him there. Let Cooper look; he wasn't going to find Parnell.

This was the sort of place he had always deserved, Parnell told himself as he looked around the room. A four-poster bed with a soft mattress and silk sheets that was even nicer than what you'd find in a high-class whorehouse. Elaborately carved chairs with spindly legs that looked too weak to hold a man's weight but were sure pretty to look at. Wallpaper with ornate gilt designs, and crystal lamps that hung from the ceiling. Soft rugs on the floor. It seemed to Parnell that to own a house like this, a man would have to have all the money in the world.

But you could never have too much money. There was always more out there for the taking, just waiting for a man strong enough and smart enough to grab it.

The sun was setting, ushering in a beautiful spring evening. Parnell was looking out at it when he heard the door of the bedroom open behind him. His partner came in, using a frilly white handkerchief to mop sweat off his face.

"It don't look all that hot out there," Parnell said mockingly.

The man shot him a hostile glance. Parnell knew that his partner didn't particularly like him, but the man sure as hell needed him if the plan was going to work.

"I've sent for the men you wanted to see," the man said. "It wasn't easy locating them and getting word to them without anyone else knowing. They're downstairs waiting for you." The man hesitated, then added, "Are you sure they can be trusted?"

"For five hundred bucks apiece, they can be trusted," Parnell assured him. "You've got the money?"

The man took a roll of greenbacks out of his coat pocket and handed it to Parnell. "Half now, half when it's over, as we agreed."

Parnell nodded. "You and me, we have to wait for our payoff," he commented as he held up the roll of money. "But it'll be a whole heap bigger'n this when it comes."

The thought of the payoff cut through his partner's anxiety. The man nodded and let a wolfish smile stretch across his face. "Yes, indeed."

Parnell put his cigar back in his mouth and moved toward the door. His partner moved aside to let him lead the way downstairs. As Parnell went down the stairs, trailing his hand along the highly polished mahogany banister, he could see into the parlor where the four visitors were gathered. Two of them he knew, having met them while he was behind bars in the penitentiary at Huntsville. The other two had been vouched for by Parnell's ex-jailmates.

Grinning around the cigar, Parnell stepped into the parlor and looked at the four men cooling their heels. He said, "Howdy, Ike, Sam," to the two men he knew.

Ike Nevers and Sam Gallagher nodded in return to Parnell's greeting. Nevers was a short, stocky man with hair the color and consistency of straw under his battered black hat. Gallagher was taller, balding, lean all over except for a potbelly. Despite the warmth of the evening, he wore a long duster.

"Good to see you again, Doyle," said Nevers. He inclined his head toward the other two men. "Meet Ed Olson and Jack Zane."

Olson was about as undistinguished looking a man as Parnell had ever seen. Two minutes after Parnell had nodded to him and said, "Howdy," he would have had trouble describing Olson if the man hadn't been sitting right there on the couch with the luxurious upholstery. Zane was chunky, with a short, dark beard.

All four of the men had one thing in common. Their features were hard and totally without mercy.

Just the kind of hombres he needed for this job, thought Parnell. He wouldn't have to worry about any sentiment getting in the way of the money they were going to collect.

"What's this about?" asked Gallagher, a hint of impatience creeping into his voice. "I rode all the way over here from Peaster."

"What were you doing over there?" asked Parnell.

Gallagher hesitated, then said, "My sister has a farm there. I been helpin' out."

"So after you got out of the pen you went to farmin'," said Parnell. He looked around at the other men. "Am I takin' any of the rest of you boys away from a plow?"

"Leave Sam alone," Nevers said. "We all got along all right inside . . . until you busted out and didn't offer to take anybody with you."

Parnell shrugged. "Big escape attempts always have something that can go wrong with 'em.'' He looked at Gallagher. ''Sorry, Sam. Didn't mean nothin' by it.''

''You know I'm a good man to have at your back,'' Gallagher said defiantly.

''Damn right. That's why I called you and Ike here and told you to bring a couple more fellas we can trust.'' Parnell took the banknotes from his pocket and tossed them to Nevers, who caught the roll deftly. ''Split that up among yourselves. There'll be that much more again when we're done.''

''What do we have to do to earn it?'' asked Jack Zane.

''Back me up on a job.''

''You plan on robbin' a bank?'' Ed Olson asked. Even his voice was quiet and faded, so that you had to listen close to understand what he was saying.

Parnell grinned and puffed on the cigar, then said, ''In a manner of speakin'. You see, here's what we're goin' to do. . . .''

TEN

Cooper watched as Dora went upstairs, then took a few minutes to finish off the mug of beer he had been nursing all evening. When he was done, he set the empty mug on the table and shoved his chair back. "Be back in a little while," he said.

"Answering the call of nature?" asked Cassidy.

"You could say that," Cooper answered cryptically, then started toward the stairs on the right-hand side of the room. He hoped to avoid Tess, who was standing not far from the bottom of the left-hand staircase.

She moved to intercept him, though, and Cooper couldn't very well change his path again without making her even more suspicious of him.

"Where are you going, Cooper?" she asked as she came up to him just as he reached the stairs.

"Just up to my room," he said, angling his head in that direction.

"Calling it a night already?"

He shook his head. "Not hardly. I forgot something."

"What?" Tess asked bluntly.

"My, ah, makin's."

‘‘I don’t believe I’ve ever seen you roll a quirly, Cooper,’’ Tess said, the skepticism plain in her voice.

‘‘Well, I don’t generally, but Harry’s running low on to-bacco, so I thought I’d loan him some.’’

Tess glanced over at the table where Cassidy and Longa-baugh were still sitting with Yance Shelby. Cooper thought he saw all three of them trying not to laugh as he stood there and endured Tess’s questioning.

‘‘I’m not a jealous woman,’’ Tess said after a moment. ‘‘So if you want to go up there and get some . . . tobacco . . . you just go right ahead, Cooper. Smoke it all you want.’’

With that she turned and strode back toward the bar, every inch the empress, at least of the Golden Garter.

Shelby, Cassidy, and Longabaugh were all laughing out loud now, Cooper saw as he glanced in their direction. Let them go ahead and laugh, he thought. He had more important things on his mind right now than the impression he made on a professional gambler and a couple of outlaws a long way from their usual bailiwick.

He went up the stairs, taking them briskly. He reached the landing, turned left, crossed the balcony at the rear of the building, and started along the balcony on the other side. From here, he couldn’t see the table where Shelby, Cassidy, and Longabaugh were sitting, nor could he see Tess. Cooper was grateful for that fact.

He had seen Dora go into one of the rooms on this side. Reaching the door, he knocked softly on it. A voice came from inside. ‘‘Who is it?’’

Cooper leaned close to the door. ‘‘Me.’’

A rapid patter of feet came from inside the room, then the door was pulled open a couple of inches. ‘‘I said five minutes,’’ hissed Dora. ‘‘It’s been longer than that.’’

‘‘I got delayed,’’ Cooper said. ‘‘Are you going to let me in?’’

Dora opened the door wide enough for him to slide through into the room. She closed it quickly behind him.

The room was lit only by a lamp on a small table beside the bed, and the wick was turned down low. In the faint yellow glow given off by the flame, Cooper saw that Dora looked tense and worried.

"Anybody see you come up here?" she asked.

"The whole saloon could have seen me come up the stairs. I don't reckon anybody knows which room I came to, though. No one else was on the balcony just now."

She took a deep breath. "Good. There's a fella named Boley, he drives a freight wagon, and he's got it in his head that I'm his personal little plaything—"

The words came out of her in a rush. She stopped short, held up a hand, and visibly collected herself. "Sorry," she muttered. "Didn't mean to start yammering. I'm just worried that Boley will show up tonight. I know he's in town."

"You said something about Parnell still being around," Cooper reminded her. "Have you seen him?"

Dora shook her head. "No, but I overheard a couple of men talking about him earlier tonight. They were supposed to have some sort of meeting with him."

"Here in Fort Worth?" Cooper asked sharply.

"It sure sounded like it," Dora told him with a nod of her head.

"Did you know either of the men?"

"No, I never saw them before."

"But when you saw them tonight, it was here in the Golden Garter?" asked Cooper.

"That's right. I brought them a bottle of whiskey and a couple of glasses, and as I was coming up to the table, one of them said to the other that they would have a few drinks before riding out to see Parnell."

"They used Parnell's name?"

Dora nodded again. "I heard it plain as day."

Cooper was tense now, too. He said, "Are they still downstairs?"

"No, they left before I got a chance to tell you what I'd heard. Just before I could get over to your table, one of the bartenders grabbed me and made me deliver a bunch of drinks."

Cooper swallowed a groan of disappointment, but he

couldn't stop the grimace that tugged at his mouth. "What'd they look like?"

"Both of them were medium height, I guess you'd say. The one who mentioned Parnell's name had blond hair. It reminded me of straw. He was clean-shaven, but the other man had a beard. Dark, and trimmed pretty close."

There might be hundreds of men in Fort Worth who could fit that description, thought Cooper. He said, "Anything else you noticed about them, anything unusual?"

"They looked like pretty rough characters," Dora said with a shrug. "That's all. And they didn't even flip me a coin for bringing their drinks to them."

"Maybe they didn't have any extra coins," mused Cooper.

If that was the case, it could explain why the two men were meeting with Parnell. He might be recruiting them for some sort of robbery. Given Parnell's history, that seemed pretty likely to Cooper.

He tried not to feel too disappointed that he had been in the same room with two men who could have led him to Parnell, if only he had known about them. "You'll recognize them if you see either of them again?" he said to Dora.

The saloon girl nodded. "Yeah, I think so. And if I see them—"

"Come tell me, as soon as you can."

She stepped closer to him. Her tongue came out to touch her lips briefly. "I will," she promised. "I would have got to you sooner tonight if I could have, Mr. Cooper, honest."

Cooper believed her. She had no reason to lie to him.

Dora came even closer, close enough so that she could reach out and lay a hand on Cooper's sleeve. Her eyelids lowered a little. "You know, as long as you're already up here . . ."

"I don't have any money," said Cooper. "I'll give you some later, for tipping me off about those two men, but until then . . ."

"I wasn't talking about money," whispered Dora. "I liked the way it felt earlier downstairs, when I leaned over your shoulder and touched you."

She was so close now that Cooper could feel the warmth

of her breath on his face. Her head was tilted back, and her lips were parted a little. It would have been mighty easy just to take her in his arms and bring his mouth down on hers.

Instead, Cooper put his hands on her shoulders, all too aware of how the low-cut dress had left the smooth, creamy flesh bare, and started to gently move her back. He shook his head.

That was when a hard fist pounded heavily on the door.

Dora jumped a little, and said, "Oh!" Her eyes widened as she looked past Cooper toward the door. A look of horror flooded into her eyes as a deep voice boomed, "Dora? Dora, honey, you in there?"

"Oh, my God," Dora said, "it's Boley."

"There's no need to be scared," Cooper told her. "Nothing happened."

"Boley's not going to believe that." Dora looked around frantically. The room was so tiny that it didn't take long. Her gaze fastened on the narrow window. "You'll have to climb out," she hissed as she turned and threw herself at the window. She flung up the pane, so that a breeze from outside billowed the gauzy curtains into the room.

"I'm not climbing out some window," Cooper started to tell her, but as he spoke the hammering on the door got harder and louder.

"Dora! I know you're in there, woman! Open up for your darlin'!"

Dora looked desperately at Cooper and pulled back the curtains.

Cooper rolled his eyes and started toward the window. Since Dora was his best lead to Parnell, he had to cooperate with her, he supposed.

But just as he reached the window and lifted one leg over the sill, the door burst open as the man out on the balcony drove his shoulder into it. "Dora!" he yelled as he stumbled into the room.

"Boley!" Dora shrieked. "Boley, don't get mad—"

The man called Boley saw Cooper then, trying to climb out the window, and his face turned red with rage. He was almost as wide as he was tall, Cooper noted, and the bottom half of his moon-shaped face was covered with bristly, rust-colored whiskers. Boley let out a roar as he charged across the room toward Cooper, moving faster than a man of his bulk had any right to.

Avoiding trouble by ducking out the window was one thing; Cooper had been reluctant to do even that much. He sure as blazes wasn't going to run from a man who was attacking him. Not that Boley gave him much choice in the matter. The fingers of an outstretched hand, each of them like an overstuffed sausage, grabbed the collar of Cooper's buckskin shirt and hauled him back into the room. Cooper felt a moment of dizziness as both feet left the floor and Boley whirled him around.

Then Boley let him go, and Cooper slammed into the wall.

He hadn't gone very far; the room was too small for that. But the impact of the collision was still enough to send Cooper's hat flying off his head and knock the breath out of him. He bounced off the wall, stumbled, caught his balance at the last second, and kept himself from falling. Even as he was trying to drag air back into his lungs, he saw a huge fist coming at his head.

Cooper ducked and let Boley's roundhouse blow go harmlessly over him. Stepping in closer, Cooper hooked a couple of quick punches to the freighter's belly. Boley looked as if he barely felt the blows, and with another bellow, he tried to snare Cooper in a bear hug. Cooper was barely able to dance back out of his grasp before the trap closed.

"Boley, don't! Stop it, Boley! You big overgrown ox!" Dora tried to grab hold of Boley's arms as she shouted at him, but he shrugged her off with little or no effort. "Oh!" she exclaimed as she threw herself at him again and this time wrapped her arms around his neck. She tightened them and hung on for dear life.

Boley didn't seem to notice the young woman's weight hanging from his neck as he threw wild, looping punches at Cooper. The Ranger dodged some of them and blocked others, but if Boley kept up this flailing attack for very long, one of the blows might get through Cooper's guard.

And one was likely all it would take to put Cooper on the

floor. If he ever went down, he knew, the very real possibility existed that Boley might stomp the life out of him with those big work shoes.

Cooper never even considered drawing his gun. Boley wasn't an outlaw, just a lovesick fool who was half-crazy with jealousy. It wasn't very smart for him to have let himself grow so attached to a woman like Dora, but there was no way to command a man's heart. It felt what it was going to feel, and devil take the hindmost.

Boley lunged at Cooper again, and this time when the Ranger darted aside, he managed to thrust a booted foot between the freighter's calves. Boley stumbled, and he had so much weight going forward that he couldn't control his momentum. He fell, sprawling across Dora's narrow bed. The bed frame broke in a couple of places with a pair of loud cracks, and it dumped the mattress, along with Boley and Dora, onto the floor. Cooper felt the vibration through the soles of his boots as all that weight landed.

Unaware that Dora was still clinging to him like a burr, Boley rolled over, trapping her underneath him. Her arms and legs were visible under him, and their flailing quickly grew frantic. Caught between Boley and the mattress, Dora was probably suffocating under there.

Cooper sprang forward and reached down to grab the front of the overalls Boley wore. There was a lot more strength in Cooper's compact body than was readily apparent. He stepped back, pulling Boley up with him. Boley seemed a little dazed, and Cooper was able to launch a fast combination of a left and a right, both punches landing solidly and rocking Boley's head back and forth. Boley's eyes grew even more glassy as he sagged toward Cooper.

Cooper stood him up with a left jab, then brought a right up practically from the floor. Boley's head snapped around and his eyes rolled up in his head. He started to topple backward.

"No!" Dora yelled.

Cooper looked past Boley and saw that she was still struggling to extricate herself from the wreckage of the bed. Boley was about to fall on her again when Cooper's hands shot out and grabbed hold of his overalls again. Boley was deadweight now, and Cooper felt himself being pulled forward.

"Get out of there!" he snapped at Dora. "I can't hold him up!"

She scrambled free of the tangle of sheets and broken bed slats. Cooper released his hold on Boley and let the freighter fall backward. Boley landed with a crash that once again shook the floor.

Cooper was breathing hard. He took Dora's arm and helped her to her feet. "Are you all right?" he asked.

"F-fine," she said. "Just fine."

A new voice came from the room's entrance, where the door Boley had broken hung crookedly from one hinge. "Well, you certainly are the gentleman, aren't you? Defending a lady that way."

Cooper looked over his shoulder and saw Tess Malone standing there. Her lovely face was set in unreadable lines, but Cooper thought he detected a coolness in her blue eyes. A couple of the burlier bartenders from downstairs, who doubled as the Golden Garter's bouncers, were standing right behind her.

Tess turned her head and said, "It's all right, boys. You can go back downstairs."

The bartenders left, but their place was taken by Yance Shelby, Butch Cassidy, and Harry Longabaugh. All three of them looked just as amused as they had earlier, when Cooper first went upstairs.

Shelby waved a hand at the unconscious form of Boley and asked with a grin, "Practicing your bulldogging for the next rodeo, Cooper? I've got a friend named Bill Pickett who might be able to give you some pointers."

Cooper ignored the gibe and looked around for his hat. It was lying on the floor, and luckily, no one had stepped on it. He picked it up, brushed it off, and settled it on his head. He turned to Dora and gave the brim of the Stetson a tug. "Ma'am."

Tess, Shelby, Cassidy, and Longabaugh stepped back as Cooper left the room. Cooper looked at Tess and said, "Sorry about the damages. I'd offer to stand good for them, but—"

"But you don't have any money, I know," said Tess. "I'm not sure what you were doing up here with Dora under those circumstances. She's either gone softhearted or softheaded, and either way, I can't have somebody like that working for me."

Cooper tensed. If Dora wound up getting fired from the Golden Garter because of this travesty, he might lose his only lead to Parnell. He looked Tess in the eye and said, "I'd take it as a personal favor if you wouldn't hold Dora to blame for this."

"And why should I do you a personal favor?" Tess shot back at him.

Cooper would have rather had this conversation without anyone else watching and listening and grinning in amusement. But he didn't have much choice in the matter, so he said, "You know I've, ah, grown right fond of you, Tess."

She laughed and looked at Dora. "You've got a funny way of showing it, cowboy." She leaned her head slightly to one side and regarded him intently for a few seconds, then sighed and said, "All right. Nobody loses a job over this. This time." She shook her head. "Hell, I can take the money to cover the damages out of Boley's pocket before he wakes up. He's always flush when he comes here."

"Thanks," Cooper said softly.

"Yeah, well, you owe me, mister. And one of these days, I'm going to collect."

"Anytime," promised Cooper.

Tess looked at Dora. "Start getting this mess cleaned up. I'll send a couple of the boys up to help you, and to drag Boley out of here."

Cooper started downstairs. Shelby fell in beside him and said, "Trouble just follows you around, doesn't it, Cooper?"

"Seems like," Cooper replied shortly.

"You know what you need? You need to change your luck, maybe play a little poker."

Shelby might be right, thought Cooper. Not about the poker; Cooper didn't have any intention of playing cards with the man.

What he needed was a change in the run of bad luck that had been following him ever since he had found himself on the trail of Doyle Parnell. Unfortunately, at the moment Cooper didn't have the slightest idea how to bring that about.

ELEVEN

Jessica Northrup put the Lexus in gear and pulled out of the parking lot at the dance school in far southwest Fort Worth. Beside her, Amber was talking in her usual mile-a-minute way about everything she had learned in class today. The nine-year-old was dressed in a black leotard and pink tights. Her long blond hair was worn in a braid that was wrapped around her head.

Jessica's hair, just as blond as her daughter's, was loose around her shoulders, and it blew around her face in the wind that came in through the open window of the car. The Lexus, of course, had all sorts of climate-control features, but on a nice spring day like today, Jessica liked to roll down the window and just let the wind blow in her hair as she drove. She'd had a convertible in college, a dozen years ago, and she had never forgotten the feeling of putting the top down, cranking the radio up, and blasting down the road. ''Rollin' down that great American highway,'' she thought, mentally quoting the lyrics of the Chris LeDoux song.

Well, those days were over and done with, she reminded herself. She wasn't a college girl any longer. She was in her early thirties, the second wife—some would cattily say the trophy wife—of the president of the largest financial institution in Fort Worth and the mother of this beautiful little girl beside her. Now it was a Lexus instead of an old Mustang convertible, dance lessons for Amber instead of philosophy classes at the University of Texas, elegant parties at the country club instead of dancing the nights away at the clubs on Guadalupe Street. That was fine with Jessica. She had made her decisions in life and was perfectly capable of living with them.

But every so often, the wind in her hair felt so damned good. . . .

She supposed she was going a little too fast, her foot a little heavy on the gas. If she'd been going slower, she might have seen the debris scattered in the road sooner as she swept around the curve in the winding boulevard. As it was, she had no chance to avoid all the nails sticking up in the boards that were strewn on the pavement.

Jessica heard at least two tires blow as she tried unsuccessfully to steer around the debris. Even with a couple of flats, the luxury car's excellent suspension and steering system allowed her to keep the Lexus under control. From the corner of her eye, she saw the old pickup parked at the side of the road as she flashed past it. The boards must have fallen out of the back of it, she thought. A couple of men were trying to pick them up before any harm was done.

Unfortunately, their efforts had come too late. The Lexus started to skid, sparks flying up from the rims of the blown-out tires. Amber cried out in fright, "Mama!"

"Hang on, baby!" Jessica called to her. She wanted to reach over to Amber, but she knew she had to keep both hands on the wheel.

With a hard jolt, the car came up against the curb. Jessica was thrown forward. The air bag inflated, cushioning her impact against the steering wheel, but she still hit it hard enough to knock the wind out of her. The air bag on the passenger side had been disabled, since Amber always rode there, but the girl was belted in securely and was stopped short of the dashboard as the car came to its violent halt. She started crying.

They were all right, Jessica told herself. Thank God, they

were both all right. She looked over at Amber, saw that her daughter was shaking and terrified but otherwise unharmed.

"Lady, lady, you okay? Are you hurt?"

The urgent voice came from outside the car. Jessica collected her wits and looked over to see one of the men from the pickup. He was bending over and peering in through the open window. The man was about her age, with a mustache and long, curly red hair. He was wearing khaki work clothes, and Jessica supposed he was part of a construction crew that was on a job somewhere in the neighborhood.

She managed to nod to him. She heard another man say, "Are they all right?"

The second man had come up on the other side of the car. He was looking in through the window next to Amber. She glanced up at him and started crying harder, even though there was nothing particularly frightening about the man. He was dressed the same as his partner and had a short beard and thick dark hair.

The man standing beside Jessica's window said, "Maybe you'd better get out, lady, and make sure you're all right."

"No, that's okay," said Jessica, starting to feel a little uneasy, even though she told herself there was no reason to. She wished she hadn't been driving with the window down, so that this strange man wasn't right here beside her with nothing between her and him. He was just a concerned citizen, she thought . . . concerned that the accident might be blamed on him, Jessica added to herself. After all, it was the nails in the boards that had fallen from his pickup that had caused her tires to blow.

She reached for the cell phone on the console between the front seats. "I'll just call the auto club and get them to come out and change these tires," she said.

The man opened the door, causing Jessica to jump a little in surprise. "We can take care of the tires," he said. "You really need to get out and make sure you're all right."

"But . . . but I've only got one spare. . . ." Jessica was getting scared now, even though there was nothing really threatening about the man's manner. She didn't like the way he had taken it upon himself to open her door, though. She wished she had thought to lock it, even after he'd come up to the window. The Lexus's engine was still running. . . .

For a second, she thought about jamming her foot down on the accelerator and driving away from there, even though she'd be riding on the rims of the blown-out tires. But before she could even decide if that would work, a van coming along the boulevard in the opposite direction suddenly swung over and pulled up next to the curb in front of her, its grille almost touching the front end of the Lexus. Jessica glanced at the rearview mirror. The two men had pulled the pickup behind the car, and it was close, too. So close that the Lexus was pinned between the two trucks.

Jessica wasn't going to wait any longer. Her instincts were screaming a warning in her head. This neighborhood was full of large estates, so large it might be a quarter of a mile between entrance gates. This was one of those stretches of road where there weren't any driveways, and the boulevard was bordered by evergreen trees that shielded the nearby houses from view. The road wasn't heavily traveled, either, and at the moment there was no other traffic on it.

The man standing beside the Lexus still had his hand on the door. It was only half-open, so Jessica suddenly lifted her left leg and slammed her foot against the door, knocking it out into the man's body. He exclaimed in pain and surprise and staggered back a step. The man on the other side of the car let out a loud curse and grabbed for the door handle. Amber screamed.

Jessica's finger jabbed the button that locked all the doors. At the same time, she grabbed the cell phone with her other hand and thumbed the button that sent a panic call to the security company her husband kept on retainer. Roger had always wanted to have full-time bodyguards assigned to her and Amber, but Jessica had refused, not liking the idea of having her privacy invaded that much.

Now she wished she had valued her safety a little more and her privacy a little less.

She leaned out of the car to reach for the handle of the open door. The man on that side of the car had recovered from the shock of being struck with the door and lunged for it at the same time. Jessica got hold of the handle and yanked with all her strength. The man had his hand on the door, but his feet weren't braced and Jessica was able to jerk it out of his grip. The door slammed.

Amber was still screaming. Jessica jerked her head in that direction and saw the second man struggling to open the door on the passenger side. He wouldn't be successful, Jessica knew. All the doors were securely locked now. She reached down to the console and flipped the switch that armed the security system. It went off immediately, since the two men were pulling on the door handles. The car's horn began to honk, and a loud, jarring siren filled the air. Jessica reached over and caught hold of Amber's shoulder, raised her voice to say over the tumult, "It's all right, honey, I promise it's all right! They can't get us now!"

She saw movement from the van that had blocked her in front. A couple of men were climbing quickly out of the vehicle, and one of them had something in his hand. Jessica wasn't sure what it was until he handed it to the man on the passenger side of the Lexus. Then she realized it was a sledgehammer.

"No," she whimpered.

The man took the sledgehammer and brought it around in a sweeping blow that slammed into the windshield. A huge spiderweb of cracks zigzagged across the thick safety glass, but the windshield didn't collapse. The man drew back the sledgehammer for another blow. Jessica and Amber both screamed as the hammer came through the glass this time and crashed into the top of the dashboard. The windshield fell in, staying together for the most part although some slivers of glass showered around Jessica and Amber.

"Unlock the doors," snarled the man with the sledgehammer, "or we'll reach in there and pull you out."

If the men did that, she and Amber would be cut badly by the edges of the broken-out windshield, Jessica realized. Where were the police and the guards from the security company? This neighborhood prided itself on its police protection, and yet here she was, the alarms on her car wailing, and there were no cops in sight.

But it had been less than a minute since this terrifying experience had begun. Time had slowed down for Jessica. In her privileged life, she had never been frightened enough to know that it has a way of doing that in moments of extreme stress.

The man handed the sledgehammer to one of the others and leaned closer to the broken-out windshield. "Come on, lady," he said. "We don't have time to fool around with you. You and the kid are coming out of that car, one way or the other."

With a trembling finger, Jessica hit the button that unlocked the doors.

Surely the men wouldn't really hurt them. This was just a robbery, she told herself. She would give them her money, her jewelry, let them take the Lexus. Anything, as long as they didn't hurt her and Amber.

The man on Jessica's side of the car jerked the door open and reached in to grab her arm. He tried to pull her out around the air bag, and she yelped in pain as the seat belt caught her. The man muttered something under his breath and leaned in to awkwardly unfasten the belt. On the other side of the front seat, Amber's door had been opened by one of the men, too, and she was crying, "Mama! Mama! Help me, Mama!" as the man reached in to unfasten her belt and drag her out of the Lexus.

"Don't hurt her!" Jessica cried as she was pulled from the vehicle.

"Nobody's getting hurt," said the man who had hold of her arm. "Just cooperate with us. You have my word you won't be harmed."

"What do you want with us?" Jessica demanded raggedly. "You can have my money, my purse, the car, anything—"

The man started tugging her toward the van. "Come on."

Jessica realized they were going to take her and Amber with them. Robbery and carjacking were one thing; kidnapping was another. Kidnap victims never came back alive, she thought.

She started screeching and flailing, fighting back with every ounce of her strength—which was considerable since she worked out four times a week, had taken several self-defense courses, and had practiced martial arts for several years. If she had kept her wits about her, she might have taken her captor by surprise and gotten loose from him, but panic made her attack foolishly, her movements out of control. The man fended off her blows, muttered, "Sorry," under his breath, and hit her hard in the face with a clenched fist. Jessica's head snapped back, and while she didn't lose consciousness, she was too stunned to fight anymore.

She was aware that someone now had hold of her shoulders while someone else had her feet. She was picked up, carried to the van, dumped unceremoniously inside through the sliding door on the side of the vehicle. Jessica heard the door slam shut and rolled over. Amber! Where was Amber? Had the men left her behind? Jessica prayed that was the case. Amber would be terrified to see her mother carried off by this strange man, but at least she would be safe.

Then Jessica heard the sobbing beside her and knew that her prayers hadn't been answered. She shook her head and looked over in the shadowy interior of the van to see Amber lying there. Jessica gathered her daughter into her arms and held her tightly. "It's okay, sweetie, it'll be okay, Mama swears it will," she crooned into Amber's ear, but she couldn't tell if the child heard her or not.

The floor of the van was carpeted. Jessica felt herself jolted as the van backed up sharply and then lurched ahead. There were no windows in the sides, only in the rear doors. And those were so grimy that they didn't let in much light.

Jessica tried to sit up and look around, but a hand on her shoulder forced her back down. "Take it easy, lady," said a voice she hadn't heard before. "You and the kid just stay put."

The van was going faster now. Jessica had no idea which direction they were traveling. She was completely disoriented. For all she knew at this moment, the entire world consisted of the interior of this van.

"Wh-where are you taking us?" she managed to ask.

"Don't you worry about that," the man looming over them said. "Just behave yourselves, and nobody gets hurt."

Jessica wanted desperately to believe the man. She couldn't bring herself to do it, though. She had always been practical, almost pragmatic.

And she knew in this moment that unless someone saved them, she and Amber were as good as dead.

Roger Northrup sat in his private office on the twenty-second floor of the bank building in downtown Fort Worth and studied the numbers on the monitor screen in front of him. The deal was shaping up nicely. He nodded in satisfaction and was clicking a mouse button to send the data to the bank he was negotiating with in Tokyo as his intercom buzzed.

He thumbed the button without taking his eyes off the screen and asked, "What is it?"

The brisk, efficient voice of his executive assistant came over the intercom. "There's a gentlemen here to see you, sir."

Northrup frowned. "I told you I wasn't to be disturbed until I had things squared away with Tokyo."

"This is a personal matter, sir, and it sounds extremely urgent." For a second, strain could be heard in the voice over the intercom. "It's the Fort Worth police, and the man said it has something to do with your wife, Mr. Northrup."

Northrup's eyes went to the large framed photograph on the desk beside the computer. He fancied himself a pretty good amateur photographer, and he had taken this shot the previous summer while he and Jessica and Amber were sailing on Eagle Mountain Lake. In the picture, Jessica and Amber had struck a similar pose, both of them laughing, sitting in deck chairs with their long, bare, brown legs sticking out in front of them and their blond hair blowing in the wind, Amber in a flower-print one-piece bathing suit, Jessica in white shorts and a blue bikini top. Northrup thought they were both incredibly beautiful, and he experienced a moment of astonishment, as he always did when he looked at that picture, that a man who was fifty years old had two such lovely females in his life.

He said into the intercom, "Send the man in," then, with a slight shaking in his knees, he stood up.

His assistant opened the door and ushered in a man in the uniform of the Fort Worth Police Department. The officer wore a solemn expression that didn't make Northrup feel any better.

"I'm Roger Northrup." He introduced himself without offering to shake hands.

"Lieutenant Wilkins of the Fort Worth Police Department," said the officer. "I'm sorry to bother you, Mr. Northrup, but we need some information."

"My assistant said this concerns my . . . my wife?"

"Yes, sir." The lieutenant consulted a small notebook he held in his hand. "Does she drive a dark blue Lexus, license number MRB-59S?"

"Yes, that's my wife's car," said Northrup. "Has . . . has there been an accident?" *Please, no. Please, God, no.*

"Well, we don't really know. . . ."

"Don't know?" Northrup exclaimed as he leaned forward. "How can you not know if my wife has been in an accident?"

"One of our units responded to reports of a car alarm going off, sir, and found your wife's vehicle parked on the side of the road, about a mile from your house. The vehicle had two flat tires and the windshield was broken out. A unit from a security company arrived right after our officers did and said that their office received a panic call from your wife's cell phone. They located the vehicle by means of the GPS transponder installed in it."

"Why are you telling me all this?" demanded Northrup, unsure whether to be angry or frightened. "What about my wife? What about my daughter? Jessica picks her up at dance class about this time—"

"We found your wife's purse and your daughter's dance bag in the car, Mr. Northrup. But there was no other sign of either of them." Wilkins paused, then said, "I'm afraid there's a good chance they've been kidnapped."

Northrup sat down without even realizing he was doing it, sagging back into his chair. The luxurious office seemed to fade around him, until it seemed that he wasn't even there anymore. Instead, he had been transported into a cold, dark place where there was no Jessica, no Amber, no sunny days sailing on the lake, no hugs and kisses, nothing but a bleak landscape of pain and loss.

Northrup cried out, a long wail that didn't even start to express what he was feeling. He was in such emotional agony that he didn't even notice the telephone ringing at first. Then, when the shrill sound penetrated, his eyes went vacantly to the phone.

Wilkins had come closer to the desk. "You'd better answer it, Mr. Northrup," he advised. "If your wife and daughter have been kidnapped, whoever has them will be contacting you with a ransom demand."

Gradually, Northrup understood what the police officer was saying. His hand shot out and snagged the receiver, as he was suddenly terrified that whoever it was on the other end would hang up. "H-hello?" he managed to rasp.

"Roger?"

Oh, Lord, thought Northrup, it's her. It was really Jessica. Relief started to flood through him. This had all been some terrible misunderstanding. "Jessica," he said.

Then a new voice, a muffled, low-pitched male voice, said in his ear, "Listen close, Northrup, and if you ever want to see your wife and daughter alive again, you'll do exactly what I tell you."

TWELVE

''Pretend you're still talking to your wife,'' Kyle Forrest said into the phone as a blindfolded and handcuffed Jessica Northrup was led from the room by Buddy after making the call.

He heard the sharp intake of breath on the other end of the line. ''What . . . who . . .'' Roger Northrup said, stumbling over the words.

Kyle's hand tightened on the phone. ''Listen to me,'' he hissed. *''Pretend you're still talking to your wife.''*

''A-all right, dear, just slow down. Now, what are you saying, Jessica?''

''That's better,'' Kyle told the banker. ''Are the police there now?''

''Why, yes, as a matter of fact, that's right.'' Northrup sounded a little stronger, a little more in control of himself now. Kyle hoped the man could keep that composure. A lot was riding on it, for all of them.

''I was afraid they would have gotten to you by now. Listen to me very closely, Mr. Northrup. Your wife and daughter are fine. They haven't been hurt. They won't come to any harm as long as you cooperate with us. Do you understand what I'm telling you?''

''Of course, dear.''

"That's very good, Mr. Northrup," said Kyle. "Are you sitting down?"

"Yes, I am."

"Look relaxed and relieved. You thought something terrible had happened to your family, and now you've found out that they're all right after all. Got it?"

"Absolutely."

"When you get off the phone with me, tell the police that someone tried to carjack Mrs. Northrup's Lexus. She and your daughter escaped from the thieves and ran home. Got it?"

"Yes." Northrup's voice was strong now, with the powerful timbre that had commanded countless board meetings.

"Mrs. Northrup and Amber are fine, just shaken up, and they just want to be left alone. The police will want a statement from your wife about the incident, but stall them until tomorrow. Understand?"

"Certainly. You must have been terrified, darling. Just rest now."

"You're very quick," Kyle told the banker. "Stick to that story. As for the men who attacked your wife, there were two of them, black, early twenties. Got it?"

"Lieutenant Wilkins is here with me right now. I'll be sure to tell him."

Kyle closed his eyes for a second, thankful that he was dealing with a man whose quick wits were making this easy. The whole thing had come damned close to unraveling because Jessica Northrup had put up such an unexpectedly stiff fight, but now he was beginning to think that they had a chance to salvage it.

"The important thing is to stall the cops and keep them from trying to talk to your wife until tomorrow."

"I can do that." Northrup sounded confident.

"As soon as you get rid of the officer who's with you now, go home. That's natural enough; you'd want to be with your wife after her ordeal."

"I can't tell you how true that is. I feel that way right now."

"I'm sure you do, and if you do everything you're told,

you'll be back together with Mrs. Northrup and Amber by this time tomorrow. I'll call you at home later with more instructions." Kyle paused, then went on, "But it's crucial that the police don't know we have your family. Absolutely crucial."

"I . . . I understand. I'll be there as soon as I can."

"Good. We'll be in touch."

Kyle cradled the receiver. He looked up and met Mitch Graham's eyes. "He's ours," said Kyle. "He'll do whatever we tell him to."

"He'd better," said Mitch.

They were in the office at North Fork, the converted warehouse. The paintball game was closed indefinitely, a sign on the door of the warehouse declaring that remodeling was going on. Buddy and Fulton were standing guard over Mrs. Northrup and the little girl, back in the storage room they had fixed up as quarters for the prisoners. The only things in the windowless room were a couple of cots and a chemical toilet. There was nothing to reveal where they really were, and whoever was standing guard would always be wearing ski masks so their faces would be hidden. Kyle and Mitch had discarded the disguises they had worn earlier, burning in the incinerator behind the warehouse the wigs and false mustaches and beards and the plastic inserts that had changed the shape of their faces. It was vital that neither of the prisoners be able to identify or accurately describe their captors.

Mitch wore a self-satisfied smirk. "Well, we pulled it off," he said.

"Not yet," Kyle cautioned. "Northrup still has to transfer the money to that Swiss bank account in the morning."

"He'll do it. Hell, a man would have to be a complete idiot to take any chances with the life of a woman who looks like that."

"We didn't pick her because of her looks." Jessica Northrup had been selected because her husband had a vast amount of money at his disposal and the computer skills with which to manipulate it as he was ordered.

"No, but it doesn't hurt to have somebody like that around. I just wish—"

"Forget it, Mitch," Kyle said sharply. He wasn't even going to allow any speculation about such matters.

He had to admit, though, that Jessica Northrup was lovely. She wasn't dressed up or anything, clad as she was in a blue T-shirt, gray sweatpants, and running shoes, and she wore only a minimum of makeup since she had just been picking up her daughter from dance class, but Kyle still thought she was beautiful. He had hated to see the look of terror on her face, the expression she had worn consistently for nearly an hour now.

And she had quite a few more hours of fear to endure before this would all be over.

"I've got to hand it to you," said Mitch, breaking into Kyle's thoughts. "You haven't said anything about Butch and Sundance for a long time now."

That's because Butch and Sundance would never have been involved in something like this, thought Kyle. He had sacrificed his ideals for the promise of more money than he could spend in his life. But it was too late to back out now.

Besides, with his share of the ransom, he would never have to worry again about whether or not he made any money from North Fork. He could even run the place at a loss from now on, if he needed to. And no one would ever be able to take it away from him. He could always come here and walk the streets of the town he had made, the town that was more of a home to him than any other place he had ever known. In the end, it would all be worth it, he told himself.

And if he kept telling himself that, maybe sooner or later he would begin to believe it.

Over the past week, Walker and Trivette had checked out everything having to do with paint in the Dallas/Fort Worth metroplex. And they weren't a bit closer to the bank-robbery gang, even though there were moments when Walker still felt as if there was something they had overlooked.

It was time to admit that the so-called lead they had gotten from Frank Kilbride was worthless, Trivette was arguing as he and Walker sat in C. D.'s Place one afternoon, having walked over from Ranger headquarters in hopes that a change of scenery would maybe prompt some new idea.

C. D. leaned an elbow on the bar as Walker and Trivette sat on stools nursing longnecks. "Seems to me," he said, "that if you're runnin' into a brick wall, the thing to do is go around it."

"What, exactly, does that mean?" asked Trivette.

"Just that there's always more than one way of gettin' where you're goin'."

"And what does *that* mean?"

"Means that when you got a dog that won't hunt, maybe it's time to teach it to do tricks instead."

Trivette threw his hands in the air. "One of these days, C. D., these little bits of down-home philosophy you're always spouting are actually going to make some sense, and I'm going to faint dead away from the shock."

Walker sipped his beer and said, "You ever catch that mouse, C. D.?"

"I'm glad you asked me that question, Cordell, 'cause I got me one of those newfangled humane traps. The little fella can go in after the bait, but he can't get back out again. Once you've got him, you take him somewhere he won't cause no trouble and let him go."

"Since when do you care about being humane to a mouse?" asked Trivette.

"All God's creatures got feelin's, Jimmy, even mice." C. D. frowned. "I got to admit, though, after playin' hide-an'-seek with this little fella for so long, I ain't feelin' too kindly toward him. Might just get me a cat if this trap don't work."

"Hide-and-seek," Walker said softly. He frowned, once again feeling that persistent tug at the back of his brain.

The cell phone that was folded up and clipped to his belt rang, and Walker put aside the thought that was trying to form. He unclipped the phone, flipped it open, and said, "Walker."

C. D. and Trivette both saw the look that came over Walker's face as he listened to whoever was on the other end of the connection, and they knew there was some sort of trouble. After a moment, Walker said, "We're on our way," and closed the phone.

‘‘What’s up?’’ asked Trivette.

‘‘A possible kidnapping,’’ said Walker as he stood up and reached for his hat. ‘‘The Rangers are being called in just in case.’’

Trivette grabbed his own hat from the bar. ‘‘Must be something big.’’

‘‘Big enough,’’ Walker said.

By the time Walker and Trivette reached the office of the bank president on the twenty-second floor of the downtown high-rise, Lieutenant Abe Wilkins was already frustrated and a little angry.

‘‘The longer we let this go, Mr. Northrup,’’ Wilkins was saying as the two Rangers were shown into the office by Roger Northrup’s executive assistant, ‘‘the greater the likelihood the carjackers will get away.’’

‘‘Would-be carjackers,’’ Northrup corrected smoothly from behind the desk. He was about fifty, well dressed, with several streaks of silver in his thinning brown hair. ‘‘They didn’t take the car after all, and my wife and daughter are safe. I don’t see why we can’t allow poor Jessica and Amber to recover a bit from their ordeal.’’ Northrup looked curiously at Walker and Trivette as they entered the room.

Wilkins grunted and turned away from the desk. ‘‘Good to see you, Walker,’’ he said. ‘‘Maybe you can convince Mr. Northrup here that he’s making a mistake.’’

‘‘Who are you?’’ Northrup asked from behind the large, glass-topped desk.

‘‘Walker, Texas Ranger,’’ Walker said with a nod. ‘‘This is Sergeant Trivette.’’

Northrup looked angrily at Wilkins. ‘‘You called in the Rangers without even checking with me first? When you got here, you didn’t even know for sure that was my wife’s car you found.’’

‘‘We knew it was registered in her name and that there were definite signs of foul play,’’ said Wilkins. ‘‘A call was put in to the Rangers just as a precaution.’’

Trivette held up a hand. ‘‘Hold on a minute,’’ he said. ‘‘Could somebody tell us what’s going on?’’

"This officer is overreacting," Northrup said as he pointed a finger at Wilkins.

"And Mr. Northrup isn't being cooperative," grated Wilkins.

"Start at the beginning," suggested Walker.

"About an hour ago, a vehicle belonging to Mrs. Northrup was found near her home. The front windshield was broken out and the car alarm was going off. The vehicle had two flat tires, also. There was no sign of Mrs. Northrup or her daughter, who she had picked up at a local dance studio a short time earlier."

Walker nodded. "So you assumed you had a possible kidnapping on your hands."

"That's right."

"But now we know that's not what happened at all," put in Northrup, "because just a few minutes after Lieutenant Wilkins got here, my wife called me. She's perfectly all right."

"You're certain it was her?" asked Walker.

Northrup frowned. "I think I know my own wife's voice."

"I already checked with Mr. Northrup's assistant, too," added Wilkins. "She was the first one to take the call, and she recognized Mrs. Northrup's voice."

"Did Mrs. Northrup sound odd in any way, as if she was being forced to make the call?" asked Trivette.

"She sounded perfectly normal to me," the banker said.

Walker nodded. "What did she say?"

"She told me that two men had tried to steal her Lexus," Northrup explained. "Carjacking, that's what you call it, isn't it?"

"That's right. Did she describe the two men?"

"She said they were black, and in their early twenties."

"What happened?"

"She said they came up while she was stopped because two of her tires had gone flat."

Trivette glanced at Walker and said, "Tires could've been tampered with, if Mrs. Northrup left the car and went into the dance studio to pick up her daughter."

"She always did that," Northrup said quickly. "She always got there a little early so she could go in and watch Amber dance.'' His voice caught a little, which was understandable considering how close his family might have come to real danger that afternoon.

''Did the men have a vehicle?'' asked Walker. ''Where did they come from?''

Northrup shook his head. ''She didn't see any other car. They were just . . . there suddenly, Jessica said.''

''Did they threaten her, or try to harm her?'' asked Trivette.

''No, they just . . . just called her names and told her to get out of the car. Jessica did the smart thing. She grabbed Amber and got out of there as fast as she could.''

''But she didn't get to a phone and call 911,'' Wilkins said. ''She could have gone to one of your neighbors—''

''She wanted to get home,'' said Northrup firmly. ''She was terrified, and she wanted to be in familiar surroundings. You can understand that, can't you, Lieutenant?''

''I suppose so,'' Wilkins admitted grudgingly. ''But once she was home, she still didn't call the police.''

''She was about to. She called me first. You know that, Lieutenant; you were here.''

''Yeah . . .''

Walker said to Northrup, ''Your wife needs to give a complete statement to the police, including descriptions of the carjackers.''

''That's what I've been telling him,'' said Wilkins.

''And I've told you what my wife said: she's too upset today, but she's perfectly willing to talk to you tomorrow.''

''If she came in today,'' said Trivette, ''she could look through the mug books, maybe work with a police sketch artist. . . .''

''Tomorrow,'' repeated Northrup.

Wilkins shook his head. ''I give up.'' He took a card from the breast pocket of his uniform shirt and handed it across the big desk to Northrup. ''Call me tomorrow, and I'll tell you when to bring your wife in.''

''Thank you, Lieutenant. We'll be there, I promise you.''

Wilkins looked at the two Rangers. ''Sorry you got called in for nothing.''

"No problem," said Trivette with a shrug.

Walker said, "Tell your wife we're glad she's all right, Mr. Northrup."

The banker nodded. "I'll do that. Now, if you'll excuse me, I want to go home to be with my wife and daughter."

Walker, Trivette, and Wilkins left the office and rode down together in an express elevator. Once they were alone in the elevator, Wilkins asked bluntly, "Do you buy his story?"

"What's not to buy?" asked Trivette. "I'm sure you've had witnesses drag their feet about making a statement when they're upset."

"Yeah, but something about this one rubs me the wrong way."

Walker said, "Like why didn't the thieves take the car after they went to the trouble of stealing it?"

"Yeah," Wilkins said quickly. "That's a good question. And would carjackers go after a vehicle with two flat tires in the first place? Can't make a quick getaway in that."

Trivette said, "Maybe they planned on changing the tires. Or using a tow truck. Were both flats on the front, maybe?"

Wilkins consulted his notebook and shook his head. "Nope, front and back on the right side."

"All they had to do was put the spare on the back and hoist the front end to tow it away."

"A couple of young black guys doing that to a car with an alarm going off?" Wilkins looked doubtful. "In that neighborhood? Not very likely."

"Well, then, you answered your own question," said Trivette. "They wanted to 'jack the car, but they got scared and ran off instead."

"After busting out the windshield because they were mad," added Wilkins with a nod. He had talked himself around to believing that version of the story. "Yeah, I guess it could have happened that way." He looked at Walker. "What do you think?"

"I think I'd keep an eye on Mr. Northrup and make sure he goes home from here," said Walker as the elevator came to a smooth stop and the door slid open almost soundlessly.

"If he does, there's not much you can do but accept his story and wait to talk to his wife tomorrow."

"Yeah, I guess that's what we'll do." Wilkins gave them a casual wave as he started across the lobby. "Sorry again for roping you in on this when it turned out to be nothing."

"No problem," said Walker.

But despite what he had said, his instincts told him there was more to the story than what they had heard. He wondered if Mrs. Northrup would show up tomorrow at police headquarters as she had promised.

If she didn't, Walker planned to start doing some digging of his own.

The kidnappers were watching him. Roger Northrup was sure of it, because the phone started ringing less than five minutes after he walked into his house.

His empty house.

Not empty of everything, of course. The expensive furniture was still there, along with the paintings on the walls and the antique vases and the sculpture and the home-theater equipment. But empty of everything that mattered.

He scooped up the phone from its base on the brilliantly polished antique sideboard. "Yes?"

"Listen closely, Mr. Northrup." The same voice as before, low and muffled. Northrup didn't say anything, just listened as he had been instructed.

"Roger? Oh, God, Roger—"

Something inside him cracked at the sound of the terror in his wife's tone and the way her voice was cut off so abruptly. "Jessica!" he cried.

A couple of seconds that felt like an eternity went by before Jessica said, "We're all right, Roger. Amber and I are fine. They haven't hurt us." She seemed to be speaking by rote, as if her captors had told her what to say. Her next words were genuine, though. "You have to do whatever they tell you, Roger. You have to. That's the only way you can save us."

"I will," Northrup said, trying not to babble in his own fear. "I swear I will."

"That's enough," the man's voice said, faint but understandable. "Give me the phone now, please, Mrs. Northrup." Under the circumstances, his tone struck Northrup as being ludicrously polite.

A second later, the man went on into the phone, "Now, Mr. Northrup, you've talked to your wife, and you know that she and your daughter are fine. Did the police believe what you told them?"

"Yes," Northrup said emphatically. "I did everything exactly the way you told me. They don't expect to see Jessica until tomorrow."

"Well, that's probably what's going to happen, because she and Amber should be back with you by then." The man paused, then said, "You're alone there?"

"Yes. There . . . there are no live-in servants, and the housekeeper is already gone for the day."

"Excellent. Now, what we need to do is establish exactly what you'll have to do in the morning in order to ensure the safe return of your family."

Northrup bit back a groan. "In . . . in the morning? No sooner than that?" He thought about the long, empty night looming before him and wanted to cry. Only the knowledge that Jessica and Amber were going through much worse gave him the strength to carry on.

"I'm afraid not. Listen carefully, Mr. Northrup. I'm going to tell you exactly what to do, and then you're going to get a good night's sleep, whether you like it or not. Because there's going to be a lot riding on you in the morning, Mr. Northrup. Twenty million dollars, to be exact, as well as the lives of your wife and daughter . . ."

THIRTEEN

Fort Worth, 1901

The hill overlooked the Trinity River about a mile from downtown Fort Worth. The big fancy houses on the bluff were visible in the distance. There were houses across the river, as well as farther west, in the neighborhood known as Arlington Heights, but this particular area was much as it had been sixty years earlier when the Comanches were the only ones who rode here. The hill was topped by a grove of oak trees, but the ground alongside the river was open and grassy, a perfect place to ride.

Doyle Parnell, Ike Nevers, Sam Gallagher, Ed Olson, and Jack Zane sat in the shadow of the trees and waited for the boy.

According to what they had been told, he rode out here nearly every day in the late afternoon, accompanied by his governess. The boy's father was a widower and had hired a young woman to look after his son. Parnell figured the young woman looked after the daddy, too, after the boy had been put to bed at night.

There were no guards watching the boy, which was a damned foolish mistake, but one for which Parnell was grateful. The boy's father probably thought it would cost too much to hire men full-time. Penny wise, pound foolish, his mama used to say. Parnell didn't remember a whole lot about his mama, and from what he did remember she had been dumb as dirt most of the time, but she had been right about that.

Nevers nudged Parnell and said, "Is that them?"

Parnell looked to the east along the river and saw a small figure on horseback trotting along the grassy bank. The rider was trailed by a buggy being pulled by a single horse. That would be the governess.

Parnell slid a small telescope from one of his saddlebags and pulled it open. He lifted it to his eye and pointed it toward the boy on horseback, just to make sure. It took him a moment to find the rider in the lens, but when he did, he saw a boy about ten years old, a little tall for his age, with handsome features and dark hair. He wore a black suit and a white shirt, lace-up shoes instead of boots, and a flat cap like some sort of foreigner would wear instead of a Stetson. Parnell grimaced in distaste at the sissified outfit. No kid born and raised right here in Texas ought to look like that.

Parnell shifted the telescope to the buggy. He saw a young woman in a gray dress, wearing a hat of the same shade with blue ribbons hanging from it. The hat had a lot of dark brown hair underneath it, and Parnell found himself wondering what it would feel like to take that hair down and run his fingers through it.

No time for that, he told himself, and anyway, that governess had to be at least twenty years old, which was older than he liked his females. He closed the telescope with a snap and said, "That's them, all right. Get ready."

Parnell, Nevers, and Zane swung up into their saddles. Gallagher and Olson climbed onto the seat of the spring wagon they had driven out here. The back of the wagon had a canvas tarp stretched tightly over it. With the three horsemen leading the way, the group of outlaws left the cover of the trees and started down the slope toward the river.

They moved at a deliberate pace, not wanting to alarm the boy or the governess. When they reached the river trail, they turned east, so that they were moving toward the boy as he rode toward them. Behind the boy, the governess flicked the reins to get the horse moving a little faster. She didn't appear to be frightened, but she was trying to get closer to the boy since there were strangers in the vicinity.

Parnell hipped around in the saddle and motioned for Gallagher to pull the wagon over to the side of the trail. It was an innocuous gesture, designed to make the governess think they were being considerate and getting out of the way. Parnell, Nevers, and Zane moved their horses to the edge of the trail, too, and Parnell gave the boy a friendly nod as the youngster rode up. In keeping with the boy's outfit, the saddle he rode was some sort of English contraption that didn't even have a saddle horn.

"Hello," the boy greeted them. His eyes were wide with wonder as he looked at their range clothes and the horses they were riding.

"Howdy, son," Parnell said in a friendly voice.

"Are you cowboys?"

Parnell pushed his hat back a little on his head and grinned. "Why, I reckon you could say that. We've punched a few cows, haven't we, boys?"

There were grunts of agreement from the other men. They weren't as glib as Parnell, so they were going to leave the talking to him.

The boy said fervently, "I wish I could be a cowboy." His expression fell. "My father won't let me, though. He says I have to follow in his footsteps, so he's sending me back East to go to school next year. I don't see what's wrong with the schools here in Fort Worth! Anyway, who needs to go to school to be a cowboy?"

"Thought you said your daddy don't want you to be a cowboy."

The boy sighed. "He doesn't. He wants me to be a banker, like him. He says I'm going to take over his bank someday."

"Could be you will."

"But I don't want to!" protested the boy. "I like to ride, and I want to learn how to rope and shoot a gun—"

"Gilbert!"

The boy grimaced as the governess called his name. She

drew the buggy to a stop in the trail, and he turned and looked angrily at her as he said, "I told you before I don't like to be called Gilbert, Emily. I want you to call me Buck."

"Mr. Vance would not be happy if he heard me calling you Buck," said the governess in a prim voice.

"Aw, but, Emily—"

Parnell interrupted the boy by tugging on the brim of his hat and nodded to the young woman. "Good afternoon, ma'am. Beggin' your pardon, but you look a whole heap too young to be this boy's mama."

Emily blushed. "I'm not his mother. I'm his governess."

Parnell had been perfectly aware of that fact, of course, but his friendly tone had lessened the woman's suspicions even more. "Me and Gilbert here been havin' a good talk," he went on. "He says his daddy's a banker."

"That's right," said Emily. "His father is Mr. Lewis Vance, the president and chairman of the board of the Trinity State Bank."

Parnell let out a little whistle. "Shoot, Gilbert, sounds like your daddy's an important man."

"He is an important man," agreed Gilbert. "But I wish you'd call me Buck."

"Miss Emily wouldn't like that," Parnell said with a shake of his head.

"Aw, who cares? She's just my ol' governess."

"Gilbert!" exclaimed Emily. "How rude! I want you to apologize at once."

Gilbert turned angrily toward her. "I won't!" he flared. "I'm tired of havin' to be nice. Cowboys don't have to be polite, and I want to be a cowboy!"

Emily was shocked by the boy's outburst. She sat there in the buggy staring at him openmouthed.

Now that he had confirmed the boy's identity, Parnell grinned and said, "If you want to be a cowboy, Buck, what you need to do is come with my pards and me."

Gilbert turned sharply toward him. "I can do that!"

"You most certainly cannot!" Emily said.

Parnell's grin widened. This was working out even better

than he thought it would. "Sure, you can come with us," he said to Gilbert.

"Are you going on a cattle drive?" the boy asked eagerly.

"Not right now, but maybe sometime."

"Gilbert," said Emily, fear edging into her voice, "I think we should go now. Your father will be expecting us to be there when he comes home from the bank."

"Aw, let me ride with these cowboys for a while," Gilbert pleaded. "Just for a little while."

Parnell moved his horse closer to Gilbert's. "You don't have to ask her permission," he scoffed. "She's nothin' but a girl. She can't tell you what to do."

"Sir! How dare you try to usurp my authority over this boy?"

"Shut up," Parnell snapped at her.

"Yeah," added Gilbert with a sneer directed toward the governess. "Shut up, Emily."

Parnell reached for the reins of Gilbert's horse. "Come along, son." It would be even better for the plan if Gilbert accompanied them willingly, rather than having to be hog-tied and gagged and stashed under the canvas in the back of the spring wagon. Of course, there was still the problem of the young woman called Emily.

"Stop that!" she cried. She snatched up the buggy whip from its holder and stood to lash out at Parnell with it. "Leave the boy alone!"

Parnell fended off the whip easily, catching it in a gloved hand and jerking it out of Emily's grip. That sharp tug over-balanced her, and she fell out of the buggy, landing hard on the dusty trail alongside the river. She cried out in pain.

"You hurt her!" Gilbert said. Suddenly he looked worried, as if beginning to realize that this was no longer some sort of adventure to be carried out in defiance of his governess. He might even be getting the idea that it never had been.

Nevers and Zane quickly moved their horses so that they were between Emily and Gilbert. She looked up at the two men looming over her on big horses and screamed.

Well, this wasn't going to work out as well as he'd hoped

after all, thought Parnell. But it would still work, and he would still wind up being a rich man.

"Sam, Ed, put the kid in the wagon," he ordered.

Gilbert looked truly scared now, and he tried to pull his horse away. Parnell had too tight a grip on the reins, however. Gilbert couldn't get loose.

Gallagher and Olson sprang down from the wagon seat and advanced on the boy. Gilbert yelled, "No!" Olson lunged forward and grabbed Gilbert's right leg as the youngster jerked his foot from the stirrup and tried to kick out at the men. Gallagher hurried around to the other side of the horse and reached up to jerk Gilbert out of the saddle. Gallagher wrapped his arms around the boy's chest under Gilbert's arms, and held him there so that Gilbert's feet dangled off the ground. Gilbert would have screamed, but Gallagher clamped one big hand over the boy's mouth as he carried him toward the wagon.

Olson went ahead of them and took several lengths of rope out of the back of the wagon. He and Gallagher worked together to quickly truss Gilbert hand and foot, then Olson shoved a rag into the boy's mouth and bound it in place as a gag.

Emily had stopped screaming when Nevers and Zane drew their six-guns and leveled them at her. She lay there on the ground, propped up on one elbow, her eyes wide with horror. When she finally found her tongue again, she looked at Parnell and said, "You'll never get away with this. What are you going to do?"

"Make that boy's daddy pay through the nose to get him back," Parnell said as he dismounted and stepped over to Emily's side. He hunkered on his heels and reached down to cup her chin in his hand. He tilted her head back a little so that he had a good look at her face. Her hat had fallen off when she tumbled out of the buggy, and some of her hair had come loose, so that several strands of dark brown hair hung around her face. "What about you?" asked Parnell. "What are you worth to Mr. Lewis Vance, lady?"

"N-nothing," she gasped. "I . . . I'm just the governess. . . ."

"Good-lookin' gal like you spendin' a lot of time with a widower, a rich older gent like Vance. I bet you figured that sooner or later you'd be the second Mrs. Vance, didn't you?"

"No!" Emily exclaimed. "I just look after the boy—"

Parnell straightened. "Ed, Sam, get over here and tie and gag this one, too. We're taking her with us."

"That wasn't part of the plan," Nevers said from horseback.

Parnell glanced up at him and said, "It is now." His eyes were ice-cold, and the false joviality was gone from his face. Now it was just hard planes and angles.

After a second, Nevers shrugged. "You're the boss," he said. He looked at Emily and licked his thick lips. "Besides, it might not be so bad havin' her around."

Gallagher and Olson jerked Emily to her feet. She might have screamed again, if she had remained conscious.

But as she looked around at the hard-faced men surrounding her, she fainted dead away.

Lewis Vance was a firm believer in coming to work early and leaving late. There was nothing at home that could be as important as the affairs of the bank. Not that Vance didn't love his son: Gilbert was the most important thing in the world to him. But it was in order to provide Gilbert with the best opportunities in life that Vance worked so hard. When it came time to turn the operation of the bank over to his son, Vance intended for Trinity State Bank to be the leading financial institution in the entire Southwest, not just the state of Texas.

So he was going over some ledgers at his desk late that afternoon when the vice-president of the bank, Henry Osbourne, came into the office with a worried look on his face. "A man just delivered this for you, Lewis," said Osbourne as he held out a rather grimy envelope. "He gave it to one of the tellers and said it concerned a personal matter."

Vance frowned in puzzlement as he took the envelope from Osbourne. His name was scrawled on it in pencil, and "Lewis" had been misspelled "Louis." Vance looked up at Osbourne and asked, "What sort of man was he?"

Osbourne sniffed in disapproval. "According to the teller, he smelled rather strongly of cows and was dressed as you might expect from someone of which that was true."

"A cowboy?"

"Exactly."

Vance understood now why Osbourne seemed so put out. Osbourne felt a hearty dislike for the cattlemen who were some of the bank's best customers. An Easterner by birth, Osbourne was much more at home dealing with the merchants who also banked at Trinity. To tell the truth, Vance didn't particularly like the smell of cattle, either, and whenever Gilbert started blathering on about wanting to be a cowboy when he grew up, he wasted no time in disabusing him of that notion. But Vance was certainly willing to put up with the ranchers and the cattle buyers, considering how much money they deposited.

Vance turned the envelope over and saw that it was sealed with a blob of wax. He picked up a letter opener from the desk and pried the wax away from the flap. Inside was a single folded sheet of paper, which Vance slid out of the envelope and unfolded.

"My God!" he exclaimed as the crudely printed words seemed to leap up off the paper and slug him in the face like a barroom brawler. The paper made a crinkling noise as his fingers involuntarily clenched it.

"Good Lord, Lewis, what's wrong?" asked Osbourne, looking even more worried now. "Is it some sort of bad news?"

Vance's face had gone stark white, making his dark mustache stand out even more than it normally did. He was breathing hard, as if he had just run a long distance. His hand shook violently as he held out the paper toward Osbourne. It slipped from his fingers before the bank vice-president could take it, but Osbourne quickly scooped it up off the desk and read the message.

Vance didn't have to see the paper to know what it said. The words were burned into his brain.

WE HAVE YORE BOY GILBERT IF YOU WANT HIM BACK ALIVE YOULL PAY US FIVE HUNDRED THOUSAND DOLL-

ERS WHATEVER YOU DO DONT TELL THE LAW OR THE BOY DIES WE WILL BE IN TOUCH

"This . . . this is incredible!" exclaimed Osbourne. "How dare they—"

Vance stood up. "I've got to go," he said.

"To the police?"

Vance shook his head and said, "No. I'm going home. This could be a hoax, an attempt to extort money. Gilbert could be safe at home with Miss Mills."

"Would you like me to come with you?" asked Osbourne. "I'd like to help if I can." Osbourne was not normally the most warmhearted individual, but he looked completely sympathetic now.

"No, Henry, you stay here and see that the bank closes normally. That's how you can help the most." Vance started around the desk.

Osbourne stopped him by saying, "Lewis . . . what if this . . . this horrible message turns out to be true?"

Vance's face was like stone as he paused and said, "Then God help the men who have my son, because no matter what else happens, I'll see that they hang, each and every one of them."

FOURTEEN

Lewis Vance drove the buggy recklessly through the arched wrought-iron gate in the stone wall that ran along Summit Avenue. A cinder-paved drive bordered by shrubs led up to the elegant three-story house that he called home. Beyond the house, the bluff dropped off steeply to the river bottoms. A wooden staircase led down the bluff to the stable where Gilbert's horse and the buggy that Emily used were kept. Every afternoon, weather permitting, Gilbert rode along the river trail with Emily following in the buggy. They had certainly gone out today, because it was a beautiful spring afternoon.

Far to the west, though, clouds were gathering. There might be a thunderstorm later in the evening. They were common at this time of year.

Vance wasn't thinking about storms as he brought the buggy to a stop in front of the house. Dropping the reins heedlessly, he leaped out of the vehicle and hurried up the steps to the large front porch. He jerked open the door and burst into the house, calling, "Gilbert! Gilbert!"

Mrs. O'Malley, the cook and housekeeper, came out of the kitchen. She wore a troubled expression on her elderly face, probably because she had noticed the note of panic in Vance's voice. She said, "Master Gilbert's not back from his afternoon ride yet, Mr. Vance. Is anything wrong? You're home a mite early today."

"You haven't seen Gilbert since he left to go riding after school?"

The cook shook her head. "No, sir, I haven't."

"What about Miss Mills?"

"Why, she's with Master Gilbert, I suppose."

Vance bit back a groan of dismay and took out his pocket watch. He flipped open the large gold-plated watch and saw that the time was almost six o'clock. It would be getting dark in less than an hour. Gilbert and Emily were always back by now. At least, he assumed they were from what he had heard, since he himself often didn't arrive home until seven o'clock or later.

"Thank you, Mrs. O'Malley," he said distractedly as he snapped the watch closed and jammed it back in his pocket. He strode down the hall toward the rear of the house, ignoring the questions the cook called after him.

Vance hurried out of the house and across the rear yard to the top of the stairs that led down the bluff. He forced himself to slow down and use the railing as he descended. The stairs were steep, and if he lost his balance and fell, he could easily hurt himself badly.

When he reached the bottom, he almost broke into a run as he went to the stable. The building was fairly small, only two stalls and a shedlike area where the buggy Emily used was kept. The stalls were empty; both Gilbert's mount and the horse used to pull the buggy were gone, as was the vehicle itself.

So there was the proof Vance needed that his son and the governess had indeed not returned. He ran out of the barn and looked to the west, raising a hand to shade his eyes from the glare of the sun, which was just about to sink into the growing cloud bank. Vance's eyes followed the line of the river, where Gilbert always rode. He saw no sign of the two missing persons.

With a taut band of fear tightening across his chest, Vance trotted down to the river and began following the path. He saw the hoofprints of Gilbert's horse on the ground, as well as the parallel marks made by the wheels of the buggy. The path twisted and turned to follow the river, and when Vance paused to look back a quarter of an hour later, he could no longer see the stable or his house perched on the bluff above it. In fact, this whole area was rather isolated, considering that about a mile away was a bustling, growing city.

As he rounded the next bend Vance saw something up ahead. He came to a stop, staring at the two horses and the buggy. The horses had wandered off the path a short distance and were contentedly grazing on the grass that grew along the riverbank.

"No!" Vance cried out.

He ran toward the horses. His shout, and the speed with which he was approaching them, frightened the animals and made them shy away from him. Vance stopped, out of breath now. He recognized the chestnut mare that his son always rode, as well as the big brown gelding that pulled the buggy.

Slowly, Vance circled the horses and the buggy. He saw no sign of Gilbert or Emily.

No, that wasn't strictly true, he realized a moment later as he came across both Gilbert's cap and one of Emily's hats. They had definitely been here.

But they were gone now, and that word echoed maddeningly in his head: gone, gone . . .

Gone.

Like a walking dead man, Lewis Vance climbed the wooden stairs and then trudged into his house. As he came into the parlor, rubbing his eyes wearily, Henry Osbourne stood up from the divan and said, "Lewis!"

Vance started in surprise, not having seen the tall, balding Osbourne in the dimness of the parlor. "Hello, Henry," he said dully.

Osbourne came across the room and gripped Vance's arm tightly. "My God, man, is it true? Has your son been—"

Vance's lips drew back from his teeth in a grimace. "Don't say it," he grated.

"But . . . it's true?"

Jerkily, Vance nodded. "Evidently," he said, keeping his

voice pitched low so that Mrs. O'Malley wouldn't overhear. "I found Gilbert's horse and Miss Mills's buggy down on the path by the river. They were both gone." He reached inside his coat. "But I found these. . . ."

He brought out Gilbert's cap and Emily's hat. "Dear Lord," Osbourne breathed as he looked down at them. "What are you going to do, Lewis?"

"I . . . I'm not sure. . . ."

"I'll return to the bank immediately and begin gathering the money," Osbourne offered. "Half a million, the note said—"

"No." Vance's voice was stronger now. "By God, no."

"But you have no choice except to pay," Osbourne protested. "The kidnappers have given you an ultimatum—"

Vance's hand tightened on Gilbert's cap. "I'll not give in to the demands of a bunch of criminals," he declared. "We'll just see what the authorities have to say about this."

Osbourne stared at him in disbelief for a couple of seconds, then said, "The ransom note made it plain that the police were not to be notified, Lewis. I believe you should think twice about this."

"Not at all," said Vance as he turned toward a side table where a telephone sat. "That's why we have the police, after all, to handle criminal matters such as this. They'll know what to do, Henry. I'm sure of it."

Thunder rumbled outside as Osbourne pulled a handkerchief from the breast pocket of his coat and mopped his forehead with it. He appeared worried, almost agitated, as he said, "You're making a mistake, Lewis."

Vance swung around to face him before reaching the telephone. "What else can I do?" the banker demanded. "I don't have half a million in cash! No one does!"

"The bank does," Osbourne said quietly.

"That's not my money."

"You could replace it, though, over time. There'd be no need for the depositors to know about it, or even the other members of the board."

"And if the bank examiners came and discovered the loss?" snapped Vance.

"I would think that risk would be worth the life of your son." Osbourne stuffed the handkerchief back in his pocket and went on, "You must do as you see fit, Lewis. This is really none of my business, after all. But I *am* your friend, and I certainly don't wish to see you hurt."

"I understand," Vance said slowly, and for a moment, he seemed to be considering what Osbourne had suggested. But then his back stiffened, and a stubborn look came over his face. "I'll not give in to such tactics," he said as he reached for the telephone. "I'm calling the police."

Osbourne nodded glumly as Vance lifted the telephone receiver from its cradle and turned the crank on the instrument. "Yes, operator," Vance said after a moment. "Please connect me to the police department. It's a matter of the utmost urgency."

Rainwater was dripping off the brim of Hayes Cooper's Stetson as he stepped into the Golden Garter that evening. His jeans and buckskin shirt were damp from the sudden cloudburst that had hit Fort Worth a little earlier. Cooper had been walking up and down the streets of Hell's Half Acre, checking at each of the livery stables and wagon yards for Doyle Parnell's horses. This wasn't the first time he had conducted such a search, but Cooper figured covering some of the same ground again was better than doing nothing. He hadn't accomplished anything, however, except to get wet when the rain had hit.

It was time to stop being so stubborn, he had decided. Even though his gut was still telling him that Parnell was in Fort Worth, tomorrow he would send a wire to Ranger headquarters in Austin and see if the outlaw had been reported anywhere else in the state. For all he knew, Parnell had robbed half the banks in East Texas during the past couple of weeks while Cooper had been searching for him here.

And on top of everything else, Tess Malone was still treating him coolly. She hadn't forgotten the incident with Dora.

That angle hadn't netted Cooper any results, either. The men Dora had seen who were somehow connected to Parnell must have been lying low, because she hadn't noticed either of them around since that one time.

Cooper heard his name being called and looked across the room to see Butch Cassidy and Harry Longabaugh sitting with Yance Shelby at the gambler's usual table. Shelby was as dapper as ever; he didn't have to worry about things like rain because he so seldom went outside. And the dry clothing sported by Cassidy and Longabaugh told Cooper that they had been in the Golden Garter since before the rain had started.

The sight of the two men made Cooper frown. He had let the whole problem of what to do about them slide while he worried about finding Parnell. But the fact remained that he had been socializing with wanted owlhoots, and he was sworn to uphold the law. It didn't really matter that Cassidy and Longabaugh weren't wanted in Texas and had apparently been living the lives of upstanding citizens while they were here. Cooper knew that he ought to march them at gunpoint back down to the county lockup at the other end of Main Street.

It was unlikely, though, that two such notorious outlaws would allow themselves to be arrested without a fight, and Cooper didn't feel much like killing either of them. Besides, there was always the possibility, remote though it might be, that he was wrong about them. What if they *weren't* Butch Cassidy and the Sundance Kid? Cooper didn't want to arrest a couple of innocent men.

"Congratulations, Cooper," the Ranger muttered to himself as he started over to the table. "You've talked yourself out of doing anything again."

"Howdy, Cooper," Cassidy greeted him as he came up to the table. "Turning into a night that's not fit for man nor beast out there."

"Best stay in here where it's warm and dry," advised Longabaugh.

"That's what I intend to do," said Cooper as he pulled out a chair and sat down.

Shelby riffled the cards in his hands and grinned. "I know a surefire way to pass the time."

"I don't know. . . ." Cooper began dubiously.

Tess Malone came up behind him, put her hand on his shoulder, and said, "I'll stake you."

Cooper turned his head to look up at her. She regarded him steadily, an unreadable expression in her blue eyes. "I reckon I probably owe you too much already," he said.

"Don't worry about that," she said with a casual wave as she left his side and went around the table to a vacant chair. "I'll sit in on the game, and you can bet what you owe me. Double or nothing, if you'd like."

"Now *that's* an interesting wager," said Cassidy with a grin. "Are you going to take the lovely lady up on it, Cooper?"

"If he does, I don't know that I want any part of that hand," commented Longabaugh.

"I'd say that particular bet ought to be between just the two of you," put in Shelby. "What do you say, Cooper? One hand of poker, double or nothing, and the stakes are what you owe Tess here. How about it?"

Cooper leaned back in his chair. There had been a time in his life when he had been pretty wild, when he had been drifting toward the wrong side of the law and would take up any dare, answer any challenge. Especially when it came from a pretty woman. But then he had pinned on the badge, and things had changed in his life. The wild side had no longer had the same appeal.

But at this moment, as he sat looking across the felt-covered table at Tess Malone, he felt the past calling to him, the siren song of the unknown, the urge to take that gamble and see what happened.

"Deal 'em, Yance," Cooper said.

Shelby, Cassidy, and Longabaugh all grinned in anticipation, but Cooper and Tess just sat there, regarding each other intently across the table, as Shelby shuffled the cards. He offered the cut to Tess, but she said, "Mr. Cooper is the guest here. Let him cut."

Cooper cut the cards. Shelby asked, "What's the game?"

Cooper looked at Tess and raised his eyebrows slightly. She said, "Five-card stud."

"Stud it is," said Shelby. "Showdown style."

He was sitting to Cooper's left, between Cooper and Tess. He dealt hole cards facedown to Tess first, then the Ranger. Tess glanced at her card, but Cooper didn't even look at his.

Tess drew an eight next, Cooper a queen. "Edge to Cooper," said Shelby. He dealt again, this time another eight to Tess, a deuce to Cooper. Shelby gave a little shake of his head as he said, "There goes your straight, Cooper."

The dealing continued, a seven to Tess and another two to Cooper. "Pair of deuces," Shelby intoned. His expression was more solemn now, and Cassidy and Longabaugh weren't grinning quite as broadly, either. The natural suspense of the game was drawing them in.

A fifth and final card landed faceup in front of Tess. It was a four, prompting Shelby to say, "Pair of eights beats the pair of deuces."

"Cooper has one more card to go," said Tess, her level gaze never leaving his.

Shelby nodded and sent the card spinning deftly onto the felt in front of Cooper. It was a jack. Shelby blew out the breath he had been holding and said, "That's it."

Tess turned over her hole card. It was the ace of hearts. A faint smile tugged at her mouth. "My eights still beat your deuces, Cooper," she said. "Looks like you're going to be into me for a lot of money if that last card isn't kind to you."

"Let's see," said Cooper, sounding a lot more calm than he felt inside. He reached out and flipped over the card that had been lying facedown in front of him.

Shelby's breath hissed between his teeth as he saw the pair of pips on the card.

Cooper let himself smile, just a little.

"Well, I'll be damned," Cassidy said softly. "Cooper won. With three deuces, of all things."

Longabaugh drawled, "Doesn't matter what the cards are, as long as you've got more of the right kind than the other fella. Or in this case, the lady."

"Well, Cooper," Tess said, "looks like we're even."

"Does that mean we start over?" he asked.

She gestured at the table. "The cards don't lie. You can't argue with fate."

Cooper felt the tension in him ease. If this was her way of forgiving him for what she thought had happened with Dora, that was fine with him. He felt a genuine liking for Tess Malone, and he sensed that with time that liking could grow into something even stronger. His smile widened . . .

Then abruptly disappeared as the front door of the Golden Garter opened, letting in a gust of wind and rain and a bulky figure in a slicker who marched straight toward the table where Cooper, Tess, Shelby, Cassidy, and Longabaugh were sitting. Detective J. P. McCormick's hat was jammed down tight on his head, and his expression was as dark as the storm clouds that had rolled in from the west earlier in the evening.

"Hello, J. P.," Shelby said as the detective came up to the table. "Care to play a little poker?"

"Not now, Yance," snapped McCormick. He gave Tess a polite nod, ever the gentleman even when he was feeling the strain of something bothering him, as he obviously was tonight. He looked across the table at Cooper and said, "I got to talk to you."

"Trouble?" Cooper asked as he straightened in his chair.

McCormick nodded. "Damn right. And if you're willin', I could sure use a hand from the Texas Rangers."

FIFTEEN

Kyle Forrest walked down the main street of North Fork, his head turning from side to side. The empty boardwalks seemed populated by dozens of people. There to his right, in front of the blacksmith shop, was Lucas McCain and his son, Mark. To the left, the Lone Ranger and Tonto. Kyle's head turned, and he saw Sheriff John T. Chance in front of the jail, along with Dude and Colorado and Stumpy. A wind seemed to blow, though none really did inside the cavernous warehouse, and the wail of the wind turned into the mournful song of a harmonica in the mouth of a man with no name who looked like Charles Bronson. The Cartwrights came out of the saloon on the corner, all four of them, even Adam. Another man with no name, this one wearing a flat-brimmed black hat and a serape, rode down the street, a stubby black cigar clenched between his teeth as he regarded his surroundings with a pinched, almost pained, expression.

And wobbling along the street on a bicycle came Butch and Etta, trailed by Sundance on horseback. Kyle stopped and stood where he was, watching raptly as they passed him by, and as they did he thought he saw disapproval in the fleeting glances they cast his way. . . .

"Kyle!"

Suddenly, the warehouse was empty again except for the buildings. The phantom figures disappeared in less than the blink of an eye. All it took to banish them was the voice of Mitch Graham calling out to Kyle.

Kyle turned and saw Mitch striding toward him. Mitch jerked his head toward the front of the building and said, "Come on. The others are waiting."

Kyle took a deep breath and forced himself back into the reality around him. "Who's guarding the prisoners?"

"Dane and Rockley. Buddy, Fulton, and Dobie are waiting for us in the office."

"What's this about?" asked Kyle. "Why did you want to talk to us?"

A smile spread across Mitch's face, and something about the expression worried Kyle. "Because I've got an idea," Mitch said. "I think you're going to like it."

Kyle wasn't so sure of that. But he supposed he could listen to what Mitch had to say.

They walked up to the office and found the other three men waiting there. Kyle went behind the desk and sat down. Buddy and Fulton were sitting on the old sofa against the wall, while Dobie perched on the edge of a chair. Mitch stood in the center of the room.

"All right," said Kyle. "Let's hear what you've got to say, Mitch."

"First of all," Mitch said, looking at Dobie, "do you know if Northrup has transferred that money yet?"

"He hadn't the last time I checked with the bank in Switzerland," replied Dobie, "but it's early yet."

"It's a lot later in Switzerland," snapped Mitch. "What if he waits until after the banks are closed over there?"

"This is the computer age, Mitch. Electronic banking goes on twenty-four hours a day."

Mitch nodded. "Yeah, I guess you're right." He glanced around at the others. "I thought while we're waiting, we might want to make an old-fashioned withdrawal from some other bank, the way we do best."

"You mean pull another job?" asked Buddy.

"Nobody would be expecting it this soon."

Kyle pressed his hands down against the top of the desk and said, "That's crazy. We're waiting for Northrup to hand over twenty million dollars to us. Why risk our lives going after a few hundred thousand?"

"Because there's no such thing as too much money," Mitch answered without hesitation. "We should take it because we can."

Kyle shook his head. "No. We have to guard Mrs. Northrup and the little girl—"

"Dane and Rockley can do that with no problem. Mrs. Northrup is so scared she's not going to give anybody any trouble. The rest of us can handle the job."

"But like Kyle said," Dobie pointed out, "we'd be risking our lives."

"It's not like we haven't done that before," said Mitch. "Besides, like *I* said, nobody's going to be expecting us to hit again so soon. It won't be much of a risk. We'll waltz in and out of there so quick nobody will be able to stop us."

Fulton said, "I guess it's something to think about, anyway."

They were doing more than thinking about it, Kyle realized. Buddy, Fulton, and Dobie were starting to look downright intrigued by Mitch's suggestion. And deep down, Kyle had to admit, there was some merit to what Mitch was saying. The job could probably be carried out fairly easily. But the risk just wasn't worth it.

"Well?" Mitch prodded. "What do you say?"

"I think we should try it," Fulton said.

"Maybe," said Dobie. "But I want to hear more details."

"Me, too," agreed Buddy. "You got a target picked out, Mitch?"

Mitch nodded. "Yeah, a little bank on the west side. It's in an affluent area, ought to be lots of money in it." He told them the name of the bank and where it was located, and the three men started to nod.

Once again, Kyle felt them slipping away from him. They were his Wild Bunch, his Kid Curry and Elzy Lay and Ben Kilpatrick and Will Carver. He had recruited them, put the group together, planned their first jobs. But Sundance had never tried to take over from Butch, the way Mitch was trying to take the gang away from him. A bitter taste rose in Kyle's mouth.

"You're all going to do this whether I agree or not, aren't you?" he said.

Mitch shrugged. "We'd much rather you were on our side, Kyle."

"All right," Kyle said, abruptly coming to a decision. "But this is the last one, understand? After this, I'm in charge again."

"Hell, you've always been in charge, partner," said Mitch with an ingratiating grin. "But you've always been willing to listen to a good idea, too, and that's what this is. I was right about grabbing Mrs. Northrup, wasn't I?"

"We don't have the money yet."

"We will," Mitch said confidently. "We will."

"When do you want to hit the bank?"

"No point in waiting. I say we go today, while we're waiting on Northrup."

"That's moving mighty fast," said Buddy.

"The sooner we hit, the more surprised everyone is going to be."

"Well, yeah, I suppose that's right." Buddy nodded. "Sounds like Mitch has thought this all out. If he thinks we can do it today, I'll go along with him."

"So will I," said Fulton.

Dobie hesitated, then shrugged. "I guess it's all right with me."

Mitch looked at Kyle, and a moment that seemed longer than it really was stretched between them.

Then Kyle nodded and said, "Saddle up."

"Any word on the Northrup case this morning?" Walker asked as he came into Ranger headquarters.

Trivette said from his desk, "I don't think there *is* a Northrup case. I talked to Abe Wilkins a little while ago. He said Northrup went straight home from the bank yesterday afternoon, like he said he was going to, then stayed in all night. Abe called the house this morning, and Northrup agreed to bring his wife in to give her statement at three o'clock this afternoon.''

Walker frowned slightly. ''Wilkins didn't talk directly to Mrs. Northrup?''

''No, and that worried him a little, too,'' Trivette replied with a shake of his head. ''Northrup claimed she was in the shower. But Abe said when he suggested that they come in at three, Northrup agreed right away, didn't act like he was stalling or anything. He said his wife was fine and none the worse for the experience.''

''What about the little girl?''

''Northrup said she wasn't going to school today, but that she was all right, too.''

Walker perched a hip on the corner of Trivette's desk and pulled thoughtfully at the lobe of his right ear. ''I don't know, Trivette,'' he said slowly. ''Something still strikes me as strange about all this.''

''Me, too.''

''Has Abe got a man on Northrup this morning?''

Trivette nodded. ''He said Northrup left the house at the normal time and went straight to the bank. I guess he wants to get in a morning's work before he takes off to bring his wife in.''

''Maybe . . .''

''You want to go see Mrs. Northrup, talk to her yourself?'' suggested Trivette.

Walker nodded. ''That's a good idea.'' He stood up. He hadn't even taken off his hat after entering the office. ''Come on.''

Trivette reached for his own Stetson.

The two Rangers were in Walker's pickup, driving west along the Overhead Freeway at the south end of Fort Worth's downtown area. To the left loomed the massive main post office and the old Texas & Pacific depot. To the right were the Water Gardens and the Tarrant County Convention Center, their modern lines replacing the rowdy red-light district known as Hell's Half Acre that had once stood there.

Walker's brain was busily sorting out the various facets of

the Northrup affair, trying to determine if there was any real reason to be suspicious. Walker was unable to pin down anything specific, but his instincts still told him it was worth a drive out South Hulen Street to pay a visit to Mrs. Northrup. He glanced to the left, at the jumble of warehouses and other buildings that filled the industrial area south of the freeway, and suddenly he caught a glimpse of a word on a sign that seemed to jump out at him.

"That's it!" Walker said as his foot went to the brake, slowing the pickup.

"What?" asked Trivette, alarmed by Walker's sudden reaction. "What's wrong, Walker?"

"The one paint-related thing we didn't check out," Walker said as he checked the traffic in the pickup's mirrors and then swerved it toward the Henderson Street exit at the western end of the elevated freeway.

"You're back to that bank-robbery business? What about Mrs. Northrup?"

"We can go talk to her after we check this out," said Walker. "C. D. kept talking about playing games with that mouse he's been after. Something about that always jogged my brain a little, but I never could figure out what it was until now." Walker took the looping exit ramp, then made the turn onto Lancaster and headed east again. This took them under the freeway and then alongside it, driving in the shadow of the elevated structure. "What kind of game do you play with paint?"

"I don't know. . . . *Paintball!*" Trivette exclaimed as the answer abruptly came to him. "We never checked out any of the paintball places in the metroplex."

"And they use bright colors, like red," said Walker.

"I don't know, Walker," Trivette said dubiously. "Seems like a thin connection to me."

"No thinner than any of the others we checked out after we busted Kilbride." Walker turned the pickup off Lancaster onto a side street and drove under a railroad overpass.

"What made you think of paintball in the first place?" asked Trivette.

Walker slowed the truck and pointed. "That."

Trivette looked up at the big sign that read NORTH FORK PAINTBALL. It was positioned on the wall of an old warehouse so that it was visible from the freeway a couple of blocks away. "You know anything about this place?" Trivette asked.

Walker shook his head. "No, but we can start here. If anybody's around, they can probably tell us where to find the other places in the metroplex where people play paintball."

Walker had to circle the block before he found a place to park. When he finally located a space at the curb, it was small enough so that he had to carefully maneuver the oversized pickup into it. The place was around the corner from the front entrance of the warehouse. Walker and Trivette got out and began walking along the cement sidewalk.

When they reached the entrance and saw the sign taped to it stating that the place was closed for remodeling, Trivette grunted in disappointment. "Guess we won't talk to anybody after all," he said. "But I can get on the phone once we're back at headquarters and find out what we need to know."

Walker rested his fingertips lightly on the door as he nodded. "Yeah."

"I guess we go talk to Mrs. Northrup now."

"Yeah," Walker said again. Still, he hesitated for some reason. Something about this place seemed to speak to him on some level, telling him that it was important somehow.

He and Trivette walked slowly around the building, and as they rounded the corner a van pulled out of the alley behind the warehouse. Walker saw a couple of young men in the front seats, and the passenger was fiddling with something in his lap. He lifted the object just for a second as he struggled with it, but that was long enough for Walker's keen eyes to focus on it.

What he saw was the breech and barrel of an automatic rifle.

Walker's hand shot out and gripped Trivette's arm. "Did you see that?" asked Walker.

"What?"

"One of the men in that van that just left had an assault rifle."

Trivette's eyes widened in surprise and speculation. "Walker, you don't think . . ." he began.

"I think we may have just gotten lucky, Trivette." Walker hurried down the sidewalk toward his pickup. "Come on! We don't want to lose them now."

SIXTEEN

Walker and Trivette raced to the pickup and piled into it. Trivette turned around and looked out the back window to keep an eye on the van, which was headed in the other direction, back toward the freeway. Walker started the engine and pulled out of the parking place in an expert turn. He tromped down on the accelerator and sent the pickup leaping ahead.

"They turned west on Lancaster," Trivette said a moment later.

"I see them," Walker replied grimly. His hands gripped the steering wheel tightly. Logically, it was too much to expect that after such a long, fruitless search, he and Trivette had found the gang of bank robbers so easily. But that was the way things worked sometimes, Walker reminded himself. Life always had a pattern to it, but sometimes that pattern was too complex for mortal eyes to see. What human beings called coincidence was often the hand of some greater, guiding force.

If that was indeed the bank robbers up there, Walker didn't want to tip them off that they were being followed. He left the pickup's flashing lights off and instead relied on his driving skills to cut the gap between him and his quarry. The series of red lights on Lancaster cooperated, and Walker was able to close to within a block of the van by the time it reached the ramp that would take it up onto the freeway.

Trivette leaned forward and squinted, trying to read the license plate of the van. "Three . . . eight . . . five . . . one . . . W . . . Z," he said. "That what it looks like to you, Walker?"

Walker nodded. "Call it in, see if there's any sort of report on it." Trivette reached for the microphone clipped under the dash, but Walker shook his head. "Use your cell phone instead of the radio, just in case they've got a scanner up there in the van."

Quickly, Trivette contacted Ranger headquarters. It took only a moment to patch him through from there to the Fort Worth Police Department's communications center, where a dispatch officer told him that there were no stolen-car reports on the vehicle in question, a Ford Aerostar van registered to a resident of one of the metroplex's suburban cities.

Trivette shook his head and said, "That's not an Aerostar, it's a Chevy Astro."

"They've switched plates," said Walker. "If the owner of that Aerostar tries to drive it today, he'll be stopped by the cops because the plates on it now will show up on the hot sheet. Advise FWPD of the switch and tell them that in all likelihood we're following a stolen vehicle."

Trivette relayed the information, then the dispatcher asked, "Do you request backup, Ranger?"

"Do we want backup, Walker?"

Walker shook his head. "Not yet. I want to see where they're going. Just give the police our location and tell them to have a couple of units in the area, no lights or sirens."

Trivette spoke to the dispatcher for a moment longer, then closed the cell phone. "They're alerted to the fact that something may be going down, but they'll wait until you give the word before closing in." Trivette paused, then went on, "Do you think they'll hit another bank again so soon? It's only been a couple of weeks. Usually it's closer to a month before they pull another job."

"Maybe they've increased their pace for some reason," speculated Walker. "Why else would they be driving around town in a stolen van with automatic weapons?''

''Yeah. You know, Walker, they were probably going out the back of that warehouse while we were standing around the front.''

Walker nodded. He knew his sixth sense had been trying to warn him about *something*. Now he thought he understood what it was.

The van drove west on Interstate 30. Whoever was at the wheel followed all the traffic laws, properly signaling his lane changes and keeping the van within a couple of miles either way of the speed limit. There was nothing about the van to draw the attention of the authorities, especially since the vehicle that really belonged to the license plates had not been reported stolen. If not for Walker's keen observation, no one would have any idea that those men were on their way to rob a bank—if that was indeed what they were up to.

Walker stayed well back, keeping several vehicles between the van and his pickup. The occupants of the van had no reason to be suspicious of the pickup, even when Walker took the same exit from the freeway. There were several high-rise buildings along the access road, and Walker knew that one of them housed a bank. There was no question now in his mind about what was going to happen. As the van turned in to the bank parking lot, Walker said tensely to Trivette, ''Call for that backup now.''

Trivette still had an open line on his cell phone. He barked the name of the bank and its location into the phone, as well as the code number for an armed robbery in progress. That would bring every patrol unit in the vicinity screaming toward the bank.

In the meantime, it was up to Walker and Trivette to delay the gang so that they couldn't enter the bank and precipitate another hostage crisis. The parking lot was elaborately landscaped. Concrete dividers separated the aisles of parking spaces, and those dividers also served as planters for rows of shrubs. Walker took a different path through the parking lot, counting on the shrubs to shield his pickup from view and keep the robbers from noticing it. He pressed down hard on the gas pedal.

Walker reached the end of the row and swung around it in a tight, tire-screeching turn. The van had just pulled up in the no-parking area at the front door of the bank. Walker's pickup came to a stop facing the van, with some thirty feet separating the two vehicles. The thieves were already climbing out of the van, carrying automatic weapons and dressed in body armor, ski masks, and helmets, as usual. Walker and Trivette leaped out of the pickup, using the open doors as cover as they leveled their pistols at the bank robbers. Walker shouted, "Texas Rangers! Freeze! You're under arrest!"

There were four of the robbers, instead of the usual half dozen, plus the man at the wheel of the van. Walker wondered fleetingly where the other two members of the gang were as the men jerked in surprise at being challenged and swung toward the two Rangers. A chattering burst of gunfire exploded from one of the automatic weapons.

Walker ducked as the glass in the window of the open door beside him shattered in a million pieces. He squeezed off a couple of shots from the Sig P-220, the slugs chipping pieces of concrete from the sidewalk at the feet of the robbers. Walker was trying to herd them back toward the van in order to keep them from entering the bank. On the other side of the pickup, Trivette had opened fire, too. He concentrated his shots on the front tires of the van, flattening both of them.

Two of the robbers made a determined dash for the bank entrance, but they were turned back by the shots of the guards, who had been alerted by the commotion just outside the doors. Walker heard screams of fear coming from inside the bank as the robbers yanked the doors open then were forced to retreat toward the van, but he was confident that no one inside had been hurt. None of the shots fired so far had been directed inside the building.

Sirens were wailing in the distance and coming closer by the second. Within a matter of minutes, the bank parking lot would be covered with police cars. The robbers were trapped unless they managed to get out of here in a hurry, and that was unlikely with the flattened tires on the van.

Crouched behind the open door of the pickup, Walker squeezed off two more shots in an attempt to keep the robbers pinned down beside the van. Suddenly, one of the men strode boldly away from the vehicle, turning to spray the glass entrance doors of the bank with automatic rifle fire. The doors exploded in a shower of sparkling glass shards under the assault. That would keep everyone inside busy hugging the floor for cover.

Walker targeted the man's legs, hoping the body armor wouldn't be quite as strong there. He saw little puffs of dust as his bullets struck the man's thighs, causing him to stagger. The bank robber didn't go down, though. He stayed on his feet and swung his weapon toward Walker's pickup. Slugs from the rifle chewed into the grille, shattering the headlights and punching through the radiator. Steam billowed from underneath the hood. As the clip of ammo ran out the gunman calmly ejected it and inserted a fresh clip.

Following the lead of their bold companion, the other robbers were now spreading out from the van, stalking stiff-legged into the parking lot. Walker's jaw clenched tightly as he saw one of the men jerk open the door of a car and reach inside to grab the terrified occupant, a middle-aged man in a suit. Walker had hoped that all the vehicles in the lot were unoccupied, but clearly, that wasn't the case. Now the gang had a hostage after all.

"Hold your fire, Trivette," snapped Walker as the robber turned and hauled the hostage in front of him. He shoved the barrel of the automatic rifle against the side of the man's head. The hostage was trembling so badly that he might have fallen down if not for the robber's hand holding the collar of his coat.

"Back off, Rangers!" shouted the robber, his voice muffled by the bulletproof visor of the helmet he wore. "I'll blow his damn head off!"

The other four robbers, including the wheelman, who had abandoned the crippled van, stood around stiffly, their rifles held ready for instant use. A couple of them looked around as police cars screeched into the parking lot, but the others had their attention focused on Walker and Trivette.

"Get all the cops out of here, or this son of a bitch dies!"

The shouted ultimatum came from the robber holding his gun to the head of the hostage. "Now!"

"Don't make things worse by killing somebody!" Walker called back to him.

The bank robber's laugh was chilling. "People died the last time out. You think one more's going to make a difference, Ranger?"

The robber was right. Half a dozen people had died in that last holdup. He and his companions were already guilty of capital murder and faced the death penalty if convicted, which they surely would be. So they had nothing to lose by killing even more people today.

"You can't get away!" shouted Trivette. "The place is already surrounded!"

That was true. Police cruisers had blockaded the entrance to the parking lot. There was no way out.

But at the same time, it was something of a standoff, because the weapons used by Walker, Trivette, and the police wouldn't penetrate the body armor of the thieves. They could stand out in the open with little fear of being shot at this point.

"Damn," muttered Trivette. "We need a grenade launcher."

"Not as long as they have a prisoner," said Walker. "We have to figure out some way to get him away from them."

The robber turned and pushed the hostage up against the car from which the man had been dragged, all the while still holding the automatic weapon to his head. "Well, Rangers, what's it going to be? Do I kill him . . . or do you let us drive away from here in this fancy new car?"

The car was big enough to hold all of them, Walker realized. And ordering the police cars to move back and let the robbers leave might save the hostage's life for a few minutes. But Walker was convinced that the robbers wouldn't hang on to the man for very long. Probably as soon as they were well away from the bank, they would shoot him in the head and dump him out of the car. Walker couldn't allow that.

The question was, how was he going to stop it?

• • •

Kevin Dalmas was as scared as he had ever been in his life, even back in the bad old days in 'Nam. He had gone on some pretty hairy jungle patrols, had survived rocket attacks, had even gone down into the tunnels to ferret out some of the Cong. But he had never had the barrel of a gun shoved against his head before, certainly not an automatic weapon that could pretty well decapitate him with one burst. Since coming home in '70 he had lived a quiet, peaceful life, rising in the business world and sliding into middle age while effectively forgetting what true violence was like. Forgetting the way fear made you sweat and how bad that sweat stank . . .

Until now, when he knew that the only thing separating him from a grisly death was a few ounces of pressure on a trigger.

In that body armor and those helmets, they looked like something out of a *Star Wars* movie. Kevin had seen them and ducked down in the front seat of his car, hoping no one would notice him. But with an unerring instinct, one of the gunmen had come for him, and now Kevin was just trying to breathe and not pass out from terror as his captor once again shoved him against the car, banging his face against the roof.

"I'll kill him!" the robber shouted, and to emphasize his point, he jabbed the barrel of the rifle hard against Kevin's temple.

Too hard, as it turned out, because the barrel of the weapon gouged out a chunk of skin and slid away from Kevin's head in the slick blood that suddenly welled from the wound.

Kevin didn't think about what he was doing as the pain burst in his head. It was like he was back in the jungle, acting on pure instinct as he shoved away from the car as hard as he could. That sent him slamming back against his captor, and Kevin's collar ripped as the robber staggered backward.

Abruptly free, Kevin dropped to the concrete of the parking lot, not even feeling the pain as the concrete abraded the knees of his trousers and scraped his skin. He rolled underneath the big luxury car he had worked so hard to own.

Maybe, just maybe, now it would save his life.

• • •

Walker saw his chance and took it. The hostage was out of the line of fire, and the robber had the hand holding the automatic rifle stuck out at his side. Walker aimed and fired in less than the blink of an eye.

The bullet hit the ring finger of the robber's right hand and blew off everything from the first knuckle on. It struck the hard rubber pistol grip of the automatic rifle and gouged out a chunk of it before tumbling upward and slicing through the fleshy part of the gunman's hand just below the thumb. The rifle went spinning out of his grasp as he screamed and grabbed his wounded hand with the other hand. The man went to his knees in pain.

But the other four were still dangerous, as Walker and Trivette discovered a second later when all four robbers opened fire. The hail of lead poured into Walker's pickup, shaking the heavy vehicle. Walker knew it was only a matter of time until the gas tank exploded, so he threw a couple of shots at the robbers and shouted over the din, "Move, Trivette, move!"

Trivette used the speed and explosiveness that had once made him an All-Pro wide receiver for the Dallas Cowboys, sprinting away from the pickup and throwing himself out full-length behind the nearest of the concrete dividers. He rolled over and twisted around so that he could poke his gun around the end of the divider and fire at the bank robbers.

Walker was on the wrong side of the truck to do that. He had to go the other direction, toward the building. There was nothing to shelter him there. All he could do was drop flat as the gas tank finally blew. Heat and impact slammed at him like the blows of twin fists. A shard of flying metal raked across Walker's back, slicing through his shirt and opening up a painful cut.

Walker was partially deafened by the explosion, and some of his hair was singed off. But he was able to push himself up on his hands and knees and fire a couple of shots toward the fleeing robbers through the leaping flames that surrounded the burning wreckage of what had been his pickup. The man he had wounded was on his feet again, Walker saw, being helped by one of his companions. A couple of them turned in circles, spraying lead all over the parking lot, while the others climbed into the car from which the hostage had been pulled earlier. Walker had lost sight of the man and hoped he was still alive somewhere out there in the hell of flame and automatic-weapons fire that the bank parking lot had been turned into.

Walker lurched to his feet as the big, heavy luxury car backed out of its parking place. The two bank robbers who were still outside the car turned their fire toward the nearest exit to the access road. One of the police cruisers was parked there at an angle, and the two uniformed officers had taken cover behind the car. One of them exposed himself foolishly as he tried to return the fire of the robbers, and he was flung backward by a burst from one of the automatic rifles.

The back doors of the luxury car still stood wide open. One of the remaining robbers dove inside as the driver gunned the engine. The last of the gang was about to follow suit when Walker fired at him. The man staggered and reached for the car door, clearly hoping to pull himself inside, but he couldn't reach it. With its tires smoking and squealing, the car leaped ahead toward the exit.

Walker and Trivette ran past the still-burning remains of Walker's pickup and saw the car gain speed. Its front bumper rammed the rear of the police car and shoved it out of the way with a grinding crash. Walker grimaced. The robbers were on the verge of getting away again, just as they had done following the standoff in downtown Fort Worth a couple of weeks earlier.

Not all of them were going to make their escape this time, however. One of the robbers had been left behind. The man Walker had wounded dropped his rifle and slumped to the pavement.

Walker and Trivette ran toward the fallen man as the car containing the rest of the gang roared and skidded onto the access road. There was an entrance ramp onto the freeway just a few yards to the west, but the car didn't go in that direction. Instead it turned the wrong way on the one-way road and roared toward the east. The access road was blocked in that direction, too, but only at the next intersection. There were other places to turn before the car reached that point, and that was exactly what it did, sliding through a sharp turn that took it into the parking lot of another high-rise, this one an office building. The lot extended all the way around the building to another street on the far side. At each of the exits was a kiosk with a wooden arm that raised and lowered to control who was admitted to the parking lot. The car burst through the arm that was lowered across one of the exits and reached the side street.

Walker found out about that later. At the moment, he was more concerned about the two men lying on the parking lot. One of them, the middle-aged man who had briefly been a hostage, was sprawled facedown on the concrete with his hands covering his head. He was shaking violently, so Walker knew he was still alive. "Check on him!" he snapped to Trivette.

Trivette ran over to the man and dropped to a knee beside him. "Sir!" he said urgently. "Sir, are you all right?"

Trivette grasped the man's shoulder and gently rolled him over, saw that the man's eyes were open and that he was conscious. "Don't . . . don't shoot me!" the man gasped.

"I'm a Texas Ranger," Trivette told him. "You're all right now. It's all over."

Meanwhile, Walker was approaching the fallen bank robber, his pistol trained on the man just in case. Walker saw a small puddle of blood underneath the man's head, though, so he didn't think the robber represented much of a threat anymore.

As he drew closer Walker could tell that his bullet had gone through the small gap between the bottom of the robber's helmet and the shoulder of the body armor the man wore. The shot had struck the robber in the side of the neck, likely severing an artery.

After all the thousands of rounds of ammunition that had been fired in the past few minutes, an eerie silence had settled down over the parking lot of the bank. Walker could hear the harsh, fluttering sound of the man's breathing. He used his foot to slide the fallen automatic rifle well out of reach, then hooked his toe under the robber's shoulder and rolled him over. The man flopped onto his back.

Walker bent over, took hold of the helmet with his free hand, and pulled it off the man's head. As he tossed the helmet to the side he saw that the bank robber was in his mid-thirties, with short dark hair. Under different circumstances, he would have looked rather clean-cut, Walker decided, and he had no doubt that this was one of the men Frank Kilbride had described to him and Trivette.

The bullet wound on the side of the man's neck was ugly and was still welling blood. Walker wouldn't have given much for the robber's chances of surviving. The man's eyes were closed, but as Walker stood over him, still covering him with the pistol, the man stirred and opened his eyes. He blinked several times before his gaze seemed to fasten on Walker.

"Sundance?" the man croaked. "Is that you, Sundance?"

Walker frowned. What in blazes was the man talking about?

"Who are those guys?" asked the robber. Then a spasm of coughing shook him and more blood flowed from his neck.

"Take it easy," Walker told the man. "Help's on the way."

"Whole damned . . . Bolivian army out there."

The man was hallucinating as he slipped closer and closer to death, Walker realized. But if he could get through to the robber, maybe he could find out where the rest of the gang had gone.

"Your friends left you here to die," Walker told him bluntly. "Tell me where they went, and we'll get them."

The man's eyes closed, and for a moment Walker thought he was gone. But then they opened again, and they seemed clearer now. In a more coherent but still steadily weakening voice, the man asked, "Who are you?"

"I'm a Texas Ranger," Walker said.

"Ranger . . . John Reid . . . only Ranger left alive . . ." The man was gone again, lost in whatever weird private fantasy was playing out in his head. He gave another racking cough and cried out, "Sundance? Where's Sundance?"

If Walker was going to get any information out of the man, he was going to have to play along with the fantasy. Casting his mind back to the movie, he knelt beside the wounded man and said, "Right here, Butch. I'm right here." He hoped he was guessing right about what was going on inside the man's deranged brain.

The man lifted a gloved hand and clutched Walker's arm. "Sorry, Sundance," he said. "Reckon I finally . . . did us in."

"What about the rest of the Wild Bunch? Did they go back to the Hole in the Wall?" Walker suddenly remembered what had happened earlier today. "Or to North Fork?"

"North Fork," the man breathed, but Walker didn't know if he was answering the question or simply repeating what he had heard. "Got to go to North Fork and get Jessica . . . I mean Etta . . . Etta Place."

Jessica. Roger Northrup's wife was named Jessica, Walker remembered. He and Trivette had been on their way to see her when he had noticed the paintball sign and gotten diverted to this botched and bloody bank-robbery attempt. Surely there couldn't be any connection between that case and this one.

But on the off chance that there might be, Walker leaned closer to the man and said, "Who's Jessica, Butch? Do you mean Jessica Northrup?"

The bank robber's fingers tightened on Walker's arm. He stared up and rasped, "You're not Sundance. You're not Mitch. He'll kill her."

"Kill who?" Walker asked urgently. "Mrs. Northrup?"

The man summoned up his strength to give a weak nod. "And the . . . little girl. You've got to . . . stop him, Ranger. I never wanted to . . . to hurt anybody. Butch Cassidy never killed anybody, you know that? Not in all the . . . the banks he robbed or the trains he held up. Never killed anybody . . ."

Walker's brain was whirling so fast it felt as if it was going to spin out of control. Unless what he had just heard was the crazed fantasy of a dying man, the bank-robbery gang was holding Jessica Northrup and her daughter prisoner at the old warehouse that was now North Fork Paintball. Could that be possible?

Walker couldn't take the risk of ignoring what the man had

said. ''We'll find the woman and the little girl,'' he promised. ''We won't let anything happen to them.''

''Good . . . Butch wouldn't have, either.'' The man's eyes drooped closed, and his fingers slipped off Walker's arm. His lips barely moved as he murmured once again, ''Who are those guys?''

Then his head fell back and he didn't stir again.

Walker looked up at Trivette, who had come up to stand over them. ''Did you hear that?'' asked Walker.

''Yeah, but it's crazy. It sounded like he said they've got Mrs. Northrup and her daughter back at that warehouse.''

''I think that's exactly what he meant,'' Walker said as he stood up and looked around the bank parking lot. It was full of police cars and fire trucks and ambulances now, with uniformed personnel rushing everywhere. The man who had been briefly taken hostage was sitting just inside the open rear doors of a nearby ambulance, an oxygen mask strapped over his face. He was breathing deeply as a paramedic checked him over. Firefighters were hosing down what was left of Walker's pickup, and police officers were leading still-frightened witnesses out of the bank building and taking their statements.

''What now?'' asked Trivette.

''We pay a visit to North Fork,'' answered Walker.

SEVENTEEN

Fort Worth, 1901

"The Texas Rangers?" Yance Shelby let out a low whistle of surprise. "You're a Ranger, Cooper?"

Cooper had seen the way Cassidy and Longabaugh had immediately tensed when McCormick mentioned the Rangers. Their attitude got even more wary as Shelby repeated the word. Tess Malone was staring at him curiously, too.

Cooper didn't see any point in trying to conceal the truth now. He gave a curt nod and said, "Yeah, I'm a Ranger."

"That's quite a secret you've been keeping to yourself, Cooper," said Cassidy. He smiled, but the expression didn't reach his eyes.

"Yeah," said Longabaugh, "I never would've figured you for a star packer, Cooper. If anything I thought you might be on the other side of the law."

"I nearly was . . . once." Cooper looked up at McCormick. Water was dripping from the city detective's hat and the slicker he wore. Whatever had brought McCormick here, it must have been something mighty serious if it had prompted him to reveal Cooper's true identity. Cooper asked, "What's wrong, J. P.?"

have been so quick to help him out, that night over at Harrigan's place."

"Yes, you would have," said Cassidy quietly. "And you know that as well as I do."

Longabaugh shrugged and reached for the bottle. He was pouring himself a drink when one of the young women who worked in the Golden Garter came hurrying up to the table. Cassidy glanced up and recognized her as the one called Dora. "Where's Cooper?" she asked. "He was here just a minute ago, wasn't he?"

"He was called away on business," said Shelby. "What do you want, Dora?"

Dora caught her full lower lip and worried it between her teeth for a moment, clearly trying to make up her mind about something. Finally she asked, "Do you know where he went?"

"Nope."

"What is it, Dora?" asked Cassidy. "What's wrong?"

"Well . . ." She hesitated again, then said, "He wanted me to keep an eye out for somebody, and I just wanted to tell him . . . the man's in here now."

Outside on the sidewalk, Cooper and McCormick paused under an awning so that the rain wouldn't fall on them. Cooper said, "What's going on, J. P.? You look pretty upset."

"Damn right I'm upset," said McCormick. "We got a young woman and a little boy missin' and most likely kidnapped."

Cooper frowned. "Tell me about it."

"The little boy's the son of a fella named Lewis Vance. He runs pretty much the biggest bank here in Fort Worth, Vance does. The sprout's name is Gilbert. The gal who's missin' along with him is his governess, name of Miss Emily Mills. Somebody grabbed 'em late this afternoon while the boy was ridin' along the Trinity not far from where his daddy lives. They got the gal at the same time."

"And they're holding the two of them for ransom?"

McCormick nodded. "Vance got a note at the bank this afternoon. The kidnappers didn't say anything about the young woman, but they demanded half a million dollars for the boy."

Cooper's bearded face was grim as he asked, "Does Vance intend to pay the ransom?"

"Nope, not a penny," replied McCormick with a shake of his head. "He don't have that kind of money."

"He could have taken it from the bank."

"Reckon that was what the kidnappers were countin' on, but Vance ain't that sort of man. Even when his own vice-president suggested that he do that, Vance turned thumbs-down on the idea."

"What's the vice-president got to do with it?"

"Nothing, really. He was there when Vance got the note and found out about what was happening. He thought Vance ought to pay up and not go to the law, like the kidnappers told him to. But he's just scared for the little boy and the woman."

Cooper nodded slowly as he thought about what McCormick had told him. Something in the story bothered Cooper, but he couldn't put his finger on what it was.

"You ever have any luck findin' that fella Parnell?" asked McCormick, breaking into Cooper's train of thought.

The Ranger shook his head. "No, you'd have heard about it if I found Parnell, J. P. With a couple of lives in danger, though, I'm going to have to forget about him for now. What can I do to help you on this kidnapping?"

McCormick squinted out at the drizzle and said, "If this damned rain hadn't come in, I'd've taken you down to the Trinity so we could see if we could pick up their trail. Nobody I ever saw could read signs as well as you, Cooper."

"But the rain will have washed out all the tracks."

McCormick nodded glumly. "I thought I'd go back to Vance's house and wait there until the kidnappers contact him again with instructions on how to pay the ransom. Then we can figure out how to set some sort of trap for 'em."

It was risky, and the delay involved before any real action could be taken would chafe at him and his fellow lawman, Cooper knew. But under the circumstances, there didn't seem to be any other way to proceed.

''All right—'' Cooper began, but then he heard his name being called and turned his head to see Cassidy coming down the sidewalk toward him and McCormick.

''It's one of those cattle buyers,'' said the detective. ''You still hangin' around with them, Cooper?''

Cooper didn't answer. He wondered what Cassidy wanted, and he felt discomfort at the idea of talking to the outlaw with McCormick right there. Cassidy had to have figured out by now, though, that Cooper didn't intend to reveal their real identities to the law.

Cassidy hurried up to them, his usual sauntering gait discarded. ''Hate to interrupt, but I've got some news for you . . . Ranger.''

Cooper glanced at McCormick and asked, ''Can't it wait?''

Cassidy shrugged. ''It's about that gent called Parnell you've been looking for. I guess we know now why you're after him. He's some sort of owlhoot, isn't he?''

''A bank robber . . . and a killer,'' confirmed Cooper.

''Well, Dora just saw the fella who was meeting with Parnell a few days ago. He's in the Golden Garter. Harry's keeping an eye on him.''

Instantly, Cooper felt torn. He wanted to help J. P. McCormick with the kidnapping case, but it might be hours before there were any developments in that matter. And it was his pursuit of Doyle Parnell that had brought him to Fort Worth in the first place. If Parnell was still around, Cooper didn't want to pass up any trail that might lead him to the bank robber.

McCormick made the decision easy for him by saying, ''You go ahead and check it out, Cooper. I don't expect to hear anything new about that other business until later tonight or in the morning. You can come on over to Vance's house later.'' He gave Cooper the address.

Cooper nodded and said, ''Thanks, J. P.'' He turned to Cassidy. ''Let's go back to the saloon.''

The two men strode back toward the Golden Garter, heads lowered against the rain. As they walked Cassidy remarked, ''They say politics makes strange bedfellows. So does packing a badge, from what I've seen.''

"You mean me and McCormick?"

"Sure," said Cassidy, sounding as if that wasn't what he meant at all.

"Justice is justice," said Cooper. "That's all that matters."

"An absolute, in other words."

"Well . . . most of the time. Every now and then, a man's got to think about what's the greater good and the greater evil."

"Then a lawman *can* compromise?"

Cooper glared down at the sidewalk, wishing he had never been put in the position of debating legal ethics with Butch Cassidy. He said curtly, "I've got a bank robber to catch. A bank robber named Doyle Parnell."

"Well, then, let's go catch him, pard," said Cassidy, sounding as jovial as ever once more. He probably figured he had won this oblique little debate.

And maybe he had, Cooper admitted to himself.

As they were nearing the door of the Golden Garter, it opened and a man came out, hunching his shoulders against the rain. He pulled his hat down tighter on his head as he turned south, toward the railroad tracks.

Harry Longabaugh came out of the saloon a moment later and inclined his head toward the man who was shuffling away down the sidewalk. Cooper and Cassidy understood perfectly what he meant, and Cooper nodded. The three men fell in alongside each other for a few steps before Cooper pointed across the street. Cassidy and Longabaugh veered in that direction, crossing the brick pavement and stepping over the streetcar tracks in the middle. Cooper stayed directly behind the man they were trailing.

It was a miserable night to be doing something like this, thought Cooper. He would have much rather been inside the Golden Garter, sipping Tess Malone's excellent whiskey and playing cards with Yance Shelby. He thought about Tess, the image of her lovely face filling his mind for a moment. The two of them had had their ups and downs, but Cooper sensed there was a genuine liking between them. Was there a chance that liking could ever grow into something even stronger?

He'd never know the answer to that question, Cooper told

himself. Soon, he would be leaving Fort Worth, no matter how the kidnapping case turned out and whether he found Parnell or not. A Ranger never stayed in one place for long, certainly not long enough to have any kind of romance that might actually mean something.

Half a block ahead of him, the man he was following suddenly stopped and turned toward the mouth of an alley he was passing. Cooper tensed, wondering what the man was doing, but then he relaxed a little as he saw another figure emerge from the alley. The light here was bad, but Cooper could see well enough to know that the second figure belonged to a woman. She held out a hand toward the man, who shook his head. A soiled dove, probably with a crib somewhere down that alley. But Cooper's quarry, thankfully, either wasn't in the mood or didn't have the money. He moved on, leaving the woman behind to spit on the sidewalk and then retreat back into the shadows of the alley.

Cooper knew she was likely to proposition him, too, so when he reached the mouth of the alley he increased his pace a little and gave a curt shake of his head to the figure that started out of the shadows. She retreated with a disappointed sigh.

The man Cooper was following walked several blocks, apparently lost in his own thoughts because he was paying little attention to anything around him. His head was down, his eyes turned toward the sidewalk in front of him. From time to time, his gait faltered, and Cooper thought he was probably drunk. Cooper debated whether to move in on the man, capture him and question him, or to simply continue following him in hopes that the man would lead him to Parnell. Cooper decided to keep trailing the man for the time being.

The man reached the Texas & Pacific tracks and crossed them east of the depot. He was near the spot where the infamous Spring Palace had been built in 1889. The huge exhibition hall had been constructed entirely of Texas products and was designed to be a showplace for Texas agriculture and industry, and that was exactly what it had been . . . until it had burned to the ground a few years later. In the time since then, warehouses and other industrial development had taken over the area.

The streets were almost completely dark now, and Cooper moved closer to the man he was following. A glance across the street showed him that Cassidy and Longabaugh had disappeared, but Cooper would have been willing to bet that they were still somewhere close by.

The drizzle had slackened off even more, until now there was just a fine, intermittent mist hanging in the air. The air had grown cooler, too, so that Cooper's damp clothes were uncomfortably chilly. He tried to ignore all that as he concentrated on his quarry.

Suddenly, the man stopped and turned, calling out in a whiskey-thickened voice, "Hey! Who's back there? What the hell do you want?"

Some instinct must have warned him, thought Cooper. The Ranger knew he hadn't made enough noise to alert the man. But it was too late to worry about that now. The man clawed beneath the long coat he was wearing and cursed.

"I see you back there, damn it! I'll teach you to follow me—"

The last thing Cooper wanted to do was kill this man. He lunged to the side as the man yanked out a gun and fired. Flame geysered from the barrel of the revolver, lighting up the night for an instant. The bullet whipped past Cooper's head.

"Hey!" someone shouted from the shadows. Cooper recognized Butch Cassidy's voice. He sprinted forward as he hoped that Cassidy and Longabaugh wouldn't open fire on the man.

They didn't. Cassidy's shout had been a diversionary tactic, and it worked. The man jerked around toward the other side of the street and let loose with another shot. That was the last one he had time for, because by then Cooper reached him and lashed out with a booted foot, kicking the gun out of the man's hand. The man yelped in pain and clutched his wrist where Cooper had kicked him. Cooper swung a hard right fist in a looping punch that caught the man on the jaw and sent him staggering backward. He tripped and fell awkwardly on the sidewalk.

Cooper heard rapid footsteps as Cassidy and Longabaugh closed in. He drew his gun and knelt beside the man he had just knocked down. Putting the barrel of the Colt under the man's chin, Cooper tipped his head back. "Take it easy if you don't want your head blown off," the Ranger warned him, although he had no intention of actually doing such a thing.

"Let's shed a little light on the subject, Harry," suggested Cassidy. A moment later Cooper heard the rasp of a match being scratched into life. Longabaugh cupped the tiny flame in his hand to protect it from the mist.

The light given off by the match wasn't much, but it was enough for Cooper to get a look at the face of the man he had captured. The man's hat had fallen off, revealing a balding head. He had a scraggly mustache and watery eyes. "What's your name?" demanded Cooper.

"I don't have to tell you anything," the man said, his voice revealing the strain of having the muzzle of a six-shooter jammed under his chin. He sounded more sober now. Being this close to death would do that. Still, he was able to bluster, "Who the hell are you, anyway?"

"I'm a Texas Ranger," Cooper told him, "and I'll ask you again: What's your name?"

The man swallowed hard. "Gallagher, Sam Gallagher."

The name was vaguely familiar to Cooper, and so was the man's face. Cooper took a guess and said, "Not that long out of Huntsville, are you, Gallagher?"

"Damn it, I ain't done nothing—"

"Where's Parnell?" Cooper cut in, hoping to startle a response out of Gallagher by the unexpected question.

It didn't work. Gallagher said, "Who?"

The match Longabaugh was holding flickered out. He lit another one, and as he did he said, "Those shots are liable to bring the police, Cooper. If you want to find out anything from this jasper, you'd better let me and Butch work him over."

"A fella hasn't been born we can't make talk," added Cassidy. He took a knife from his pocket and opened it, began idly cleaning his fingernails with the long, shining blade. Gallagher's eyes couldn't help but follow the movements of the knife.

Cooper knew they were bluffing, so he played his part. "I don't know," he said reluctantly. "I'm a lawman, after all. . . ."

"What you don't know about can't bother you," said Cassidy. "Just take a walk for a few minutes, Cooper. We'll find out where Parnell is. Then we'll take care of Gallagher here."

Longabaugh lowered his head and blew out the match with a puff of air. Darkness dropped over Gallagher's frightened face like the jaws of a trap snapping shut.

"Hold on!" exclaimed Gallagher. "Mister, you're a Ranger. You can't let these . . . these crazy sonsabitches torture me!"

"Where's Parnell?" Cooper asked quietly.

"He's holed up in a warehouse a couple of blocks from here with the others. It wasn't my idea to snatch that kid, Ranger, honest!"

Cooper stiffened. "What did you say?"

"The kid, that banker's kid." Once Gallagher had broken, he had broken good. He was almost babbling now. "It was all Parnell's idea. Me and Ike and Ed and Jack just helped him because he promised us five hundred bucks apiece." Gallagher moaned. "I knew it was a bad idea, I just knew it. I should've stayed on the farm."

"Yeah," said Cooper, "you should have."

He could hardly believe what he had heard. In looking for Doyle Parnell, he had inadvertently found the gang that had kidnapped young Gilbert Vance. He had no trouble believing that Parnell would do such a thing. Parnell was plenty vicious.

"Cooper, what's he talking about?" asked Cassidy.

That was right, Cooper reminded himself, Cassidy and Longabaugh hadn't heard J. P. McCormick's explanation about the kidnapping. Cooper took his gun away from Gallagher's throat and stood up, hauling Gallagher upright with him. "Where's that warehouse?" he asked.

"Two more blocks on down this street, on the right," said Gallagher. "It's brand-new, just built."

"How many doors?"

"One in the front and a big one in back. And around on the right side, in a little alcove, there's a small door that you can't see from the street."

"That might be our best bet, Cooper," said Cassidy.

"*Our* best bet?" repeated Cooper.

Longabaugh laughed. "You don't think we're going to miss out on the fun, do you, Cooper? We may not know exactly what's going on here, but you're not going in that warehouse without somebody to back your play."

"A couple of somebodies," added Cassidy.

Cooper shook his head. "I'm going in alone. I may be able to slip in and get the prisoners out without the gang knowing about it. That'll be the safest." He shoved Gallagher at Cassidy. "You two stay here with this piece of scum and turn him over to the police. Tell them to send for J. P. McCormick, and when he gets here, tell him everything that Gallagher told us."

"You expect *us* to work with the law?" Cassidy asked, sounding as if he could hardly believe what he was hearing.

"That's right," said Cooper. "You're my friends, aren't you?"

"Damn it, Cooper, that's not fair," protested Longabaugh.

Cooper ignored him and said to Gallagher, "That little boy and the woman had better be all right."

"They were fine when I left earlier tonight," Gallagher said. "I swear it, Ranger."

The rain had grown a little harder. Cooper nodded and turned to walk away.

"Be careful," Cassidy called after him.

"I always am," Cooper replied before he vanished into the rainy night.

Longabaugh had hold of Gallagher's collar. In the distance, someone was blowing a whistle. The city police were finally responding to the report of shots being fired near the railroad tracks.

"Sundance," Cassidy said quietly, "are we going to stand

here in the rain and let Cooper have all the fun?''

Longabaugh's pistol slid from its holster. ''Hell, no, Butch,'' he said.

Gallagher realized what was happening and started to cry out, ''No, don't—''

The butt of Longabaugh's pistol thudded against his skull. Gallagher's eyes rolled up in his head, and he sagged in Longabaugh's grip. Longabaugh let him fall, and Cassidy bent over Gallagher to yank the kidnapper's belt loose and tie his hands with it.

Cassidy straightened with a grin. ''Now,'' he said, ''let's go find Cooper.''

EIGHTEEN

Doyle Parnell lifted the bottle of whiskey to his mouth and drank deeply, the liquid inside the bottle gurgling as the level dropped. He lowered the bottle with a satisfied sigh and wiped the back of his other hand across his mouth. Nobody was going to search for them here, he thought as he looked around the inside of the warehouse. They were as safe as if they were inside a bank vault. That thought made him laugh out loud.

The warehouse had been recently built and had never been used, so the place was still clean. There was an office area in front, then a big, cavernous main room with a row of small cubicles along the right-hand wall. Each cubicle had a bin in it where small items could be stored. The only windows in the place were high, right under the ceiling. The lamps that were lit inside the warehouse had been shaded so that little if any of their glow would reach the windows. From the outside, the place looked dark and deserted, and that was just how Parnell and his partner wanted it to look.

The prisoners were sitting huddled on the floor in one of the cubicles. Emily had her arm around Gilbert, who had realized that this wasn't a game after all, wasn't an adventure to be relished. Rather, it was deadly serious business . . . business that was going to make him a rich man, thought Parnell.

Parnell was sitting on a crate that somebody had hauled in. Jack Zane was standing guard in front of the cubicle where the prisoners were being kept, and Ike Nevers and Ed Olson were sitting on crates along with Parnell. Nevers held out a hand and said, "Pass over that bottle, would you?"

"Sure, Ike," said Parnell as he handed the bottle to Nevers. Parnell didn't want any of them getting too drunk, but he figured a little tonsil lubrication wouldn't hurt anything. They were safe as could be here in this warehouse. They had driven the wagon straight here from the Trinity River that afternoon after grabbing the young woman and the kid, and nobody had paid any attention to them. Parnell had the key to the warehouse; it had been given to him by his partner, who had picked this as their hiding place. He had unlocked the big rear door and driven the wagon inside. The prisoners had been taken out from under the tarp, still bound and gagged so that they couldn't move or make a sound. Then Zane and Olson had returned the wagon to the wagon yard where they had rented it earlier in the day. The gang's horses were stabled in a livery barn a block away.

This was where they would stay until the ransom had been paid, all of them except Gallagher. Parnell had sent him out to circulate around Hell's Half Acre and see if anybody had heard about the kidnapping. The kid's father had been instructed to keep quiet and not notify the police, but it was impossible to predict what somebody would do in a situation like that. Vance could have started hollering to beat the band, and the whole town might be talking about the kidnapping by now. If that was the case, Parnell wanted to know about it.

Nevers downed a healthy slug from the bottle of whiskey, then inclined his head toward the cubicle where the prisoners were. "I say we have us a little fun with that gal."

This wasn't the first time Nevers had made that suggestion. Parnell grimaced and said, "She's scared enough now that she's keeping her mouth shut. You go to maulin' her and she's liable to start screamin'."

Nevers gestured at the thick walls of the warehouse. "Who's going to hear her in here?"

"There'll be time enough for that later, after we've got the money."

"Before we kill the two of 'em, you mean," said Nevers.

Olson sighed. "I wish we didn't have to do that."

"Well, we don't have any choice about it," said Parnell. "They've seen all of us, and I don't hanker to hang or even go back to prison." He shot a glance at Nevers. "But be quiet about it, Ike. We don't want to spook 'em any more than we have to. As long as they think they're going to get out of this alive, they're more likely to cooperate."

"Yeah, yeah, sure," groused Nevers. "That gal sure is pretty."

"Later," snapped Parnell.

Nevers squinted at him. "You sure you don't just want her all to yourself, Parnell? You want to cut us out on that, too, just like you're cuttin' us out on most of the money?"

Parnell's jaw tightened. He hoped he wouldn't have to shoot Nevers before the night was over. "That ain't it at all," he said. "Besides, the man who works out the plan always gets the biggest share, you know that." Nevers didn't have to know that this hadn't been Parnell's plan at all, but rather that of his partner.

"Maybe if you don't want the girl, you'd rather have the little boy instead," said Nevers with an ugly grin. "I've heard things about you, Parnell, about how you like your meat young and tender."

It was all Parnell could do not to grab his gun and put a slug in the middle of that smirk on the face of Nevers. He'd never messed with little boys in his life. With an effort, he controlled his anger and said, "Just drink your whiskey, Ike. Talkin' too much is going to get you in trouble."

Nevers grunted and lifted the bottle to his mouth again.

Parnell slipped his watch from his pocket and opened it to check the time. He frowned a little. Gallagher should have been back by now. The farmer was probably sitting in some saloon getting drunk. Parnell didn't mind about that, as long as Gallagher kept his eyes and ears open and his mouth shut. He should have chosen somebody else for the job, Parnell told himself. Olson, maybe. Ed was mighty sobersided, especially for somebody who was an outlaw and a gunman. He would have done the job and come right back. But Parnell hadn't even known Olson until the start of this job, and Gallagher was an old cell mate.

Well, it was too late to worry about such things now, Parnell decided as he put his watch away. Nobody was going to find them here, and even if they did, this warehouse was a good place to defend. Hell, they could hold off an army from in here.

But Parnell hoped they wouldn't have to. All he wanted was to get that money, kill the girl and the kid, and get as far away from Fort Worth as he possibly could.

"It'll be all right, Gilbert, you'll see," Emily whispered into the boy's ear as she sat beside him. He was huddled close against her side, both because it was chilly in the warehouse and because he was frightened.

That was all right. She was frightened, too. In fact, she had never been so scared in her entire life. She wished now she had stayed on the family farm near Jacksboro.

Emily Mills had seen what such a life had done to her mother, however, aging her before her time and draining all the vitality and hope from her. It was doing the same thing to Emily's older sisters. They had married and started families of their own, and already Emily had been able to see the same defeat and despair creeping into their eyes.

So when the opportunity had cropped up for her to come to Fort Worth and attend a local business college, she had leaped at it. One of the storekeepers in Jacksboro, a middle-aged widower, had offered to pay for her tuition and room and board, and she had agreed that when she completed her course of study, she would return and keep his store's books for him.

Of course, he wanted more than that, and Emily knew it. She had seen the way his eyes followed her around the store every time her family came into town. He thought that when she returned to Jacksboro and went to work in his store, it would only be a matter of time until she married him. And that was all right with Emily. Marriage to him would certainly be better than staying on her parents' farm or marrying some other farmer.

Once she was in Fort Worth, however, she had realized that if she was going to set her cap for a businessman, she could find one even more successful—and more handsome—than some old storekeeper from Jacksboro. She had looked around and then answered an advertisement in the *Telegram* from someone who was looking for a governess. That someone had turned out to be Lewis Vance, and as soon as she had seen him, Emily had known he was the one. That awful man—Parnell, that was what she had heard some of the others call him—had been right: Emily planned to move smoothly from being Gilbert's governess to being his stepmother. Lewis had already made it plain on more than one occasion that he desired her. So far she had deftly fended off his advances. . . .

Now she wished she had given in to him. If she had gratified his needs, he might be more likely to pay the ransom these horrible outlaws were demanding.

Surely he would pay, she thought as she tightened her arm around Gilbert's shoulders. After all, this was his son. He loved Gilbert, and he was fond of her. He would come up with the money.

"I'm cold," Gilbert whimpered. "And I'm hungry."

"I know," Emily told him. "We'll be going home soon, and then you'll be warm, and there will be plenty to eat."

"You promise?"

"You have my word on it, Gilbert."

He leaned his head against his shoulder. "You're nice, Emily. I . . . I'm sorry I was mean to you earlier. I just wanted to be a cowboy. But I shouldn't have said those things."

"Shhh," she said. "It's all right."

"You're not mad at me?"

"Not at all."

"I'm thirsty, too."

Emily raised her voice a little and said, "Sir?"

The stolid, bearded outlaw who stood just outside the tiny space where they were confined turned his head and looked at them. "What is it?" he asked.

"Could . . . could we have some water?"

"Not now," the man said. His tone wasn't particularly sharp, but there was no sympathy in his eyes. They were as cold as the concrete floor on which Emily and Gilbert were sitting.

Despite her youth and inexperience, Emily was no fool. She had begun to fear that the men would not let her and Gilbert go, whether the ransom was paid or not. After all, she knew what all five of them looked like, and she had heard several of them address each other by name. She could describe them to the authorities if she was freed.

She alternated between wild hope and utter despair, thinking one moment that her assurances to Gilbert were true, that they would indeed be all right, then a moment later plunging into the abyss of certainty that the men intended to kill both of them no matter what happened.

At least none of them had tried so far to molest her. That would have been horrible beyond words, to be forced to submit to them right in front of Gilbert. Death might almost be better.

Almost . . .

"Damn it, Sam should've been back by now! Something's gone wrong."

Parnell listened to what Ike Nevers said and was secretly afraid that Nevers was right. It was getting late now, on toward midnight. The hours they had all spent in here in the warehouse had passed slowly, stretching nerves tighter with every minute that passed. And Nevers had been drinking too much, too. He had finished off one bottle and started another.

"Hey, Ike, remember that fella Jimbo who was in the pen with us?" asked Parnell, hoping as much as anything else that he could distract Nevers.

"Jimbo," Nevers said with a frown. "I don't remember any Jimbo."

"Sure you do," said Parnell. "He's the fella who thought he was a chicken. Remember how we'd all be out in the yard and all of a sudden Jimbo would flop down on his hands and knees and go to peckin' the ground with his nose?"

Nevers let out a harsh laugh. ''Oh, yeah,'' he said. ''Jimbo. Craziest son of a bitch I ever did see.''

Parnell laughed, too, and said, ''The guards would have to come out there and haul him up on his feet again, and Jimbo would let out the dadblamedest squawkin'. It was a sight to see. Almost as funny as when he'd flap his arms and try to fly. I never will forget the way he'd run across the yard a-flappin' and a-squawkin'.''

Olson smiled. ''Sounds crazy, all right. What happened to him?''

''Ol' Jimbo?'' said Parnell. ''One day he up and flew out of the prison, of course. Even a chicken can get up in the air if he tries hard enough and long enough.''

Nevers howled with laughter and slapped his thigh as Olson frowned, realizing that he had been taken in by the story. ''Flew out of the yard,'' said Nevers between laughs. ''Damn, I'd've like to see that!''

Jack Zane came over from the row of cubbyholes along the warehouse wall. ''The woman and the kid are complaining about being thirsty,'' he said. ''Can I give 'em something to drink?''

Nevers held up the bottle of whiskey he was holding. ''Give 'em some of this who-hit-John. Make 'em forget all about what's comin' to 'em later.''

Parnell shook his head, serious again. ''No whiskey. I put my canteen there in the office. You can get it for them, Zane. But hurry it up. I don't like leavin' them over there without anybody watchin' them.''

''They're too scared to go anywhere,'' said Zane. ''Besides, where would they go? We got this place locked up tight.''

That was true. All three doors, front, back, and side, were locked.

''Hurry up anyway,'' said Parnell. ''I get nervous when there's a bunch of money on the line.''

Zane nodded and walked toward the office at the front of the warehouse. Up there it was even darker, because the weak glow from the lamps didn't reach that far. The ceiling of the warehouse was in shadow, as were all four corners. If a man

McCormick jerked his head toward the front door of the Golden Garter. "Come along with me and I'll tell you," he said.

Cooper scraped back his chair. As he stood up he looked across the table at Tess and said, "Thanks for the game."

She met his gaze squarely. "Sometimes you're playing a game and you don't even know it," she said cryptically.

Cooper didn't have the time to try to puzzle out what she meant by that. Instead, he followed J. P. McCormick toward the door and then out onto the sidewalk. A steady drizzle was still falling, visible for a moment through the open door.

Then the door closed, and the four people around the poker table were left looking at it. After a moment of silence, Shelby said in a wondering voice, "What do you know? A Texas Ranger!"

"I need a drink," said Tess as she stood up.

Ever the gentlemen, Shelby, Cassidy, and Longabaugh also got to their feet. When Tess had gone to the bar, they sat down again. Shelby picked up the cards and began idly shuffling them. Without looking at Cassidy and Longabaugh, he said, "Well, I imagine that came as quite a surprise to the two of you."

"What do you mean by that?" snapped Longabaugh.

"A pair of notorious outlaws such as yourselves drinking and playing poker and generally befriending a member of the West's most famous outlaw hunters."

"We're cattle buyers," grated Longabaugh.

Butch Cassidy picked up the bottle at his elbow and splashed whiskey into the empty glass in front of him. He said, "Oh, give it up, Harry," and tossed back the drink. "Shelby figured out a long time ago who we really are, and I'd lay odds that Cooper did, too."

"Then why didn't he arrest us?"

"On what charge? We haven't broken any laws in Texas. Sure, they could hold us while a bunch of badge toters from up north came down here and argued over us, but you know these Texans. Live and let live, that's their motto. Why should they do Idaho's work?"

"I still wish we'd known," Longabaugh said. "I might not

looked into the darkness for too long, he'd swear that he saw things moving around there, thought Parnell. It was natural for a man's eyes to play tricks on him, especially when he was tense.

That was probably why he didn't pay attention to the faint movement he saw until it was too late.

NINETEEN

Mitch Graham was raging.

It wasn't just the pain of his wounded hand that had driven him half-mad, although that was bad enough. It was the sheer frustration of having a perfectly good plan go up in smoke for no logical reason that he could see. They hadn't even gotten in the bank, for God's sake! All they had done was pull up in front and start to get out of the van Fulton had stolen earlier in the day, and then suddenly those two Texas Rangers had been there, ruining everything.

"Son of a bitch, son of a bitch, son of a bitch!" yelled Mitch as he slammed his good hand against the door of the stolen car.

"Take it easy, Mitch," Buddy said as he tried to wrap a field dressing around Mitch's injured hand. Everything past the first knuckle on one of the fingers was gone, shot away by one of the Rangers, and the rest of the hand had been torn up pretty good by the ricochet. Mitch had lost quite a bit of blood, and the blood loss and pain might have sent him into shock if Buddy hadn't pumped a hypo full of stimulants and opiates into him. The combination was a dangerous one, but it would keep Mitch functioning for a while and that was the way they needed him now, especially with Kyle gone.

Fulton was behind the wheel, of course, and Dobie was beside him in the front seat. Mitch and Buddy were in the backseat. Dobie had helped Mitch into the car after Mitch was wounded by that Ranger, while Kyle and Buddy covered them. Buddy had been able to leap into the car as Fulton roared away, but Kyle had gone down, hit somehow by one of the Ranger's shots. Buddy figured that the bullet had found one of the small gaps in the body armor. Bad luck, that was all it was.

Dobie twisted around in the front seat and looked back at Mitch and Buddy. All of them had taken off their helmets. Dobie's face was white with fear and covered with beads of sweat. "We should've gone back for Kyle," he said. "We should've gone back."

"We couldn't go back," Mitch practically snarled at him. "It was too late. Kyle knew the risks, just like the rest of—*damn it!*" He jerked his wounded hand away from Buddy. "What are you trying to do, rip off the rest of my fingers?"

"I'm trying to stop the bleeding, Mitch," replied Buddy with more patience than he actually felt. "Don't want you passing out."

"I'm not going to pass out," snapped Mitch. "Somebody's got to do the thinking around here."

"Yeah," said Dobie, "Sundance would've taken over for Butch—"

Mitch's left hand shot out and grabbed the collar of the fatigue shirt Dobie wore under the body armor. He jerked hard, pulling Dobie halfway over the front seat. Dobie yelped in surprise and pain.

"Shut up!" Mitch shouted. "I don't want to hear any more of that Butch-and-Sundance shit! I put up with it from Kyle because we were friends, but it's over now! Understand?"

Buddy reached across Mitch's body to tug at his arm. "Let go of him, Mitch," he urged. "It's not going to do us any good if we start fighting among ourselves."

With a grimace, Mitch let go of Dobie's collar, which he had been twisting until it cut into the smaller man's neck. Dobie slumped back down in the front seat, gasping for breath. "I . . . I'm sorry, Mitch," he said raggedly. "I won't say . . . anything more about it. . . ."

"Kyle's gone," Mitch said. "Maybe he's dead, maybe the cops got him. I don't know, and it doesn't matter. It's up to us now to save our own skins. Fulton, get us back to that damn warehouse."

"That's where I'm headed, Mitch," Fulton replied from behind the wheel of the stolen luxury car.

They had made it from the bank parking lot that had almost turned into a death trap, through the parking lot of the other building, and into the maze of residential streets lined with large, expensive houses that lay north of the freeway, where Fulton had given the pursuing cops the slip with some fancy driving. The right front fender of the car was badly crumpled where it had knocked the police car out of the way, but other than that the vehicle was the sort that looked right at home in this exclusive neighborhood. They had stopped on a tree-shaded street and swapped license plates with a BMW that some fool had left parked at the curb. It had taken Fulton only a minute to make the switch. Mitch had considered just stealing the BMW, but that would have taken longer.

They cruised into the even more high-class neighborhood known as Westover Hills, then reached State Highway 183. This took them up through River Oaks, where Fulton veered onto White Settlement Road. In less than ten minutes, they were approaching downtown Fort Worth again, and so far they hadn't even *seen* a cop car, let alone been chased by any.

Buddy finished taping the bandage in place around Mitch's hand. Mitch had subsided a little and was no longer shouting and thrashing around. He was still muttering curses under his breath, however.

"We'd better start thinking about what we're going to do," suggested Buddy.

Dobie turned again to look into the backseat. "What do you mean?" he asked. "We just go on like before, don't we? When we get back to the warehouse, I'll log into the Swiss system and see if that money's been deposited in our account yet."

"You're forgetting something, Dobie," said Mitch. "If Kyle's alive, he may have talked to the cops."

Dobie shook his head. "No, Kyle wouldn't do that," he insisted. "He's our friend, he wouldn't sell us out."

Mitch's mouth twisted in a scornful grimace. "Wise up, Dobie. Kyle never wanted to grab the woman and the kid in the first place, you know that. He felt sorry for them. Hell, I think he halfway fell in love with the woman."

"I agree with Dobie," said Buddy. "Kyle wouldn't tell the cops anything."

"Are you sure of that?" asked Mitch. "Sure enough to risk your life on it?"

Fulton looked at them in the rearview mirror. "You got to ask yourself one question about what Kyle would do," the wheelman said. "I know you don't want to hear it, Mitch, but Kyle would do whatever he thinks Butch Cassidy would've done."

Mitch nodded curtly. "You're right. He's always been hung up on that code-of-honor garbage."

"The cowboy way," muttered Buddy.

Mitch looked sharply at him and asked, "What did you say?"

"Never mind," Buddy said with a shake of his head. "It's not from a movie, anyway, but I guess you're right about how Kyle looked at things." He sighed. "Kyle might tell the cops about us, might even tell them about the warehouse. I don't like it, but there it is."

"That's right," said Mitch. "That's why we've got to get rid of the woman and the little girl."

Dobie swallowed hard. "You mean kill them?"

Mitch gave an ugly laugh. "Hell, it's what we were going to do all along, isn't it?"

"That's not what Kyle had in mind," Buddy said slowly. "That's why he made sure they never saw us or heard our names. He always planned to let them go without hurting them."

"Kyle's not running things anymore. I am. And I say we don't leave any loose ends dangling behind us." Mitch looked at Dobie. "You can take your computer gear and set it up anywhere, can't you?"

Dobie shrugged. "Anywhere with a power source and a phone line."

"So there's nothing in that warehouse we really need in order to collect the ransom."

"Just the prisoners," said Buddy.

Mitch waved his uninjured hand. "We don't need them. Northrup's going to pay up. He doesn't dare stall. I say we give the woman and the little girl a bullet in the head and then torch the place as we leave."

"I don't know, Mitch. There's been a hell of a lot of killing—"

Mitch's left hand dipped into a pouch attached to his left thigh and came up with a small pistol. He turned in the seat and brought up the gun, leveling it into Buddy's face.

"Then one more kill won't make a difference, will it?" he asked quietly.

For a long moment, Buddy didn't say anything. Then he rasped, "You do what you want, Mitch. But it's not going to be on my head."

Mitch laughed as he lowered the gun. "Fine. Just stay out of my way." He had said it before, and it was just as true now:

Anybody who got in Mitch Graham's way was a dead man . . . or woman, as the case might be.

Jessica Northrup had never known a man who was more interested in money than in sex. She felt sure there were men in the world like that, but she had never encountered any.

She had never been forced to compete with the seductive power of twenty million dollars before, either.

Still, she wasn't going to give up. She called, "Hello? Could . . . could we have something to drink?"

She heard the door into the tiny room open, and she arched her back slightly, the movement so small that it might have gone unnoticed, yet enough to make her breasts stand out more prominently against the soft fabric of the T-shirt. She had been trying for the past ten minutes to think erotic thoughts so that her nipples would harden and be visible through the sports bra and the shirt. She wasn't sure if she had been successful in that effort or not.

Her wrists were tied together in front of her, and her ankles had been lashed together, too. Another rope linked the bonds at her wrists and ankles, so that she could lift her arms but was unable to reach the knot of the blindfold at the back of her neck. She was sitting up with her back against the wall. She could feel Amber's hip pressing against hers as Amber sat beside her, and hoped that her daughter took some small comfort from the human contact. Jessica knew that she did.

"Here," a muffled voice said. Jessica felt a plastic cylinder pressed into her hands and recognized the shape as a water bottle. She lifted it to her lips and drank deeply, once again thrusting her breasts out so that her captor couldn't miss them. What was wrong with the bastard? Why didn't he reach down and fondle them? Jessica wanted him to.

Because when he did, she would know where to aim her kick. Both feet, right into the balls.

Either that, or let him do what he wanted, she hadn't decided which. But she was perfectly willing to use whatever advantages she had on her side in order to save her life and the life of her daughter.

The man stepped back, however, after giving her the water bottle. Jessica heard the shuffle of his feet against the concrete floor. Trying not to sigh in dejection, she turned her head toward Amber. "Honey, are you awake? Do you want something to drink?"

"Yes, Mama." The fear in the little girl's voice was heartbreaking.

"How can you do this?" Jessica said to her captor, anger forcing the words out of her before she could stop them. "What kind of monster are you? How can you live with yourself when you've terrified a defenseless little girl?"

"Mama," Amber said desperately, "it's all right, Mama. Don't make the man mad. I'm not scared, really."

Brave little girl, thought Jessica. Braver than her mother, maybe, when it came right down to it. Because she didn't know enough yet about the ways of the world to know that some men are capable of absolutely anything, no matter how bad.

Anything.

Jessica turned, fumbled around with the water bottle, found Amber's hands, and pressed the bottle into them. Her fingertips lingered for a second on the backs of her daughter's small hands.

A moment later the muffled voice said, "That's enough." Jessica heard him move closer. He was probably bending down to take the water bottle from Amber. Jessica thought about lashing out with her feet. She couldn't kick very well, not tied up the way she was, but if she could manage to sweep the man's legs out from under him and make him fall . . .

What then? she asked herself. What then? How could she, tied up and blindfolded, overpower a fully grown, obviously dangerous man? All her self-defense and martial-arts courses weren't worth much at a time like this.

She thought there was only this one man, or at the most two, guarding her and Amber. She had heard the others leave, and they hadn't come back yet. He had to have a gun, and if she could get her hands on it and get this damned blindfold off . . .

Too late. She heard him stepping back, then heard the door close. As usual, she had thought too much and not acted quickly enough. She wished she wasn't half-paralyzed with fear.

And then things got even worse, because she heard the rumble of the big overhead door in the rear of the warehouse being raised and knew it could mean only one thing.

The others were back.

The crumpled fender was probably good camouflage in an industrial area such as this; otherwise a luxury car would have looked out of place. Anybody who noticed the car probably thought it was being taken to a body shop by a mechanic. That was what the men inside the car hoped as Fulton turned onto the driveway behind the warehouse and rolled up to the door.

Dane was waiting just inside. He raised the door, rattling

the chains that controlled it. He had been expecting the others to return in a different vehicle. The van would have been swapped for another stolen vehicle before they came back to the hideout. But he wasn't expecting to see his fellow bank robbers in a long, heavy luxury car, let alone one that looked as if it had been through a firefight.

Quickly, he lowered the warehouse door and then turned to the others as they were getting out of the car. "Something went wrong," he said. It was a statement, not a question. Then he noticed that there were only four of them, not five. "Where's Kyle?"

"Dead or in the hospital or in jail, depending on how bad he was hit," replied Mitch, who had been wounded himself if the bloody bandage on his right hand was any indication.

"Damn," breathed Dane. "Did you take down the bank?"

"We didn't even get in the door," Mitch said disgustedly. "A couple of damned Texas Rangers showed up and ruined everything. It was almost like they knew who we were and trailed us there."

"You don't think that's what happened, do you?"

"I don't know, but we're cutting our losses and getting out of here anyway." Mitch turned to Dobie. "Get in the office and find out if that money's in our account yet."

Dobie nodded. "Sure thing, Mitch." He hurried toward the front of the building.

Mitch looked at Dane. "What about the prisoners?"

"No problem," Dane said with a shrug. "They're not going to give us any trouble. They'd better hope Northrup comes through for them, though."

Mitch just gave him an odd look and said, "Too late for that." He turned away and headed for the office. Buddy trailed behind him.

Dane looked at Fulton and asked, "What did he mean by that?"

"You won't like the answer. I didn't." Fulton shook his head. "But there's no other way."

Inside the office, Mitch and Buddy stood behind the chair where Dobie was sitting. A computer and monitor were set up on a folding metal desk in front of Dobie. His fingers played over the keyboard, and the faint, high-pitched sounds of a modem connecting could be heard coming from inside the computer. Different screens popped up on the monitor, each of them prompting keystrokes from Dobie that caused them to disappear too fast for Mitch and Buddy to read them. "You sure you know what you're doing?" asked Buddy.

"Trust me," said Dobie. "This is maybe the one area in life where I absolutely do know what I'm doing."

A moment later, a screen that was blank except for a small box in the middle appeared. A cursor was blinking in the box. Dobie typed in the complicated sequence of letters and numbers that formed the password for that account, and another screen popped up. This one was full of columns of numbers.

"Damn it!" exclaimed Dobie.

"No twenty million, right?" Mitch asked tightly.

"I don't understand it," said Dobie. "It would have been so easy for Northrup. He should have done it long before now."

"Maybe he called in the police and the FBI," said Buddy.

"Then he's a damned fool," Mitch said savagely. "Doesn't he love his wife and daughter? Does he *want* them to die?"

"You said they were going to die either way, Mitch," Buddy reminded him.

"Northrup doesn't know that!"

Tentatively, Dobie said, "Maybe we should give him a little while longer before we do anything."

"No, I want to get out of here now." Mitch leaned over and once again took the pistol from the pouch on his thigh. "Close up shop, Dobie. You can check the Swiss bank again later, after we've gotten settled somewhere else."

"What are you going to do, Mitch?" asked Buddy, although he thought he already knew the answer.

Mitch laughed. His eyes were wide and shining, showing the effects of the drugs Buddy had given him earlier. "I'm going to take care of business," he said. "I don't imagine any of the rest of you want to do it. While I'm at it, get some gasoline and spread it all around the inside of the warehouse.'' He strode to the door and paused to look back at the others. ''North Fork's going to burn,'' he said, ''and I'll be glad to see the damned place go up in flames.''

TWENTY

Fort Worth, 1901

Cooper struck a match, shielding the tiny flame with his hand to protect it from the rain as well as to keep the glare from being seen. He had worked his way around the warehouse, searching for the little alcove where Gallagher had said the side door was located, and he had finally found it. Now he had to figure out how to get in.

The door was narrow, and short as well, barely wide enough for him to pass through it if he could get it open. Cooper was unsure why the builders of the warehouse had even included it, unless it had something to do with the city's fire code. He studied it quickly, before the match flickered out.

He put his hand on the knob, tried it. Locked. That came as no surprise. He slipped his bowie knife from the sheath on his left hip and, working by feel in the darkness, slipped the point of the razor-sharp blade into the lock. This was delicate work and the heavy bowie wasn't the ideal implement, but after a few minutes of quiet, careful manipulation, Cooper felt the tumblers of the lock flip open.

He put the knife away and tried the knob again, turning it a mere fraction of an inch at a time. This time the knob turned, and Cooper felt the door move slightly, opening inward. He eased it open even more, bending so that he could slide quickly through the aperture. As soon as he was inside the warehouse, he closed the door quietly behind him and stood utterly still, letting his senses search the darkness around him.

He was in a narrow gap between two wooden partitions. His shoulders almost brushed the walls on each side of him. Cooper tipped his head back and saw that the partitions didn't go all the way to the high ceiling. They ended a couple of feet above his head.

The corridor formed by the partitions ran for about ten feet in front of him, then opened up into the big main room of the warehouse. A faint yellow glow came from that area, providing enough illumination for Cooper to be able to see that this cubbyhole where he stood was empty. He heard voices but couldn't make out the words. They had a hollow, echoing quality, no doubt due to the high ceiling. After a few moments, Cooper moved toward the opening in front of him, lifting each foot carefully and then putting it down with equal caution. He moved soundlessly on the concrete floor, not allowing the soles of his boots to scrape against it.

He could hear rain drumming on the roof of the building and was grateful for it. It would help to cover up any noise he made inadvertently. When he reached the end of the corridor formed by the partitions, he reached up and removed his Stetson, then leaned forward gingerly to ease an eye around the corner.

To his right, maybe twenty feet away, stood a bearded man. He had his left side turned toward Cooper. Across the room, three more men sat on wooden crates and passed around a bottle as they talked in low tones. A kerosene lamp had been placed on the floor near them, and another lamp was burning on the floor toward the front of the building, near a door that probably led into an office.

Cooper stiffened as he heard a woman's voice. *Emily Mills?* He couldn't see a woman anywhere in the warehouse. The man to his right turned and spoke to someone behind him. A moment later, the woman said something else, and the man let out a long sigh. He started walking across the big room toward the men who were sitting on the crates.

Cooper thought he had it figured out. Here along the wall of the warehouse, small storage areas had been partitioned off. The entrance he had used was located between two of those storage areas. He wondered how far they extended and whether or not they were open at the top.

The best way to find out was to take a look, he thought. He replaced his Stetson and moved back next to the door where he had come in. Bending his knees slightly, he sprang upward and reached with both hands to grasp the top of the partition on his right. He lifted both feet behind him to keep his boots from banging against the wooden wall.

Cooper got a good grip the first time and was able to hang there for a second before he pulled himself up and chinned his head over the top of the partition. The shadows were thick here, but his keen eyes were able to tell that the storage areas did have plank ceilings on them. Cooper pulled himself higher, threw his left leg up, got a toehold, and with a quick heave rolled his body onto the planks.

The partitioned area extended almost all the way to the front wall of the warehouse, he saw as he paused where he was to study the layout. It ended a couple of feet short of the wall, leaving a gap much like the one into which the side door opened. Cooper could also see across the big main room, to where the bearded man stood talking to the other men.

The bearded man was probably a guard, Cooper thought. He was able to catch a couple of words of the conversation, and they seemed to confirm that guess. The prisoners wanted something to drink, and one of the other men gestured toward the office and said something about a canteen.

Cooper's intense gaze fastened on that man. *Doyle Parnell.* Cooper was sure of it. Being this close to the man he had been after for so long, the man who had gunned down innocent people in the course of his bank robberies, the man who had given Cooper the bullet graze on his hip that still ached a little, made the Ranger want to leap down off the balconylike structure and confront the outlaws. His hand practically itched with the need to reach for his Colt.

But there was Emily Mills and Gilbert Vance to think of. Cooper had to make sure they were safe before he did anything else.

They were somewhere below him, probably tied up. He knew they weren't gagged because he had heard the woman speak. Cooper began crawling along the top of the shedlike storage area, being as quiet as possible about it. From the corner of his eye, he saw the bearded man start walking toward the office. Cooper was reasonably confident that he could not be seen up here, even if one of the outlaws was to look straight at him. The shadows were just too thick for that.

Suddenly, when he was about halfway to the front of the building, he heard them again, the woman's voice and the boy's, coming from right below him. They were talking in quiet tones, and even though they both sounded frightened, the woman was trying to reassure the boy. He paused, just for a second, then resumed his crawl. He wondered if they had been able to hear the faint dragging of his clothes against the wooden ceiling and asked themselves what it was.

Moving a little faster now, Cooper reached the end of the storage area, grasped the edge of the partition, rolled off, and dropped the eighteen inches or so to the floor. His knees flexed when he landed, and his left hand went out to steady him against the wall. He was only a few feet from the door into the office, which was now open. Cooper took his hat off and dropped it behind him, then risked a glance around the edge of the partition. Parnell and the other two men had brought out a deck of cards and dragged another crate between them to serve as a table. One of the other men was shuffling the cards.

None of them was even looking toward this dark corner of the warehouse.

Cooper heard footsteps nearby and drew back. The bearded man came out of the office, carrying a canteen. He had taken only a step when Cooper moved silently out of the darkness, striking with deadly speed and accuracy. Cooper's left arm circled the man's head and closed over his mouth to prevent any outcry, while his right hand palmed out the Colt and reversed it. As he jerked the man back into the pitch-dark area between the warehouse wall and the wooden partition, Cooper slammed the butt of the gun against his skull. The man sagged loosely in his grip, out cold. He dropped the canteen.

Cooper's left hand shot out and snagged the strap of the canteen before it could hit the floor and make a racket. He pulled the unconscious man deeper into the shadows and lowered him to the floor. He had to move quickly now. There was no time to waste.

As Parnell had hoped, the poker game had distracted Ike Nevers from the woman. Nevers liked to play cards, but he wasn't very good at it. He had to concentrate on what he was doing just to stay even. It would have been easy as pie for Parnell to win back that two hundred and fifty bucks he had paid Nevers. Hell, he thought, he could have taken markers from Nevers and cleaned him out of the rest of the money he had been promised. But Parnell didn't want to do that, so he took it easy, folding at times when he could have kept playing, calling sometimes when he should have raised. The main thing was just to keep Nevers occupied.

Parnell glanced over his shoulder and saw Jack Zane moving along the row of storage cubicles, canteen swinging from his hand by its strap. It wasn't going to hurt anything to let the governess and the boy have a drink of water. Parnell liked to think that he had a little of the milk of human kindness left in him, though it had soured for the most part.

Yeah, he thought, there was nothing wrong with showing the prisoners a little consideration now. It wasn't like that would stop him from killing them later.

Cooper forced himself to walk at a normal pace. He carried the canteen by the strap in his left hand as he walked toward the cubbyhole where Gilbert Vance and Emily Mills were being held. Now that he was out in the open, he could see how the place was set up.

Luck had been on his side. The man who had gone to fetch the canteen from the office had a short beard, just like Cooper. The kidnapper's beard was dark brown instead of the reddish hue of Cooper's beard, but in this dimly lit, cavernlike warehouse, that detail would probably go unnoticed unless someone was really close to him. The man's hat fit well enough, and despite the fact that he was thicker through the body than Cooper, so did his coat. Cooper saw Parnell glance at him, then look away, obviously fooled by Cooper's masquerade.

To Cooper's left, another of the cubbyholes opened up, and inside, sitting on the floor with their backs against a storage bin made of thick boards, were the woman and the boy. As Cooper turned toward them they looked up at him with eyes made wide by fear. The light was bad over here, too, and they might not even realize he wasn't the man who had formerly been standing guard over them.

He stepped into the cubicle and unscrewed the cap on the canteen. As he bent over and held the mouth of the canteen to the young woman's lips, he whispered, "Don't say anything, Miss Mills. I'm a Texas Ranger. I'm here to help you."

She jerked and caught her breath. "A Texas—"

Cooper said, "Shhh. You'll be all right. Just pretend that I'm one of them." He glanced at the boy, whose eyes had grown even wider, only with amazement now. "You have to be quiet, Gilbert," Cooper went on. "Don't let them know. Can you do that?"

Gilbert Vance's head jerked in a nod.

"Go ahead and drink," said Cooper as he held the canteen to Emily's mouth. She did so, and then Cooper gave Gilbert a drink as well. Then he straightened and capped the canteen as he moved out of the cubicle. He kept his head down so that the brim of the unconscious outlaw's hat would continue to shield his face.

Cooper had left the man tied and gagged securely, so he wasn't worried about any interference from that source. He resumed the same position the bearded man had occupied earlier and took advantage of the opportunity to study the situation. What he needed was some way to get Emily and Gilbert out of the warehouse without the others being aware of it, but try as he might, he couldn't see any way of doing that.

Then, before Cooper could ponder the problem any longer, someone started pounding on the front door of the warehouse.

Parnell threw his cards down in disgust and swung toward the front of the building. "What in blazes . . . !" he exclaimed. Instinct brought him to his feet and sent his hand to the butt of his gun. He drew the Colt as he swung around toward the office.

Nevers and Olson were on their feet, too, with guns in their hands. Parnell jerked his pistol toward the office and said, "Nevers, go see who it is."

"Got to be Gallagher," said Nevers. "He's the only one who knows we're here."

"You'd better hope you're right," snapped Parnell. He threw a glance over his shoulder at Zane, who had also drawn his gun and was standing tensely in front of the cubicle where the prisoners were being kept. When Parnell looked back at Nevers, the man hadn't moved. Irritably, he said, "Well, go on."

With a muttered curse, Nevers moved toward the office. It was a small, walled-off area with a door that led into the warehouse proper and another that opened onto the street. That was the one still being pounded on. The door into the big main room was open wide, so the men inside could plainly hear the knocking.

Nevers stepped into the office and went to the outside door. He called, "Who is it?" then moved quickly aside, a habit of long standing developed so that no one could hit him by firing a gun through a door.

"It's jus' me—Gallagher," came the reply in a whiskey-thickened voice. "Open up and lemme in, damn it." The words were muffled by the door but audible in the office.

Nevers turned his head and called to Parnell, "It's Gallagher."

Parnell gestured again with his Colt. "Don't just stand there, let him in."

Gun still drawn, Nevers reached down with his other hand and twisted the key in the lock. As soon as the tumblers clicked over, the door burst open, slamming into Nevers as he tried to leap back out of the way. He didn't make it. The door caught him on the shoulder and sent him staggering back through the office.

After that, it was inevitable that all hell was going to break loose.

Cooper had stiffened. He didn't think that Cassidy and Longabaugh had had time to get in touch with J. P. McCormick and have the police sent here. Besides, knowing that Cooper was probably inside, McCormick would likely just surround the place with his men and wait to see what happened. He wouldn't just waltz up to the front door and knock so brazenly.

Once he had drawn his gun, because all the others had, there was nothing else he could do except wait. One of Parnell's men went into the office and called back a moment later that the man demanding entrance was Gallagher. Cooper knew that was impossible. Gallagher couldn't have gotten away from Cassidy and Longabaugh. This had to be some sort of trick. . . .

So Cooper was expecting trouble, and he got plenty of it as two men knocked the kidnapper aside and rushed into the warehouse. Even in the dim light, Cooper recognized Butch Cassidy and the Sundance Kid as they leveled their guns at Parnell and the other outlaw. Cassidy shouted, "Hold it right there!"

Parnell yelled, "Go to hell!" and started shooting.

Cooper's left hand swept up and knocked the hat off his head. He didn't want Cassidy and Longabaugh mistaking him for one of the kidnappers. He shouted, "Texas Rangers! Drop it, Parnell!"

Parnell swiveled toward him and snapped off a shot. Everybody was shooting now, and the echoing roar of gunfire inside the warehouse was deafening. Cooper spun around and ducked back into the cubicle. He jammed his gun in its holster and bent to grab Gilbert Vance under the arms. He came upright, hauling the boy with him, and dumped him roughly into the storage bin. The thick walls of the bin would stop any stray bullets, Cooper hoped.

Emily was already struggling to her feet as she saw what Cooper had in mind. Cooper grabbed her arm and practically flung her into the bin, regretting the roughness with which he had to handle her. A few bruises were a lot better than a bullet hole, though. "Stay down!" he barked at the two prisoners, then whirled back toward the furious gunfight that was going on in the warehouse.

There had been plenty of gun battles in which a lot of powder had been burned and a lot of lead flung without any of the participants ever getting hit. So far, that seemed to be the case here. Cassidy and Longabaugh had scrambled back into the office, taking advantage of whatever cover its flimsy walls might afford them. Parnell and the other two outlaws were hunkered behind the crates they had been using as chairs a few minutes earlier. Parnell twisted to fire again at Cooper, and as the bullet whipped past the Ranger's head, he realized that he didn't have any cover at all in this open cubicle, short of climbing into the bin with Emily and Gilbert. Cooper didn't want to draw any more fire toward them, so instead he sprinted to his left, toward the back of the warehouse.

Parnell rolled over and fired at him. If Cooper got behind the kidnappers, he and Cassidy and Longabaugh would have them in a cross fire. One of Parnell's desperate shots clipped Cooper on top of his left shoulder, the impact of the bullet sending him tumbling off his feet.

Cooper grunted in pain as he slammed into the hard floor of the warehouse. He managed to hang on to his gun as his momentum sent him rolling over a couple of times.

While the other two kidnappers poured covering fire toward the office, Parnell lunged to his feet and sprinted toward the cubicle where Emily and Gilbert lay cowering in the bin. Cooper knew Parnell probably intended to use them as hostages to get out of here. He pushed himself to his knees and fired two quick shots, forcing Parnell to veer away from the cubicle.

Parnell ducked instead toward the gap between the partitions, heading for the side door where Cooper had gotten into the warehouse. Cooper grated a curse and forced himself to his feet as Parnell disappeared into the shadow-cloaked gap.

Cooper didn't think the wound he had suffered was very bad, but for the time being, his left arm was numb and hung uselessly at his side.

He would go after Parnell in a minute, he decided. Right now he had to make sure that Emily and Gilbert were safe, and that meant taking care of the other two outlaws. He leveled his Colt at them and yelled, "Give it up!"

One of them, a smaller, deceptively mild-looking man, turned toward Cooper and fired. The bullet whined past Cooper's ear. Cooper squeezed the trigger of his gun, feeling the Colt buck against his palm as it roared. His slug caught the outlaw in the shoulder and sent him flying backward. The man landed on his back and skidded across the floor.

The final member of the gang roared his defiance and came to his feet, emptying his revolver toward the office. Cassidy and Longabaugh fired at the same time from the office door, their bullets driving into the outlaw's body and crumpling him. His hat fell off, revealing a shock of strawlike hair. He writhed for a couple of seconds on the floor, then stiffened and lay still, a pool of blood slowly spreading beneath him.

Cooper hurried across the room and kicked away the gun that the surviving outlaw had dropped. The man had passed out, but he was still alive. Cooper looked up as Cassidy and Longabaugh emerged from the office. Cassidy called, "You all right, Cooper?"

Cooper ignored the question and pointed toward the cubicle where Emily and Gilbert were hidden in the bin. "The woman and the little boy are over there," he said. "Take care of them." He turned toward the door where Parnell had made his escape.

"Where are you going?" Longabaugh called after him.

"To finish this," said Cooper.

As he stalked toward the door he flipped open the cylinder of his Colt and dumped the empty cartridges. Awkwardly, since he had the use of only one hand, he took fresh cartridges from his shell belt and thumbed them into place, then snapped the cylinder closed. After holstering the gun, he stripped off the coat he had taken from the outlaw he'd knocked out earlier and tossed it aside.

The small side door was open and flapping a little in the chilly wind. Cooper paused and looked back at Cassidy and Longabaugh before he went after Parnell. "I don't suppose you sent for McCormick before you came busting in here," he said.

Cassidy shrugged. "There wasn't really time. We left that fella Gallagher tied up where the law could find him, though."

Cooper nodded curtly. He was on his own again, chasing Doyle Parnell once more.

The difference was, this time Parnell wasn't going to get away.

Inside the warehouse, Cassidy and Longabaugh lifted Emily and Gilbert from the bin. Cassidy used his knife to cut the ropes around their wrists and ankles. Emily was unsteady on her feet after having been tied up for so long, but Cassidy was clearly glad to help support her.

"What happened to the other man?" she asked breathlessly. "The Texas Ranger."

"He's gone after the last of the kidnappers," Cassidy told her.

"By himself? Against that horrible outlaw?"

"The odds are even," said Longabaugh. "That's all a fella like Cooper ever asks for."

The rain had stopped, but the air was still cool and heavy with dampness. The numbness in Cooper's shoulder was starting to wear off, to be replaced by a dull ache. He walked along the street toward the railroad tracks, stopping occasionally to listen. He knew that Parnell couldn't be far ahead of him.

He heard the sudden patter of running footsteps, the rasp of harsh breathing. Parnell burst from cover in the mouth of an alley and ran across the street at an angle in front of Cooper, twisting to fire twice at the Ranger as he did so.

One of the bullets chipped fragments of brick from the pavement at Cooper's feet while the other whined off harmlessly into the night. Cooper didn't draw his gun but kept coming on steadily, relentlessly, behind Parnell. The wind suddenly freshened, and the clouds that had covered the sky all evening began to shred. A few stars peeked through the gaps, then the moon itself, casting a silvery glow down over the scene. Cooper could hear raucous music coming from Hell's Half Acre a few blocks away.

Parnell reached the Texas & Pacific tracks and started hurrying across them. His foot caught on one of the rails and he was thrown down, falling hard on the cinders of the roadbed. He yelled, "Son of a bitch!" then scrambled up again, looked over his shoulder. Cooper was even closer now.

"In the name of the state of Texas, you're under arrest, Parnell," Cooper called to him.

Parnell yelled an obscenity and fired again as he stumbled past the rest of the railroad tracks. If he could reach Hell's Half Acre, he could vanish there. Cooper would never find him. He had given the Ranger the slip before, and he could do it again. . . .

Cooper drew his gun, aimed by moonlight, and fired. The bullet creased Parnell's right thigh and sent him spinning to the ground. Parnell howled in pain but managed to roll over and come back up on one knee. He drew a deep breath and struggled to his feet. There was no way he could outrun Cooper now.

"Come on!" screamed Parnell as he beckoned to Cooper with his left hand. "Come on, Ranger! Damn you—"

Less than twenty feet separated the two men now. Still yelling curses, Parnell jerked his gun up and pulled the trigger. Cooper fired a split second earlier, his bullet driving into Parnell's chest and throwing the outlaw backward, so that his shot went almost straight up into the air. Parnell thudded to the pavement.

Cooper strode over to him, gun still trained on him just in case he was shamming. Cooper didn't think that was likely, but he hadn't lived this long by being careless. He kicked Parnell's gun away as he saw the outlaw staring up at him. Dark trails of blood dribbled from both sides of Parnell's mouth as a racking cough shook him. But then he laughed and said, "You . . . you're a damned fool . . . Ranger. . . . Now you'll never know . . . who came up with the plan. . . ."

"I've got a pretty good idea," said Cooper. He spoke a name.

Parnell's eyes widened in surprise, then stayed that way as he died.

Cooper holstered his gun. The night's work wasn't over yet.

TWENTY-ONE

Begin Transfer? No Yes

Roger Northrup stared at the words on the monitor screen. All he had to do was press one key, and twenty million dollars would be on its way to Switzerland. Twenty million dollars, vanishing into a hiding place where the only ones who could ever retrieve it were the animals who had stolen his wife and daughter. Twenty million . . .

And all it would take was one keystroke.

It had required all of Northrup's considerable expertise and the power of his position at the bank either to override or circumvent all the safeguards that were supposed to make such a thing impossible. Of course, he wouldn't get away with it for very long. Even with all his tricks, once he pressed that key, flags would begin to pop up on computers all over the building. In less than a minute, security would be on the way to his office. But it would be too late. The money would be gone. And Roger Northrup would be facing years in prison.

But Jessica and Amber would be safe. That was all that mattered, he told himself. His eyes filled with tears as his finger hovered over the keyboard.

He had delayed all day, hoping against hope that the phone would ring and Jessica's voice would tell him that she and

Amber had gotten away from the kidnappers. Either that, or by some miracle the monsters had been caught and his wife and daughter had been freed. But those were futile hopes, and Northrup knew it. The only way to save them was to push that key.

And even that might not do it, he knew. He would be relying on the word of vicious criminals. He had no other assurance that they would free Jessica and Amber once they had the money. They might even already be—

No. He wouldn't allow himself to think it. They were all right, and he would save them by pressing that key. . . .

No Yes

The door of Northrup's office opened. He looked up, gasping audibly in surprise, as a very attractive blond woman in a dark blue suit walked in, followed by several uniformed policemen. "Mr. Northrup," she said, "my name is Alex Cahill. We have to talk."

Sweat rolled down Northrup's face. "No!" he cried, half-crazed. "Stay away!" His face contorting, his finger jabbed at the Y key on his computer.

But instead of the command that had been there a moment earlier, now the words *Connection Terminated* glowed mockingly at him. He stared at them in horror for a second, then slumped forward over the keyboard, sobbing uncontrollably.

Walker and Trivette borrowed a car from one of the police detectives who showed up at the bank. As they wheeled out of the parking lot past the burned-out wreckage of Walker's pickup, Trivette said wryly, "You sure do lose a lot of trucks, Walker."

Behind the wheel of the borrowed car, Walker shrugged. "Occupational hazard," he said.

He got onto the freeway and drove quickly toward downtown Fort Worth. Before leaving the bank, the Rangers had learned of the bank robbers' successful getaway. Walker had also spoken to Alex Cahill by cell phone and alerted her to the possibility that Roger Northrup might attempt to transfer a large amount of money from his bank, if he had not already done so.

Following Walker's orders, by this time the Fort Worth Police Department would be establishing a discreet cordon around the old warehouse where North Fork Paintball was located. Walker didn't want the cops to move in just yet, so their instructions were to block off the streets and wait. Walker wanted to see if he could get into the warehouse and free the prisoners before any sort of armed assault took place. One thing was almost certain: the kidnappers wouldn't surrender peacefully. They were well armed, and they had demonstrated on numerous occasions that they didn't mind using the weaponry.

Trivette shook his head. "I never would have dreamed that the same bunch we've been after for those bank robberies would turn out to be behind Mrs. Northrup's kidnapping. We didn't even know for sure that she had really been kidnapped! Quite a coincidence, eh, Walker?"

"I'm not sure I believe in coincidence," Walker said slowly.

Trivette frowned. "What do you believe in, then?"

"Fate."

Ever since he had seen that old warehouse earlier today, Walker had experienced the oddest sensation, as if someone was trying to talk to him but he couldn't quite make out the words. Once he and Trivette had discovered that the bank-robbery gang was using the place as their hideout, he had been willing to chalk up the eerie feelings to his instincts trying to warn him about it. But he was beginning to sense that it was more than that.

A few minutes later, Walker and Trivette arrived at the police barricade near the warehouse. The captain who met them there said, "We've evacuated everybody we could find in a four-block-square-area around the place. Quietly, of course, so that we wouldn't alert them if they're actually in there."

"You don't know for sure that they are?" asked Trivette.

The captain shrugged. "There hasn't been any activity at all, so we can't really say."

"The gang might not have come back here," mused Walker. "But the hostages could still be inside."

"Only one way to find out, isn't there, Walker?" Trivette said with a grin.

"I can send a tactical unit in with you, Ranger," the police captain suggested to Walker.

Walker shook his head. "Trivette and I will go in alone at first," he said. "But be ready to move if we give you the word."

The captain nodded.

Walker and Trivette slipped full clips into their pistols, then started toward the warehouse on foot. Walker recalled that the east side of the building was blind except for the high, filthy windows just under the roof, so they approached from that side. If the gang was inside, they might have a lookout posted. On the other hand, if they believed their hideout hadn't been discovered, they might be careless.

Either way, Walker and Trivette were going in.

As they drew closer to the warehouse Walker felt that odd sensation again. He frowned. It was almost as if someone was calling his name, but only in his mind. He glanced at Trivette. Clearly, his fellow Ranger didn't hear anything out of the ordinary. Trivette's face revealed the strain of trying to rescue a pair of defenseless hostages from a gang of vicious killers, but that was all.

A calmness crept over Walker. That had always been one of his advantages in combat, going all the way back to his time in Vietnam and even earlier, to the rough-and-tumble days of his adolescence on the Cherokee reservation. His mind was clear, and his pulse beat perhaps a little faster than normal but not out of control. He was fully aware of his surroundings and his own body. It was an almost Zen-like clarity.

The Rangers darted from parked car to parked car, using them as cover as they approached the warehouse. Suddenly, when they were only a few yards away from the building, Walker stopped and held up a hand, motioning for Trivette to do likewise. Walker frowned as he stared hard toward the building. The voice in his head was louder than ever, but he still couldn't make out the words.

Then, suddenly, he knew what he had to do.

In a crouching run, he came out from behind cover and veered toward the building, heading for the corner. Trivette followed. Walker made his way across the back of the warehouse, catfooting along as quietly as possible, especially as he passed the big door. When he reached the far corner, he ducked around it. Trivette joined him a second later.

"Walker, what are you doing?" hissed Trivette. "If they had opened that door while we were right there—"

"Up here," Walker said, motioning along the western wall of the building. He started along it, and Trivette followed.

Abruptly, they reached an alcove, so narrow that it was difficult to see from a distance, especially since it was clogged with what looked like a hundred years' worth of trash. Walker moved through the debris carefully. At the end of the little passage, crates had been stacked against the wall of the building. Walker lifted the top one down and passed it back to Trivette, who set it on the cracked concrete sidewalk. Walker removed another box, and this time he was rewarded by the sight of a door. As he handed the box to his fellow Ranger, Trivette asked in a whisper, "How did you know this door was here?"

Walker just shook his head. He didn't want to take the time to explain that he hadn't known about the door. Something had told him to look behind those crates; that was all he knew.

In a matter of minutes, Walker and Trivette had cleared the area in front of the door. It looked as if it hadn't been used in decades. Walker bent and looked at the lock. There were some scratches around the keyhole, but they were covered with rust. He grasped the knob, tried gingerly to turn it.

The knob moved.

Trivette shook his head in disbelief as Walker opened the door. This was the luckiest break they could have gotten. From the looks of this door, the gang never used it. They might not even be aware of its existence.

Walker and Trivette both bent over slightly as they entered, since the door was short as well as narrow. Trivette eased it closed behind them.

They found themselves in pitch darkness. Walker moved forward slowly, his left hand extended in front of him, the

Sig P-220 in his right. He could hear faint noises: the sounds of someone moving around, an occasional snatch of a voice. Someone was in here, all right, and Walker had no doubt it was the bank robbers.

His left hand encountered a wooden barrier. Walker explored it quickly by touch and decided that someone had nailed boards over the end of this little passage. They hadn't done a perfect job of it, though. He was able to get his fingers into the gap between two of the boards about waist level, and one of them moved a little as he pushed on it. He clipped his gun back onto his belt so that he could use both hands on the board.

In a matter of moments, Walker had worked the board back and forth until it was loose. Carefully, not wanting to betray their presence by the squealing of nails being pulled, he put steady pressure on the board until one end of it came free. He was able to pull the other end loose then and maneuver the board back through the gap he had created. He laid it on the floor.

Dim light slanted into the passage where Walker and Trivette found themselves. Walker bent over to peer through the opening. There was another wall of some sort about twenty feet away, but there were windows in it, and light came through the glass. Shadows played over the windows, and Walker knew they came from people moving around inside the warehouse.

"Give me a hand," he whispered to Trivette as he grasped the next board down from the one he had already removed. The quarters were cramped, but the two Rangers managed to work the board back and forth until it also came loose. The boards were one-by-sixes, so when they had pried another one loose, they had an opening almost eighteen inches high. That was enough room for them to crawl through, one at a time.

Walker stood up and looked in both directions. The second wall extended in both directions, but not all the way to the ceiling. Trivette studied the layout, too, and whispered, "What in the world?"

"False fronts," said Walker. "The other side probably

looks like buildings." Gun drawn, he moved to the nearest window. Flattening his back against the wall, he bent over to glance through the glass. What he saw surprised him.

On the other side of the window was an old-fashioned boardwalk, and beyond it was a dirt street. On the other side of the street were buildings. Well, the facades of buildings, anyway, he decided. There was probably nothing behind them, just like on this side. He saw signs advertising a barbershop, a doctor's office, and a gunsmith. Walker craned his neck to peer in the other direction and saw what appeared to be a larger street crossing the one that ran between the phony buildings. On the corner of the intersection was the batwinged entrance to a saloon.

"It's a Western set," Walker breathed.

"What?"

"A Western set, like they used to use to film TV shows," explained Walker. "They've set it up this way for paintball games. People can pay to have Old West gunfights or reenact their favorite TV series or movie."

Trivette nodded in understanding. "And that robber who was killed seemed to be obsessed with the Old West. Butch Cassidy and the Sundance Kid, in particular. He must have been the boss. They used this place as a cover for what they were really doing."

It made sense—of a sort. Walker had been a lawman long enough to know that there was no telling what a twisted criminal mind might come up with.

He was still looking through the window when he saw a man move into view on the other street. The man had an automatic rifle slung over his shoulder, and he was carrying a red plastic gas can. Walker grimaced. "They're getting ready to torch the place," he whispered to Trivette. "We've got to find Mrs. Northrup and her daughter."

"If they're here," said Trivette.

Walker nodded. "They're here."

Staying in the shadows behind the false wall, the Rangers moved toward the center of the building. They came to another wall, this one with a door in it. Walker tried it, eased it open. He found himself in a recreation of a general store.

The buildings that fronted along the larger street obviously had interiors. They were built to a smaller scale than real life, so that they would fit inside the cavernous warehouse. Walker's hat brushed the ceiling as he stepped inside the emporium. He took it off and set it aside.

Walker and Trivette walked quietly to the front of the store. They knelt at the window and looked out. From here, Walker could see the office area in the front of the building. Several men stood there. They no longer wore the body armor; instead, they were clad in the fatiguelike outfits they had worn underneath the armor earlier. All of them were armed with automatic rifles.

"Where are the hostages?" asked Trivette.

Walker shook his head. He didn't see Mrs. Northrup or the little girl. He prayed they weren't already dead.

The four men near the office had gas cans, which they tossed aside. Walker could tell the cans were empty. That meant they had already spread the gas around the building. He took a deep breath and caught a faint whiff of the sharp, distinctive odor of gasoline.

Both he and Trivette tensed as another man suddenly appeared, prodding a blindfolded woman and little girl ahead of him at gunpoint. Both the woman and the girl were blond, and Walker knew he was looking at Jessica and Amber Northrup. He hoped that someone had gotten to Roger Northrup in time to stop him from turning over the ransom money to the kidnappers, but that really wasn't very important at the moment. What mattered was the safety of Mrs. Northrup and her daughter.

It appeared that their time had run out. The man holding a gun on them with his left hand had a bloodstained bandage around his right. That would be the one who had threatened to kill the hostage on the bank parking lot, Walker realized. He seemed to be in charge, and Walker already knew that he was ruthless.

If Walker and Trivette were going to make a move, it was now or never. . . .

• • •

The Northrup woman and her daughter were both crying. Mitch Graham didn't care, but the others looked bothered. With a grin, Mitch said, "What's the matter? You wish I'd killed them where you didn't have to watch it?"

Buddy ignored the question. "We're ready to go," he said. "All we have to do is touch off that gas, and the whole place will go up."

Mitch nodded. "Good. What about the computer?"

"All loaded up," said Dobie. "Maybe by the time we get set up somewhere else, Northrup will have made the transfer."

Clutching her daughter to her side, Mrs. Northrup spoke up in a frightened, yet courageous voice. "Why don't you just go away and leave us here?" she asked. "You don't have to kill us. We don't know your names, or even what you look like—"

Mitch lifted the automatic rifle he held in his left hand. "Sorry," he said, but everybody in the place knew that he didn't mean it. The other men turned away. . . .

A voice shouted, "Texas Rangers! Drop your guns!"

Inside the general store, Walker and Trivette saw the kidnappers suddenly turn around, jerking their weapons up as if they were under attack. Mrs. Northrup snatched her daughter up into her arms and began running blindly along the street. Walker had no idea what had spooked the gang, but he knew he and Trivette had to get out there if the hostages were going to have any chance to survive.

"Come on, Trivette," he barked as he sprang to the door that led onto the boardwalk. Slamming into it with his shoulder, he knocked it open and lunged out onto the planks. "Mrs. Northrup!" he shouted, hoping she could follow the sound of his voice. "Over here!"

She turned toward him, and Walker fired past her as one of the kidnappers tried to bring his rifle to bear on the fleeing hostages. Walker's bullets sizzled close enough to Mrs. Northrup's head to make her cry out involuntarily, but they found their target, drilling into the chest of one of the men and throwing him backward. The other kidnappers scattered, firing wildly down the street of the Western town. Slugs kicked up dust around Jessica Northrup's feet, but she kept running.

Trivette bounded out into the street to intercept her. He grabbed her arm and said, "Texas Rangers, ma'am. Hurry!" He steered her toward the open door of the general store as Walker threw more shots at the kidnappers to keep them occupied. The window of the emporium exploded, blown out by a burst of automatic-rifle fire. Trivette practically flung Mrs. Northrup through the door and dove into the store after the woman and the little girl.

Walker ducked into the emporium, too, as more bullets chewed splinters from the wall of the building. "Take them back out the way we came in," he snapped to Trivette. "I'll keep the rest of them busy."

Trivette hesitated, clearly not liking the idea of leaving Walker to fight it out with the remaining four kidnappers, but only for a second. Then he nodded and yanked the blindfold off Mrs. Northrup. "Come on," he told her. "Let's get you and your daughter out of here."

They ran out the back door of the emporium. Walker threw a glance over his shoulder and dimly saw his partner and the former hostages making their way quickly along the passage behind the false wall of the buildings on the side street. In a matter of minutes, they would be safely out of the warehouse, and the police could move in.

In the meantime, Walker had to deal with the remaining kidnappers. He couldn't fort up and stay in one place; these fake buildings weren't constructed sturdily enough to stand up to steady fire from automatic weapons. He had to move and keep moving if he was going to have a chance.

He went out the back door of the emporium, which sat on the corner of the two streets. Once he was back behind the false wall of the side-street buildings, he kicked one of the doors open and dashed out into the open. Somebody yelled, "There he is!" and bullets ripped up the dirt behind him. One of the false storefronts on the other side of the street had a large window in it, and Walker launched himself through it, shattering the glass and plunging through the opening to sprawl behind the wall. He rolled over and came up on his knees to fire back through the broken window.

One of his shots clipped a kidnapper on the arm, making the man stagger. Walker saw that, then he was up and running again, heading back for the main street. Slugs made a sieve out of the storefront he had just left.

Meanwhile, Trivette had helped Mrs. Northrup and her daughter through the opening he and Walker had made in the entrance to the boarded-up passage. He hustled them to the old, unused door and flung it open. Daylight flooded in, almost blinding them.

"The police are waiting," Trivette told Mrs. Northrup. "Keep moving. They'll come to you."

"Thank you," she said breathlessly. "But . . . aren't you coming with us?"

Trivette cocked an ear at the shooting that was going on inside the warehouse. "I'm going back for my partner," he said grimly.

At the moment, Walker was still on the move. He found himself in a blacksmith shop that fronted on the main street. It had a set of double doors that stood wide open, and Walker was edging toward them when one of the gang suddenly appeared there, ready to spray the inside of the building with bullets. Walker flung himself headlong toward a big anvil that was set on a sturdy pedestal. He hoped the anvil was real.

Bullets sparked and ricocheted off the anvil as the gunman opened fire. Walker fired around the pedestal, and with a loud cry the kidnapper flipped backward.

Back up the street, Trivette emerged from the general store. From the sound of the shooting, Walker had moved to another part of the Old West town. Trivette hoped he could get behind the kidnappers so that he and Walker would have them in a cross fire. But as his boots thudded on the planks of the boardwalk, he heard a curse to his right and swung in that direction to see one of the gang lining sights on him. Trivette leaped desperately off the boardwalk toward a water trough that sat a few feet away in the street. A burst of gunfire shredded the air where he had been an instant earlier.

Bellied down behind the water trough, Trivette snapped a

shot at the gunman, who ducked back into a doorway. Trivette glanced around. There was no place for him to go. If he stood up, the kidnapper would riddle him. He was pinned down, at the mercy of the much-better-armed criminal. Trivette ducked as the man stepped out of the doorway and opened fire again.

Suddenly, the sound of the shots changed. Trivette risked a look and saw that the gunman had swung around and was firing madly along the boardwalk in the other direction. He was firing at nothing, as far as Trivette could see.

No, not nothing. Trivette caught a glimpse of two figures in the shadows. He couldn't see them very well, but he thought the figures were those of two men wearing—of all things—derby hats.

Whatever was going on here, Trivette had to take advantage of it. He came up on his knees and lined his pistol on the rifleman's back. "Drop it!" Trivette shouted.

The man didn't drop his weapon. Instead he tried to turn and bring the automatic rifle to bear once more on Trivette. Trivette fired, a fast doubletap, and the slugs tore through the gunman's side. He dropped the rifle as the impact of the bullets drove him off his feet. He landed in a loose-limbed sprawl. Trivette slowly rose to his feet, keeping his gun trained on the fallen man.

Then froze as a ring of cold metal was suddenly pressed against the back of his neck.

Down the street, in the blacksmith shop, Walker came to his feet and moved toward the entrance, the Sig held ready in his fists. Instinct warned him, and he pivoted and dropped into a crouch as one of the men opened fire on him from across the street. The man was on the boardwalk, and his shots sliced through the air above Walker's head. Walker fired, his shots catching the man in the midsection. The kidnapper doubled over and went backward into the window behind him, crashing through it. His knees caught on the sill and hung there. Walker saw his feet kick spasmodically for a second, then go still.

Walker slapped a fresh clip into the butt of the pistol, then moved cautiously into the street. He spotted movement from the corner of his eye and swung to the right.

The last member of the gang stood there, some twenty feet away. His right arm, the one with the bandaged hand, was wrapped tightly around Trivette's neck, holding the Ranger in place in front of him. In his left hand he held a high-caliber pistol with the muzzle pressed against the side of Trivette's head. He grinned past Trivette's left shoulder and called out, "Drop the gun, Ranger, or I'll blow his head off!"

Walker lowered his gun slightly but didn't drop it. "You sure like to take hostages, don't you?" he said tautly.

"I do whatever I have to," the man replied. "Right now I plan to kill the two of you and then burn this place to the ground."

Hoarsely, because of the arm pressed across his neck, Trivette said, "You still won't get away. The police have the warehouse surrounded."

"Then I'll burn it down around me and go out in a blaze of glory." The man laughed, insanity creeping into the sound. "My partner Butch would have liked that."

He snapped the barrel of the pistol away from Trivette's head and pointed it toward Walker, his finger tightening on the trigger. Walker heard someone say, "Blaze of glory, hell!" and a pistol boomed. The kidnapper cried out in pain. Trivette drove an elbow back into his belly and tore free, shouting, "Take him, Walker!" as he dove out of the line of fire.

Walker tried to ignore what he saw from the corner of his eye as he fired. The kidnapper managed to get one shot off, but it was sandwiched between two blasts from Walker's gun and went harmlessly into the ground. Both of Walker's bullets slammed into the man's chest and drove him backward. He fell, arms and legs spraddled out, and managed to heave one gasping breath before he died.

Walker made sure of that, then turned to help Trivette to his feet. "You all right?" he asked.

Trivette nodded. "Sorry I let him get the drop on me, Walker. That was good shooting. That first one was a hell of a shot."

Walker didn't say anything. He didn't tell Trivette that he hadn't fired that first shot, the one that jarred the kidnapper enough for Trivette to break free. Nor did he say anything about the man who *had* fired the shot, the man standing on the boardwalk with a smoking Colt .45 Peacemaker in his hand. Walker had caught just a glimpse of him, just enough to see the long hair under the Stetson, and the beard, and the buckskin shirt from another time. . . .

The front door of the warehouse crashed open under the impact of a battering ram wielded by the FWPD tactical unit, and Walker and Trivette went to meet them and tell them it was all over.

TWENTY-TWO

Fort Worth, 1901

It wasn't over.

That thought resounded through Hayes Cooper's head as he carried the little boy through the front door of Lewis Vance's house. Gilbert had a blanket wrapped around him, and he was holding tightly to Cooper's neck. Behind Cooper came Emily Mills, and trailing her was a grim-faced J. P. McCormick.

"My God!" exclaimed Lewis Vance as Cooper strode into the banker's parlor. Vance sprang up from the chair where he had been sitting, dejected. His eyes lit up as he saw the small figure huddled in Cooper's arms. "Gilbert!"

Gilbert started squirming, and Cooper lowered the boy to the floor. Like a shot, Gilbert was in his father's arms, hugging him desperately. Vance returned the embrace, tears of joy and relief beginning to run down his cheeks.

On the other side of the parlor, Henry Osbourne turned away from the fireplace where he had been standing, warming his hands. He stared at the four people who had just come into the room.

"Emily!" Vance said as he turned toward her, still holding

Gilbert. He freed one arm to draw the governess into the hug as well. She rested her head against his shoulder.

That made a pretty good family portrait, thought Cooper as he looked at them . . . if that was what they all wanted. They'd have to work that out among themselves. The hostages had been returned safely, and his job was done.

Almost.

Vance kissed Emily on the forehead, then looked up, still blinking back tears. "I . . . I don't understand," he said. "Detective McCormick, who is this man?"

"Ranger Hayes Cooper," said McCormick, "the best damn lawman in the whole state of Texas. He rescued your boy and the young lady from that bunch of owlhoots who'd kidnapped 'em."

"Ranger Cooper, I . . . I can't thank you enough—" Vance began.

"Have you gotten instructions from the kidnappers about how to deliver the ransom?" asked Cooper, cutting into Vance's declaration of gratitude.

The banker frowned. "As a matter of fact, I have, just half an hour ago, in fact. One of the kidnappers called on the telephone and said that I was to have someone I trusted bring the money to the pavilion at Lake Como. . . ."

The resort pavilion, built over the waters of Lake Como on the western outskirts of Fort Worth, would be deserted on a night like this. Not a bad place for a ransom delivery, thought Cooper.

"Were you going to pay the ransom?" he asked.

Vance's frown deepened. "Honestly, I don't know," he said "I didn't want to give in to the kidnappers, but I was growing more and more frightened for Gilbert and Emily. That's why I summoned Henry here."

Osbourne cleared his throat and looked uncomfortable.

"I wanted to ask his advice one more time," continued Vance, "and if . . . if I decided to pay, there's no one I would have trusted more to deliver the money. . . ."

"There's your mistake, right there," said McCormick.

"I beg your pardon?"

Cooper nodded toward the bank vice-president. "Osbourne

planned the whole kidnapping. It was his idea from the start. He brought a man named Doyle Parnell here to Fort Worth to put together a gang and carry out the plan.''

Osbourne gaped at Cooper for a second, then exclaimed, ''You're insane!''

Cooper ignored the man's angry declaration and went on to Vance, ''None of the actual kidnappers could have called you. For the past three-quarters of an hour, they've all been either dead or in jail. So they had to have someone else working with them who didn't know what had happened at their hideout.''

''But . . . but that doesn't mean it was Henry,'' sputtered Vance.

''Lewis, this man had obviously lost his mind,'' Osbourne said haughtily. ''I know you're grateful to him for rescuing Gilbert and Miss Mills, but you shouldn't believe anything else he says.''

''Who delivered the note to you that said your son had been kidnapped?'' Cooper asked Vance.

''It was delivered to the bank by a man who immediately left.''

Cooper shook his head. ''No, I asked who handed it to *you*?''

''Why . . .'' Vance glanced over at Osbourne. ''Henry did.''

''Did the note say anything about Miss Mills being kidnapped along with Gilbert?''

Vance shook his head. ''No. No, I'm certain it didn't.''

''That's because when Osbourne wrote it, he didn't know that Parnell and the others had taken Miss Mills with them,'' said Cooper. ''That wasn't part of the plan.''

McCormick said, ''Where do you live, Mr. Osbourne?''

Osbourne hesitated before answering, then finally said, ''Quite near here, actually. Two blocks down the street.''

''So you know the area,'' said Cooper. ''You know the habits of Mr. Vance's family, too.''

''This is all highly circumstantial,'' said Vance. ''I told you, I trust Henry.''

''He's been hiding Parnell in his house,'' Cooper went on

inexorably. "The rest of the gang met Parnell there. The ones who are still alive can identify the house . . . and Osbourne."

Slowly, Vance turned his head toward Osbourne. "Henry . . . ?" he said.

Osbourne stepped back quickly and reached under his coat. He had barely gotten his fingers around the butt of a small pistol when Cooper's fist crashed into his jaw and knocked him back against the mantel. The pistol fell from his hand onto the hearth in front of the fireplace.

McCormick moved in, grabbed the collar of Osbourne's coat, and hauled him stumbling toward the door, where he turned him over to a couple of blue-jacketed police officers who were waiting there.

Vance stared down at the gun Osbourne had dropped. "Good Lord," he breathed. "Henry would have tried to shoot all of us. I . . . I can't believe it."

McCormick dusted his hands off as he came back into the room. He said, "Well, Osbourne might've *tried* to plug us, but if he'd actually gotten that gun out, Cooper here would've ventilated him good and proper."

Vance turned toward Cooper. "Ranger Cooper, earlier I started to say that I could never thank you enough for bringing my son back to me. Now it appears I have even more for which to be grateful to you."

Cooper smiled as he took the hand Vance extended toward him. "Just doing my job," he said.

"And doing it exceptionally well, I'd say."

Gilbert looked up at Cooper and asked, "Mr. Cooper, are you a cowboy?"

McCormick clapped a hand on the boy's shoulder. "Son, Hayes Cooper is something even better'n a cowboy. He's a gen-u-wine Texas Ranger—and they're the best!"

"A Texas Ranger," said Yance Shelby with a shake of his head. "I still can't get over it."

"Were you ever going to tell us the truth?" asked Tess Malone.

They were standing at the bar in the Golden Garter with Cooper and J. P. McCormick. Cooper and McCormick were nursing beers while Shelby toyed with his ever-present deck of cards. It was the next day, a beautiful spring afternoon. The storms of the night before were long gone.

Cooper took another sip of beer and placed his mug on the bar in front of him. "When the time was right," he said to Tess, answering her question.

"And when might that have been?"

Cooper grinned at McCormick. "Well, thanks to J. P. here, we'll never know."

"I figured that kidnappin' was more important than whatever you were after, Cooper," said the police detective. "I reckon that was a mite presumptuous of me, but it worked out all right. I didn't have no idea we were both after the same fella."

"Luck was on our side," Cooper said with a nod.

Luck . . . and a couple of gents from up north.

As that thought was going through Cooper's head the front door of the Golden Garter opened and the two gentlemen in question strolled into the saloon. They looked as dapper as ever as they came across the room to join the foursome at the bar.

"Howdy, Cooper," Butch Cassidy said. "Better come along with us."

"Where are you going?" asked Cooper.

Longabaugh looked at Cassidy and said, "Somebody's got it in his head that we ought to have our picture taken."

"There's a photography studio right down the street," said Cassidy with a grin. "We're going to meet some friends of ours there and have a nice group portrait made. Thought I'd send a copy to a pal of mine out in Winnemucca, Nevada."

"I'd better not come along," Cooper said dryly. "This face of mine might break the camera."

"Oh, I doubt that," said Tess. "I think it's a rather handsome face."

That comment brought laughter from Cassidy, Longabaugh, Shelby, and McCormick. Cooper grinned good-naturedly and shook his head.

"Well, if you're sure, I guess we'll be moving on," said Cassidy. He sketched a salute to the curled brim of his derby and turned to leave. Longabaugh nodded farewell and followed him.

"Stay out of trouble," Cooper called after them.

Butch Cassidy paused in the doorway to look back with a jaunty grin. "Not likely, pard," he said.

"Seem like a couple of pretty good fellas," McCormick commented when they were gone. "I never was sure they were tellin' the truth about bein' cattle buyers, though."

"Well, whatever line of work they're in, they turned out to be good friends," said Cooper quietly. He glanced at Tess and Shelby. The three of them would keep the secret that they shared.

McCormick turned back to his beer. "You should've got your picture made," he said to Cooper. "Famous fella like you."

Cooper shook his head. "I'm not famous, J. P."

"Well, one of these days, I reckon you will be," declared McCormick. "If there's ever a place where they put the pictures of the best Rangers to carry the badge, that's right where you belong. . . ."

Walker tapped the frame of the photograph hanging on the wall beside him. "And Hayes Cooper is here to this day, along with all the other Rangers in the Hall of Fame."

The group of children gathered in front of him burst into applause. The one called Ricky said, "That was a great story, Ranger Walker. I'm glad you finally got to finish it for us. Are you sure you told us all of it?"

Walker thought back over the yarn he had just spun for the group of schoolchildren. He'd left out a lot of the more unsavory parts, which had meant skipping over some of the things about Hell's Half Acre and the people who had lived and worked there. But he nodded anyway and said, "That's all there is to tell."

The teacher didn't have to urge the children to crowd around Walker as they thanked him and told him good-bye. "Until next time," Walker said as they left the Texas Ranger Hall of Fame.

He left the Hall himself a few minutes later and drove back

to Ranger headquarters in his new pickup. He hoped this truck would last longer than some of the ones he'd driven in the past.

Trivette's desk was littered with papers when Walker came into the room. He looked up from the documents and said, "I don't suppose you want to help me with this mess of reports on that bank robbery and kidnapping gang, do you, Walker?"

Walker hung his Stetson on the hat tree and moved behind his desk. "You're better at that sort of thing, Trivette," he told his partner.

Trivette grunted. "I thought you'd say that." He picked up one of the papers in front of him. "Say, here's something interesting. Ballistics report on the bullets taken from Mitch Graham's body. There were three slugs, and I figured they all came from your gun."

That odd feeling was coming over Walker again. "They didn't?"

"No, two out of the three did, but the third one didn't match your gun, my gun, or any of the weapons recovered from the warehouse." Trivette frowned, then asked, "Walker, did you see anything . . . funny . . . in there?"

Walker took a deep breath and said, "Nope, not a thing. How about you?"

Trivette hesitated slightly, just enough for Walker to catch it, before saying firmly, "No, of course not."

"Trivette . . . what caliber was that bullet the ballistics lab can't account for?"

"See for yourself." Trivette stood up and handed Walker the report.

Walker looked down at the paper. The best the technicians in the ballistics lab could do was make a guess, but it appeared that the unidentified bullet had come from a Colt .45 Peacemaker. . . .

AUTHOR'S NOTE

Butch Cassidy and the Sundance Kid, along with several other members of the Wild Bunch, actually did visit Fort Worth in 1901, following their robbery of the First National Bank in Winnemucca, Nevada. They spent several months in Fort Worth, and did in fact have their portrait made at John Swartz's photography studio in the area known as Hell's Half Acre. This famous photograph includes Butch Cassidy, Harry Longabaugh, Ben Kilpatrick, Will Carver, and Harvey Logan, alias Kid Curry, and ultimately contributed to the downfall of the Wild Bunch when copies of it began to be circulated among law-enforcement officers and Pinkerton detectives.

The rest of this novel involving Butch Cassidy and the Sundance Kid with Texas Ranger Hayes Cooper is, of course, fiction.

The actual Texas Ranger Hall of Fame and Museum is located in Waco, Texas, at Fort Fisher Park where Interstate 35 crosses the Brazos River. The museum contains the finest collection of Texas Rangers memorabilia in existence, as well as other exhibits pertaining to the Old West and frontier law enforcement. It is well worth a visit. The Web site for the Texas Ranger Hall of Fame and Museum can be found at www.texasranger.org.